To Wed
in Texas

To Wed
in Texas

Jodi Thomas

BERKLEY BOOKS, NEW YORK

TO WED IN TEXAS

A Berkley Book / published by arrangement with
the author

The Penguin Putnam Inc. World Wide Web site address is
http://www.penguinputnam.com

ISBN: 0-7394-0730-9

BERKLEY®
Berkley Books are published by The Berkley Publishing Group,
a division of Penguin Putnam Inc.,
375 Hudson Street, New York, New York 10014.
BERKLEY and the ''B'' logo
are trademarks belonging to Penguin Putnam Inc.

PRINTED IN THE UNITED STATES OF AMERICA

TO WED
IN TEXAS

ONE

DANIEL MCLAIN WRAPPED HIS ARMS ACROSS HIS chest and fought to keep warm. He stood on the cold, damp dock and watched an ancient trunk being unloaded off the day's only steamboat. Dark, brooding clouds reflected his mood while the boat's whistle echoed to the far bank covered in cypress trees. His massive strength could no more help him now than he could hold back the impending storm. He was alone.

If he were a swearing man, this would be the time for a few carefully chosen words.

He'd been talked into coming to a Texas town so wild, federal troops were pulled from along the frontier to handle the riots. Law was nonexistent. The worst of men, both Northern and Southern, poured through the streets as though it were the only hole in the dike. Corruption spilled like sewage, fouling even those trying to mend the country's cavern-wide rip. Prison corrals, not fit for pigs, held innocent men while the guilty walked free, bragging of their crimes.

Daniel shoved the old trunk, engraved with his late wife's maiden name, into the bed of his wagon. "Hell," he mumbled low enough he hoped Heaven wouldn't hear. As if he didn't have enough problems, the trunk from May's aunt had arrived without the old woman attached.

He had his hands full trying to stop war from breaking out. Thanks to one old maid who'd missed the only boat from Shreveport, he had no one to keep his three-year-old daughters out of harm's way.

As rain broke free from above, Daniel closed his eyes and fought back the loneliness that shook from his very core. "Why'd you have to leave me, May?" he whispered for the hundredth time since his wife died. If she'd known how hard his life would be, would she have fought a bit longer to survive? He lived through his war injuries to come back to her. Why hadn't she lived through childbirth?

Maybe this mess was his fault? He could have said no to his best friend's request. He could have stayed in the small religious community near Dallas, teaching and writing papers on brotherly love. But, no, his belief in justice wouldn't let him. There comes a time when every man has to stand and fight for what's right, even when it's not his battle. For if he doesn't fight, he has to live with a slice of the guilt that comes with injustice.

This time . . . this place was Daniel's stand.

He slapped the horses into action and set his jaw. Somehow, he would do what had to be done. And amid the chaos, he'd raise his daughters. Then, when his days were over, he'd hold his head high when he went to meet May again. He had no doubt there was a Heaven with her waiting, for he was living in Hell.

Karlee Whitworth fought to stretch her cramped leg amid the scratchy woolens and once-starched cottons that surrounded her like a stagnant tornado. If she'd realized her stay in the trunk would be so long, she would have removed more of the clothing before climbing inside.

"Help," she whispered, knowing no one would hear her. "I'm trapped in here! Help!"

The swaying had stopped hours ago, so she knew she was no longer being transported. She'd recognized the rocking of the ship last night, then felt a shifting when moved to a wagon. The uneven bumpy ride had seemed endless before she'd felt the trunk lifted and set on solid ground. But where? A night and a day must have passed while she waited.

What if the baggage housing her had been set aside in some storeroom? It might be weeks before her cousin's husband picked it up! Karlee wasn't even sure Aunt Rosy had sent him word she was coming in Rosy's place. The last letter he'd probably received had listed plans for the old aunt to make the trip.

Rosy and Violet, her old maid sister, had hatched up the idea of Karlee going to help the widowed husband of her first cousin and presented it to Karlee as a surprise. She was packed before the shock had time to wear off. The entire clan seemed in such a hurry to get rid of Karlee, they probably hadn't thought of posting word of her arrival.

What if she had to wait days until someone noticed the shipment? When Reverend Daniel McLain finally opened the chest addressed to him, he'd find nothing but the bones of Karlee Whitworth, an unknown cousin-in-law, amid her wrinkled clothing.

Karlee pounded against the inside of the trunk in earnest. "Help!" she screamed knowing the fabric around her muffled her cries.

She listened, praying to hear any human sound. Riding in the trunk had seemed such a good idea in Shreveport when she'd run out of money. But now, it was more likely to fall into the category of half-baked schemes. She always had trouble telling good ideas from half-baked schemes. In the beginning, they were twins. In the end, opposites.

Maybe there *was* something wrong with her brain. Her aunts had whispered often enough that Karlee was "perplexing, at best." They used the phrase as though talking of an incurable illness to be tolerated. The whole town seemed to agree, for gentlemen callers were as scarce as fleas on a catfish.

Maybe her aunt hadn't sent word of her arrival for fear the good reverend would turn her down. Announcing a "perplexing, at best" cousin-in-law might be rather like wiring ahead of a plague's arrival.

Since her parents' deaths when she was six, more than one relative had refused to take a turn at raising her. But the matronly aunts had taken precautions this time. They'd provided what they hoped to be enough money to make it to Jefferson, Texas, and not a dime more. No return passage. The reverend would have to take Karlee in.

But she was no charity child. She was years past grown, and she'd come to help. Surely, he'd understand and allow her to earn her keep. That is, if she ever got unpacked.

Hometown headlines flashed through Karlee's mind, "Crazy old maid dies in box left in warehouse. No kin. No one to care."

She pounded harder.

Her plan had seemed so simple. She'd watched the docks knowing the codes used by the workers, thanks to her father, who'd been a captain. He had explained to her that most of the workers couldn't read, so playing cards were placed on all unaccompanied freight to indicate destination. Jefferson was known all along the waterways as the King of Spades.

Karlee had simply taken a card from the deck in her pocketbook and stuck it on the trunk already addressed to Daniel McLain. Then she climbed inside, planning to sleep the night away and wake at her destination.

But the dockhand had slapped the latch closed when he'd loaded the trunk.

Now, she might sleep forever! Karlee pounded again, then waited, hoping, praying.

After a few seconds, something, or someone, pounded back!

She let out a cry, expecting the lid to open, but nothing happened. The tiny sliver of light between the top boards was too small to see through. She felt like a Jack-in-the-box waiting for the tune to end.

Karlee knocked again.

A rapping echoed her cry.

She tried once more with three sharp taps.

Three answered, but nothing more.

Karlee's hopes began to fade as, again and again, the rapping came and she answered, but nothing happened. Whoever was on the other side was toying with her but allowing no freedom.

Pulling into a tight ball, she tried to look at the bright side. If she died in this box, she wouldn't have to worry about all the wild stories she'd heard of Jefferson. Rumors were told that a man could rape and kill without even going to jail in this town called the porthole to Texas. Riverboat trash, outlaws, thieves, carpetbaggers and angry rebs populated the booming port.

Oh, well, in this coffin she didn't have to worry about the criminals. She'd simply starve to death in her warm, dark prison.

She knocked again. She'd rather take her chances among the outlaws than die in silence.

A devil knocked back without touching the latch.

"Girls, stop knocking on the trunk," Daniel ordered from the stove where he was trying to make pancakes.

The twins looked up at their father without the slightest hint of planning to follow such an order. They had his blond hair and their mother's brown eyes. As soon as he returned to the cooking, they returned to knocking on the tattered old box he'd brought in.

A few minutes passed before Daniel lifted one daughter off the ground with a hand clamped over the back of her overalls. She squealed and wiggled as if on a carnival ride, but showed no fear of her only parent.

"I said . . . ," Dan couldn't help but smile. "Stop knocking on your great-aunt's trunk."

"But, Daddy," the child on the ground corrected. "It knocks back."

Daniel raised an eyebrow as he lowered the other girl to the ground. "It does? Next you'll be telling me it talks as well."

Both girls nodded, sending their curly hair flying around their faces.

Daniel pictured May's plump little Aunt Rosy being stuffed into the trunk and shipped. Impossible.

"Can we open it?" one twin asked as the other knocked once more on the lid.

"No," Daniel answered. "It belongs to . . ."

The faint sound of a rapping froze his words.

TWO

∞

DANIEL FLIPPED OPEN THE LATCH ON THE OLD
trunk. An explosion of fabric rocked him backward. As
he sat on the floor watching, a mass of red hair pushed
through the dull-colored clothing, looking more like a
huge ball of yarn than a woman's head. Daniel forced
his mouth closed as the boxed creature stretched and
climbed, none too gracefully, from the trunk. Her arms
and legs were long and grew stronger with each movement. The clothes she wore were wrinkled and thread-
bare.

Bright green eyes glanced at him a moment before the
woman yelled, "Clear the decks!" at the top of her lungs.
In a mad dash, she ran across the room and out the back
door as if her hem were on fire.

Daniel raised to his knees and fought to keep his balance as the twins rushed toward him. He rocked his
daughters in strong arms. They all three stared out into
the night where she'd vanished. The low howl of the
wind and the blackness beyond the door seemed to erase
any hint of her passing. She could have been a mythical
creature born to full life before them and disappeared
just as quickly, if he believed in such things.

"Who was that, Daddy?" the twin on his right knee whispered.

"I'm not sure," he answered honestly, feeling very much as though he'd just opened Pandora's box. "I think it was a woman." Of course it was a woman, he corrected mentally. He might have been a widower for years, but he hadn't yet gone blind. "One thing I know, that wasn't your mother's Aunt Rosy."

"Lock the door before she comes back, Daddy!" The other twin stretched and clutched his neck. "I'm afraid."

"No, let's wait and see if she returns. You've nothing to fear." He only hoped he spoke the truth. Women, even normal ones, tended to make him speechless. And he had a strong feeling this one was not within shouting distance of normal.

He lowered his voice to a calming tone. "From the speed she left, she may be halfway to Shreveport by now." He lifted the twins as he stood. "We might as well eat supper. If she's not back by the time we finish, I'll go outside and try to find her. It wouldn't be right not to look after whoever, or whatever, Aunt Rosy shipped us."

The twins dove into their pancakes with zest as Daniel poured himself a cup of coffee and watched the door. A hundred questions drifted through his mind. Answers were way outnumbered, which wasn't all that unusual if May's family was involved.

Quirkiness seemed the only common batter in the mix where the Whitworths were concerned. Even Aunt Rosy, who'd offered to come help, was a woman who liked to do most of the talking and *all* the thinking in a conversation. She not only was free with telling you what she thought, but if given a moment, she'd tell you what you should think also. Her sister, Violet, hadn't ended a sentence in years as far as Daniel could tell. Even when she paused, she began again as soon as possible by starting with an "and" or a "but" or her favorite, "furthermore."

One thing he knew, whoever this woman was, she'd been sent by the aunts. But had they packed and shipped the fiery redhead to help him, or to sweep her off their doorstep? From the glance he had of her, he guessed her to be mature, mid-twenties, maybe. She didn't seem a bad looking woman. He'd noticed no deformities. Except, of course, her hair. She seemed too thick of body to be stylish, no eighteen-inch waist, he guessed, but not fat. He'd also noticed an ample chest packed into a properly tight bodice.

Judging from the speed with which she ran, she must be healthy enough.

"Reverend McLain?"

The woman was back, standing just inside the doorway, her dress and hair whirling in the night air.

Daniel stood slowly, forcing himself not to look at the way her clothes clung about her in the wind. "Yes, I'm Daniel McLain," he answered in his most formal voice.

The stranger leaned her head back and shook her hair as though enjoying the wind's combing. "Good," she said. "I'm in the right place. That's something at least. Sorry about the sudden exit, but sometimes, it's a 'clear the decks' you know, no time to stop and chat."

Daniel had no idea what she was talking about. Her chatter reminded him of years ago when seminary students were required to visit the insane wards. One poor man flashed to mind. Daniel prayed to God with the ill soul for an hour before the man informed Daniel that he *was* God and had grown tired of listening.

The stranger before him glanced at Daniel as if she thought him slow of mind and whispered, "You know, the privy?"

"Oh." Daniel cleared his throat. Men and women weren't supposed to address such subjects. May had made him blush when they first married by simply saying she needed to take a walk outside. He suddenly felt very much older than his twenty-four years.

Changing the subject seemed the safest defense. "And who are you, Madam?"

"It's Miss," she answered as she moved into the room, twisting her hair in one thick braid at her shoulder. "I'm the spinster, Karlee Whitworth, your wife's first cousin. I don't mind being unmarried, but I do get tolerably tired of being called Miss. Everyone in town knows I'm an old maid, but they still seem to say the word 'Miss' a little louder when they introduce me."

"Well, Miss . . . I mean . . ."

"Karlee," she helped. "Call me Karlee. After all, we're almost related."

She walked past him and sat down across the table from the twins. "And these must be your daughters. They do look alike. What are their names?"

Daniel frowned. "I just call them twin. When I want one, I usually want the other."

The strange woman jumped from her chair once more, and Daniel wouldn't have been surprised to have heard her yell "clear the decks!"

But this time she headed straight toward him like a warrior on the attack. "You mean you haven't named your daughters? They're almost four by my count, and you still just call them 'twin'?"

"I've been busy." Daniel forced himself not to step back with her advance.

She was tall; half a head more, and she'd be his height. And she stared directly at him without any respectable fear or feminine shyness. Even for a Whitworth, he decided, she was a strange one.

"How busy does a man have to be to name his children?" She shook her head and several strands of hair mutinied from her braid.

He studied her carefully, putting the pieces together.

He'd been a fool to ask Aunt Rosy for help. She'd probably notified the one person he didn't want to know he was having problems, his wife's sister. If Gerilyn knew he needed help, she'd be on the next boat from New Orleans trying to take the twins away. She'd made it plain more than once that she wasn't interested in helping him raise them, she was interested in having them as her own. She must have sent this strange woman to check on things.

"Have you heard from Gerilyn lately?" he asked casually without answering Karlee's question.

"No," she answered, leaning her head a little to the side. "Should I have? I only met your wife, May, and her sister once when we were about eight. I stayed with their family for a month. But as you know they already had their hands full of girls and didn't need me moving in."

Before he could answer, gunshots rang from just outside and the sound of horses' hooves gave rhythm to the night.

Karlee's green eyes sparkled with sudden fear, but she didn't move.

"We're only half a block from the docks. Trouble always rattles after dark. But tonight it sounds like it's headed straight for us. Grab the blankets!" Daniel signaled with his head toward a pile of quilts as he tucked a twin beneath each arm. "And run, Spinster Karlee."

She didn't question, but followed as he hurried through the small house almost void of furniture. He not only didn't have time to name his children, he obviously didn't bother with shopping. No extra chairs, no rugs, no curtains. Only the basic furniture needed to function.

They entered the wide entry hall built in the center of the house. With one mighty shove of his shoulder, Daniel slid a panel along one side of the foyer. A row of rifles lined the once-hidden section of wall and a hastily cut trap door scarred the floor. For a man of the cloth, he seemed ready for anything.

Daniel lifted the lid. "Climb inside! You and the twins will be safe. I made this hiding place yesterday, just in case it was ever needed."

Karlee glanced down at the hole that looked little more than four feet deep and coffin width. She was in no hurry to be locked away again.

"What about you?"

"I'll face the men. There's a group of troublemakers looking for a reason to act. I've dealt with them before. If they're not too liquored up, I should be able to send them on their way."

"I'll face them with you, Reverend."

"Get in there and be safe, Spinster Whitworth!"

The sternness in his voice sounded like an old man. He couldn't be much older than her, Karlee thought. But he obviously was a man not given to bending.

"I think not," she challenged.

As always when emotion rose within him, Daniel's throat closed. He couldn't force the angry word out.

Karlee had no such problem. "I wouldn't climb in there if it were the only way to Heaven. And you're not putting your no-name daughters in that hole while I've strength left to fight. We'll face the drunks together, for I'll not be boxed again. And that's my final word, Reverend."

Daniel almost laughed in amazement. He might be a preacher by calling, but he'd spent most of his life being a blacksmith by necessity. He could easily send her to meet her Maker with one mighty blow, if he were a man given to violence. She might not be a thin woman, but he was well twice her size.

"You have no idea what's going on in this town. The preacher who built this house was shot in the streets."

Karlee raised her chin. "Well, if they've come down

to murdering women and children, I might as well go now and avoid the dread of dying."

Daniel took a deep breath and reminded himself he was a man of peace as he handed over his daughters to a woman he felt sure could fight off a war party. "Stay out of sight," he ordered trying to gain back a few degrees of control.

The spinster nodded once and was wise enough not to smile at her victory. She hurried back to the kitchen with the twins in tow as Daniel slid the panel closed once more and moved to the front door.

Before the kitchen door completely closed, Karlee heard boots stomping across what had to be a long front porch. She leaned her back against the hallway door, but angry shouts from the front of the house rattled it.

She had to think of something fast without frightening the twins. With a forced laugh, she grabbed the corner of a quilt she carried and waved it across the clean end of the table. "Would you like to live in a tent?"

The twins forgot about anyone beyond the kitchen and ran to crawl beneath the homemade tent.

Karlee arranged the blankets around the table. "Now if you'll both be real quiet, I'll give you a surprise."

She heard them laugh and knew she'd found a game. They'd be safe beneath the table.

A sudden rattling at the back door reminded her that she might not be so secure. Frantically, Karlee searched for something to use as a weapon. She wouldn't go quietly to her death in this nowhere town, and no one would hurt her little cousins as long as she breathed.

Karlee scanned the L-shaped kitchen. In a corner furthermost from the door was a fireplace, but no tools to use for weapons. The large room was furnished with a rocking chair, four chairs and a table long enough to seat ten. Nothing more.

Just as the door creaked open, Karlee grabbed the

still-warm skillet dotted with burned pancake dough. She stepped behind the door as an enormous, hairy man poked his head through the opening like some huge bear checking a new den.

Karlee raised the iron skillet and swung with all her might, figuring a skillet was like a gun. She wouldn't have picked it up if she hadn't planned on using it.

The bearded man took the blow to the side of his head without even time for surprise to register on his face. For a moment, he just stood still, like a mighty oak unaware of a final ax cut.

Karlee lifted the skillet, prepared to hit him again. But slowly, he crumbled, open-eyed and out cold.

She moved around him, her weapon ready, pride straightening her shoulders.

Two blonde heads popped out from beneath the blanket, their eyes curious at the sound.

"Our surprise!" they both shouted as they crawled from the blanket tent. "Uncle Wolf!"

"Uncle Wolf?" A sickness settled over Karlee thick as cold molasses.

The girls jumped on what they thought was their sleeping uncle.

A fine brew, Karlee thought, another great idea soured into a half-baked scheme. The curse of her life had followed her to Texas.

THREE

DANIEL TOOK ONE LOOK AT WOLF HAYWARD sprawled across his kitchen floor like some bear rug children had dressed up to resemble a man. Without hesitation, he knew who was to blame. The Spinster Whitworth. Daniel had faced a dozen drunks on the porch without striking a blow. She'd managed to clobber his best friend.

Without looking in Karlee's direction, he knelt to check Wolf for a pulse. Daniel needed no explanation. The skillet in her hand and Wolf on the floor said all that needed saying.

Daniel let out a long-held breath. At least the huge man was still alive. Blood pounded beneath the layer of skin and hair at his throat.

As Daniel walked to the pump, Karlee followed like a orphan pup, but he didn't say a word to her. Wolf was the one person he could trust in this town. Daniel had come to Jefferson at the hairy ranger's request. She'd probably scrambled the man's brains.

The more he saw of this old maid, the more he believed she must have been stuffed in the trunk by his wife's aunts and put on the first boat. But he couldn't remember them disliking him so.

"I'm sorry," she whispered from behind him. "I didn't mean to kill Uncle Wolf, whoever he is."

Daniel drew water and fought the urge to keep an eye on her and the weapon. He was starting to fear what she might do next even more than he worried about the mob forming outside. She was a woman whose only talent seemed to be unpredictability.

"Is he your brother?" She leaned over the counter at his side.

Her action tightened her dress over her ample chest, forcing him to concentrate on not looking. "No," Daniel managed to mumble.

"Well, he's no kin of my side of the family. I'd have remembered someone with that much hair. With the wind blowing, I thought he was a walking willow come to call. So, if he's not your brother, or from your wife's kin, why do the girls call him 'uncle'?"

Daniel forced the words out slowly. "He's my brother Adam's wife's older brother."

"Oh." Karlee nodded as if his words explained everything. "I guess that's why he never shaves and lurks about the back door after dark. Being a brother to your brother's wife must be a trying job with no time to visit a barber or learn manners."

Daniel looked at her then. Her face was front-row serious, but her bright green eyes danced with mischief. He wasn't sure if she were attempting to tease him, or a concentration of the "odd" traits had cursed her double in a family where everyone was half-off. He used to tell his wife that he'd definitely got the "pick of the litter." This wife's cousin seemed more likely the "bottom of the barrel."

Lifting a bucket from below the pump, Daniel moved across the room, thinking he'd tell her as soon as there was time that he had no sense of humor left. It was buried with May. If . . . if he ever had a moment's peace with this redhead shadowing his every step.

He splashed first a little, then all of the water over the huge man on the floor.

Wolf jerked and roared loudly. He scrabbled from the waterfall, then shook his head like a wet dog and looked around for answers.

The twins giggled at him, then darted beneath their blanket tent.

Karlee slowly moved the frying pan behind her skirt and stayed well protected at Daniel's back.

"What happened?" Wolf asked as he took Daniel's offered hand.

"You just met my wife's cousin. She's used to folks who knock." Daniel glanced at Karlee. "Miss Whitworth, I'd like you to meet Wolf Hayward. He's a friend and the best Ranger Texas ever had."

Wolf took a wide swipe of his hand over his shoulder-length hair and full beard before making a deep bow and erasing any improvements he might have made in grooming. "Thank you for not killing me, Miss Whitworth. You are right, a man oughta knock before poking his head in a home. I'd been drinking some tonight, I must confess. You sobered me right up."

The Southern drawl to his voice made Karlee smile as he continued, "My mother always said drinking would lead a man down the path to Hell, but I swear when you hit me I saw the Pearly Gates of Heaven there for a minute. You may have given me the only glimpse I'll have. For, unlike the reverend here, I'm not a peace-loving man."

Karlee laughed. She'd expected anger, or maybe even an attempt at reprisal, but not appreciation.

Wolf pointed to the twins playing beneath the blanket. "Did you come to help out with the wee wild ones?"

Karlee stared at Daniel. "We haven't had time to talk about it, but if the reverend will allow me, I'd like to help. I haven't been around children much for the past few years, but I'm sure I could learn."

Daniel started shaking his head before words could come out. "I don't think so. I can manage fine without assistance." He'd look somewhere else for help. He didn't need Karlee scrambling up his household. He was a man who lived with order. He doubted she'd ever heard of the word or its meaning.

Wolf looked at Daniel as if he'd been the one whacked with the skillet. "Now, Danny boy, wait just a minute. With Willow married and in a family way, she don't have the time or the energy to chase after them two. You've got your hands full with this town. You can't cook and clean and take care of them while you're trying to settle things with a town full of men used to fighting. There ain't enough hours in the day."

Wolf glanced at Karlee and winked, obviously considering himself a great orator. "I've been in the McLain family a long time, since before the twins were born. Danny's smart with books and strong as an ox, but he don't take to change well. That's one of the reasons I had to sign on as the third big brother, the kid needs a lot of looking after."

"I do not." Daniel frowned. "And I think I'm a bit old to be referred to as 'the kid.' " Wolf was more irritating than Wes or Adam. At least they'd been born to the big brother role. Wolf had adopted it and, like every role he'd played as a spy in the war, he played this one well.

Wolf walked across the room as though pacing off the space between his thoughts. When he returned to the same spot, he looked past Daniel straight to Karlee. "Miss Whitworth, do you suppose you could use that skillet to make up another batch of pancakes? I haven't had food worth eating in a week."

Karlee nodded and went to work. Daniel groaned,

thinking it was almost too obvious what Wolf was planning. But a few home cooked meals wouldn't change his mind. He'd seen enough of the spinster to know she didn't belong here. He wanted an older woman who'd cook and clean and take care of the twins . . . and stay out of his way.

An hour later Wolf finished off his plate. He tried to smile his thanks, but Daniel knew he'd have to wait another day for any "food worth eating." Somehow she'd managed to make a dozen pancakes without any of them cooking up round. Two had been stuck together in the flipping, and Daniel had almost laughed aloud when Wolf pushed his fork into the pair and batter oozed out around his plate.

Several of her creations had jumped skillet into the fire. They were now burning on the coals, generating a smoky, sweet smell throughout the kitchen. He thought the odor blended nicely with the smell of burned coffee beans caused when she'd returned an empty pot to the fire by mistake.

"I could cook up another plate," Karlee offered as she removed the empty one from beneath Wolf's nose.

"No, thanks," Wolf forced down the last bite. He had his cup halfway to his lips, before he reconsidered and sat it back down. "I couldn't eat another one or take another swallow of your coffee if there was a gun at my head."

Daniel stood suddenly and stormed from the room.

Karlee and Wolf stared at one another, then watched the door leading to the rest of the house as if he'd return momentarily. But Daniel's footsteps sounded on the stairs. A door closed somewhere on the second floor with a slam.

Wolf frowned and Karlee felt her hopes sink. Daniel didn't want her here. He'd probably pay to send her back to the aunts when he discovered she'd arrived penniless.

After the meal she'd fed Wolf, the hairy man would no longer be on her side. They'd likely take up a collection to have her on the first boat so there would be no chance she'd cook breakfast.

Karlee forced herself to face Wolf. The least she could do was thank him; he'd given her a chance, which was more than the reverend had done. "I . . ."

Wolf's raised hand stopped her. When he moved his finger to his lips, she heard a strange sound. Low, rumbling, like thunder trapped in a faraway canyon.

The eerie sound continued, growing louder.

"What is it?" Karlee whispered.

Wolf smiled as the sound rattled from above. "It's laughter," he whispered. "Laughter from a man who hasn't laughed in far too long."

The hairy man winked at Karlee. "You're staying, Cousin Karlee," he mumbled. "If you're still willing. I think you might just be the medicine this family's been waiting for."

"I'm willing," she answered, wondering if she might be wiser to think about it for a while. This was unlike any household she'd ever been in. Guns behind sliding doors, drunks arriving unannounced, a Ranger who thought of the place as home.

But one thing seemed blended in the very air here . . . adventure. To Karlee, who'd spent the past few years taking care of aging aunts, the desire to breathe deep overwhelmed her.

An hour later the twins were tucked into bed and the kitchen was clean of all but the smells. Daniel had returned and talked to Wolf, but he hadn't said a word to Karlee. By the time the men left, she was starting to believe she was invisible.

She'd been a fool to hope, she thought. A fool to dream that this place would be where she'd stay for a while. When would she learn that all places were temporary?

She moved out the back door and welcomed the darkness of the moonless night. When she'd been a child, she really believed that she could stand in a room full of people and be unseen. After her parents died, she moved from relative to relative. A few, she soon realized, never took the time to learn her name, but simply counted the days until they could pass her on.

Silent tears rolled unchecked down her cheeks as she remembered a Christmas when all the gifts had been passed out and none were for her. When someone noticed, they'd said it was all right because she'd be moving the next day. But there was nothing waiting for her at the next home. She was just the poor relative each family took in as part of their Christian duty. The relative never remembered at holidays. The child without a birthday.

Karlee slipped to the darkest point at the corner of the house and pressed her body against the painted wood. She didn't belong here either. There was no adventure waiting here. One night changed nothing. As always she was too different, too strange, too alone. She pushed harder as if she could move into the frame of the house and finally belong somewhere. Maybe being invisible wasn't so bad. If she were invisible no one could hurt her.

She could just vanish. No one would notice. No one would care. Maybe, years after she was gone, one of her relatives would wonder, "whatever happened to that funny little redhead who couldn't do anything right?" But no one would answer, or think of her again.

Karlee closed her eyes, wishing that there was a real place called "Nowhere" where people who were "nobodies" could go. She'd go there and be happy with all the other invisible people.

From house to house she was always given the chores no one wanted to do. The clothes no one wanted to wear. She'd been a fool to believe this time would be any different. The aunts had pushed her toward Texas not because they thought it would be better, but only to have her move on, out of their lives.

Adventures only happened in books and belonging anywhere was too much to ask for.

Fighting down a cry, Karlee faced the truth. Here was no different than anywhere else. She didn't belong.

"Miss Whitworth?" a voice said from behind her.

She closed her eyes and concentrated on being invisible.

"Karlee, are you all right?"

Pushing harder into the side of the house, she tried not to think about having to face the reverend. Karlee knew what he was going to say. She'd heard good-bye a hundred times in her life. Maybe he'd tell her how much she was needed somewhere else. Or maybe he'd say he couldn't afford to feed another. Or maybe he'd just tell her it was time for her to go, as if somewhere in the overall makeup of the world there existed a chart of when she had to leave a place.

"Miss Whitworth?"

She sensed him standing just behind her. He shifted nervously, but she couldn't bring herself to make it easy for him. Not this time in her life. This man she barely knew would have to say what most had only hinted at when they handed her a ticket or loaded her suitcase in the back of a wagon.

He'd have to tell her to go.

Karlee waited, tears dripping off her face and onto the white frame of the house.

But Daniel didn't say a word. He waited, her short intakes in breath the only break in the silence of the darkness.

Finally, he rested his hand on her shoulder, at first so lightly she wasn't sure it was there, then firmer, comfortingly in an awkward way.

She tried not to shake with her grief. Over the years she'd learned to cry quietly, so that no one would know. But when he touched her, he could feel her sorrow, she knew he could.

His body leaned closer until she felt the heat of him through her clothes and his breath brush over her damp cheek. His hand moved hesitantly against her face, stroking her hair back away from her eyes.

The palm of his hand filled with her tears as he turned her face slowly toward him.

Karlee moved into his arms as though it were the most natural act in the world. She'd never felt a man's arms around her. The warmth of him. The experience of being enclosed in strength as he leaned against her.

He held her to him, letting his calm warmth seep into her. She leaned her head against his shoulder and breathed deep. There was a rock-solid feel to him that made her believe the world might settle into place enough to allow her to grow roots and belong.

"We have to talk," he whispered without easing his hold around her.

"I know," she answered wanting the closeness to never end.

"Are you sure Gerilyn didn't send you?"

Karlee let out a little laugh that sounded more like a hiccup. "If you mean your late wife's sister, no. She hasn't spoken to me in years."

Karlee didn't add that Gerilyn's quick tongue had cut her to the bone when they'd met once several years back. "Gerilyn considered herself the grand lady of the family. I seem to be the embarrassment to her. Even the few times she invited the aunts to a holiday, she made a point of not including me in the invitation. We'd have nothing to say to one another even if we did meet."

She felt his hand brush her shoulder slightly in comfort. "I believe you," he finally said. "But she's told me often enough that this is no place for a woman or children for that matter. And she's probably right. The town may break out in war at any moment." He rested his hands at Karlee's waist.

"So I've heard."

"It's not fair to ask you to stay." He pulled a few inches away. His light grip at her waist kept her from moving against him once more.

Karlee lowered her head, realizing what he was trying to say. "I understand. I can't cook and I'm not even sure I can take care of children. I tend to act before I think and . . ."

"I know," he chuckled. "In truth, I'm not an easy person to be around either. Wolf complains that I make hailstorms look cheery most days."

Karlee brushed away her last tear, thinking she'd like to get to know this man if things were different. He made her feel calm and protected even though she could see the banked turmoil in his eyes. He was a man whose kind soul showed in his eyes.

"To be honest." He let out a long breath. "All I care about is my daughters. I died inside a long time ago, but they keep me going each day. If Gerilyn knew I needed help, she'd fight me for the twins in every court from here to New Orleans."

Karlee touched his arm, knowing he was showing her more of himself in the shadows than he allowed most people to see in sunlight. Despite all his strength, he was a man wounded so deeply he had to remember to breathe.

"I'd never tell her." Karlee guessed Daniel had his secrets but there was a goodness about him anyone should be able to see. She'd never want to hurt him.

He placed his hand over hers. "That's why, despite the trouble here, I'm asking you to stay and help me raise the twins. With you, a relative here, Gerilyn wouldn't stand a chance."

"What?" Karlee tried to see his face in the darkness.

"Stay," he said. "Help me protect the twins, Karlee."

"Say it again." She closed her eyes so that all her energy could concentrate on listening.

"Stay, Karlee," he repeated. "Stay with me."

FOUR

KARLEE FELT SUDDENLY SHY AS SHE FOLLOWED
Daniel up the stairs. He carried her huge trunk as if it
were no more than a carpetbag. He didn't fit the mold
of what she thought a preacher should look like. Maybe
it was his size, or the quiet air about him, but she'd never
have guessed him a reverend.

At the small second floor landing, he turned left and
entered the first door. "The twins' room is larger and
has a small bed in it where Willow always slept, but I
thought you'd like the privacy of your own room."

Karlee set the lantern down on a small chest of drawers. He hadn't lied, the room was small yet neat and
clean. Through the window, she could see a barn in the
back and a garden plot, newly plowed, waiting for
spring. Everything about the house was plain and simple
as though it had been built only a short time before. A
house to look like a home, she thought—walls, white
paint, a porch—but something was missing. Somehow
this little place with its square rooms and blank walls
was not a home.

Daniel put the trunk down at the foot of the bed. "I've
only been living here a few months." He seemed to have
read her mind. "The house came with my assignment to

the church. The preacher who came before me was killed
and his mother should have gotten the house, but she
disappeared. After a few months they passed it along to
me."

"Before that I lived with a farm family outside of
town and rode a circuit to preach every Sunday." He
glanced around as though it were the first time he'd been
in the room. "I hope you have everything you'll need
up here."

"Thank you, I'll be fine." She tried to hide the awkwardness of the moment by straightening the lace-
trimmed pillows on the bed.

"Main Street is only a few blocks from here." He
moved closer to the window. "Willow always walked
with the twins, but if you like, I'll hitch the wagon before I leave each morning. I'll tell the bank and all the
merchants Monday that you're to charge whatever you
need to my account." He hesitated, as though choosing
his words carefully. "The climate is warmer here. You
may want to buy a few new dresses."

Karlee looked at her threadworn "best" dress. She
couldn't remember ever having had a new dress. It had
taken great skill to cut this one down to fit her after Aunt
Violet tired of it.

When she didn't say anything, Daniel paced in front
of the window, making the room seem smaller. "Charge
the things you need to me, but I'll have the bank open
an account in your name. I'll deposit ten dollars a month.
You'll need your own funds."

She was speechless. No one had ever offered to pay
her. Most thought just giving her a roof over her head
should be payment enough. Except for the times she
traveled, she'd never had any money.

He frowned at her. "That might not be enough. I was
just guessing."

"No!" Karlee answered. "It's very generous. I read

somewhere the cowhands make that a month in Texas."
In truth, she'd read everything she could get her hands
on about Texas.

"Corralling longhorns may be easier than keeping up
with the twins," Daniel guessed. "But it's your money
to use or save as you choose. I'll pay for anything you
need while you're here."

On impulse, Karlee closed the distance between them
and hugged him lightly, placing her cheek against his
for the briefest of moments.

The muscles in his arms tightened beneath her fingertips. A twitch along his square jaw line reacted to her
touch. He stepped backward so fast he almost toppled
over the trunk.

Karlee froze. She'd done something wrong. She'd
been too personal. Should she apologize? Should she try
to explain? How could she take back her action? They
might have touched in the darkness when he'd com-
forted her, but this was in the light, and in her bedroom.

She wished desperately she were alone. Then she
could dig into her trunk and find one of her favorite
books. She could lose herself in a story and no longer
have to worry about doing the proper thing. In her stories, the characters knew what to say and do. In real life,
when Karlee didn't show affection, the aunts had ac-
cused her of being cold and heartless. When she did,
they'd laughed at her and called her childish.

"I'm sorry." She steeled herself to face the conse-
quences of her action.

"No." Daniel held up a hand. "It's not your fault." He
glanced at the window as though wishing for an escape.
"I'm not used to anyone hugging me."

"It won't happen again," Karlee promised.

"You did nothing wrong." Daniel took a deep breath.
"I think it quite normal that people living under the same

roof would occasionally touch. In a proper way, of course."

Karlee watched him closely. "Of course," she whispered. He was justifying her action, letting her get away without criticism. He wasn't going to make fun of her.

"We have to figure out how to make this arrangement work." His words were painstakingly slow. "I've had no woman in my house since my wife died. I want no woman in my life now. I only want someone to care for the twins, nothing more. There are things I must do here, times I'll be away."

"I understand." Karlee felt the room suddenly grow warmer. "I didn't come here, Reverend McLain, for any purpose other than the children." How could he think she'd been making an advance? She'd never done anything like that in her life. Even when she'd thought of it a few times with young men, her aunts had lectured her in shifts for hours.

A proper young lady never flirts, she'd been drilled. The lesson always ended with a list of reasons no man would ever look her way. After all, she had no family, no money and no land. She was taller than almost every man she met, a trait no husband would want, not to mention the curse of her red hair.

"Well, good night."

He looked every bit as uncomfortable as she felt.

She raised her head with another idea. "Maybe we should shake hands on our bargain? . . . to keep everything proper."

Daniel offered his hand. "I like that idea, Spinster Whitworth."

Karlee placed her hand in his. "To working together, Reverend McLain."

He held her fingers for only a moment then turned and vanished from the room.

She remained still until she heard his footsteps end at

the bottom of the stairs, then unpacked. Within minutes, the room was hers. Hers! She'd placed a coverlet her mother hand quilted across her bed and, for lack of a shelf, lined her books up along the windowsill. A jewelry box with a broken lid held handkerchiefs atop the chest. Her few clothes fit easily into the drawers. And her hatbox filled with yellowed letters was shoved beneath her bed.

Slipping into a nightgown almost twice her size, she quickly crawled beneath the covers. Monday, if she lasted that long, she'd buy a nightgown and ship this one back to Aunt Rosy. Her aunt had made such a production of giving it to her when Karlee packed, as if it were a great sacrifice and Karlee hadn't known that it was really her oldest gown.

She'd also select material for a new dress on Monday. And scraps, if the stores in Texas had scrap barrels. She'd make her dress and the twins each a cloth doll with button eyes. She might not be able to cook, but she could sew. It would be a delight to make a dress from clean, new material.

Karlee closed her eyes, smiling into the darkness. At the end of the month, if she lasted that long, she'd use just a few cents of her own money to buy a comb for her hair. A real comb, not just pins. She'd save the rest of the money, for in thirty days she'd no longer be penniless. She'd be a woman of means.

Daniel stood on the porch just below her room. He could hear her moving around, moving in. He'd been so sure he wanted her gone from his life. Only minutes ago when he'd returned from town, he planned to ask her to leave, but then he had seen her silently crying in the shadows.

Daniel rubbed his forehead with his fist. She wasn't some old woman or slow-witted girl he could easily fool.

She wouldn't be tricked, or satisfied with half-truths. He was insane to allow her to stay. She'd be good with the twins, but it was only a matter of time before she saw the lie that was his life.

How long could he explain the riders at night as drunks? Or call Wolf just a friend and nothing more? One night she'd hear him leaving, or maybe she'd hear the sound of the hidden gun case sliding open. Some time she'd see blood on his shirt or a bruise only a fist could have made and she'd guess there was more to the preacher than met the eye. When she figured it out, he'd know for sure if she were an ally or an enemy.

Then, if she stood with Gerilyn, this woman moving a floor above him might have the power to destroy his world.

FIVE

KARLEE SPENT MOST OF THE NIGHT PRACTICING THE speech she'd say to Daniel. She'd promise to learn to cook and do her best with the twins and go to church, and keep house, and try not to kill any of his friends or relatives. She'd promise anything. This place might be the end of the world, but he'd made her a fair offer and she planned to live up to her half.

By the time she'd dressed in her wrinkled Sunday best and headed downstairs, Daniel had gone to church. He left her breakfast of oatmeal and bread warming by the stove and Wolf watching the twins.

Disappointed, Karlee sat down at the table with her bowl in hand. Finally, someone had asked her to stay, and she couldn't even remember saying thank you to him.

"What's the matter, Carrot Top?" Wolf lowered his huge frame into the chair across the table from her. A twin, dressed in white, climbed on each of his knees. "You sorry you didn't get to cook breakfast?"

"No. I only wanted to talk with Daniel. And please don't call me Carrot Top." Once, she thought, I'll ask him nice once. "I hate that name. I don't call you Root-brain or Tree head."

She smiled at the twins, wondering if anyone usually brushed their curls before church. They were so beautiful, so perfect, like an angel mirrored before her.

"I'll try to remember." Laughing, Wolf fed one twin a biscuit half topped with jelly. "As for Daniel, if he were here you could talk to him, but there's no guarantee he'll listen . . . or answer. From the stories his brothers tell, he never put more than a few words together in his life. Seems May, his wife, was the only one he ever really talked to."

"But he's a preacher." She thought about how hard it had been for Daniel to say all he did last night in her room.

Wolf nodded. "He's more a teacher. Always studying and writing papers. When he started preaching, folks said he would look straight down at May on the first row and talk to her like there was no one else in the church. They say his words were blessed, making a body feel closer to Heaven just from listening."

Wolf buttered another biscuit and handed it to the twin on his left. "I ain't one to get within shouting distance of a church, but those who do say he still stares at the third place on the first pew like he was talking the whole time to his dead wife."

An invisible icicle slid along her spine. "That's spooky." She didn't want to think the man who'd held her last night might be a little mad. He hadn't said a word of comfort, but when he'd touched her he'd made her pain and loneliness go away.

"Maybe." Wolf scratched his head. "I seen so much during the war, I ain't saying nothing's spooky now days."

Karlee leaned closer, her breakfast completely forgotten. "Like what?" She'd lived with her aunts when the conflict ended. They'd allowed no stories of war told at their table. And this man, who looked like he might be the first person she'd ever met to have fleas and not mind, would never have been allowed in the aunts' house.

The corner of Wolf's lip lifted at her interest. "Once," he whispered as if afraid to continue too loudly, "I saw a Yankee private, his head blown half off in battle, get up and walk off the field like he was out for a stroll."

Karlee leaned closer. "What did you do?"

Wolf straightened. "I cocked my rifle and followed him for a spell. Pretty soon, he stuck his hands in his pockets and started whistling." Wolf paused, his bushy eyebrows dancing.

"And?" Karlee couldn't wait.

"Well, I circled around the Yank, not wanting to shoot him in the back unless I had to. The sight of his face, half-missing from the cheek up, blood sloshing out with each step, stopped me cold. I never seen anything like it."

Karlee closed her eyes, almost smelling the blood.

Wolf's Southern voice was low and slow as it drifted to her. " 'Course, I can't be positive, him only having one eye and all, but I think he winked at me as he passed." Wolf stared directly at her and winked. "I guess that proves Yanks don't need more than half a brain."

Karlee jumped to her feet as she realized he'd been pulling her leg.

Wolf had the sense to look alarmed amid his chuckling. "I didn't mean nothing," he mumbled as fast as the words could fight their way past the mass of hair around his mouth. "I was just joshing."

She took a deep breath and pushed aside the thought of hitting him with the frying pan again. "Well, I'm more gullible than most, I guess." She straightened, deciding not to fight the war all over in this kitchen. "But Daniel did talk to me last night. In fact, he asked me to stay."

One eyebrow shot up. "The truth?"

"Truth. I've been asked to remain and help." Karlee nodded once. "In fact, he wants me to stay as long as I like." She added the lie for good measure.

"Well, I'll be. The only woman Daniel has let within a hundred miles of him is Willow. She took over the twins' care at birth. Every other woman you would have thought was poison."

"Willow?" She remembered Daniel saying someone named Willow sometimes slept on the bed in the twins' room. "Where is she, now?"

Wolf set one of the twins down gently. "We all thought Willow had a mountainsize heart and a child's mind, but there was enough woman in her for one man to love. She married one of the Buchanan boys last fall and will be calving by summer. They live down by Big Cypress Bayou in a house full of relatives. I'm sure you'll meet her. She doesn't let more than a day pass without dropping by to see the twins. You'll probably see her in church this morning."

Karlee glanced at the open window, trying to guess the time.

Wolf read her mind. "Daniel will ring the bells when it's time to start for church." As if drawn by his words, a bell began to toll.

"I'll be saying good-bye," Wolf mumbled as he stood. He picked up his rifle as though it were an extension of his arm. "The twins are all yours."

"But where . . ."

He moved to the door. "Just follow the bells, and you'll find the church." He vanished without another word, not bothering to close the door behind him.

Karlee stared at the twins. One was crying because Wolf left, the other was busy spreading grape jelly from her finger to her white dress.

"Twins!" She hated not calling them by name. "Want to go to church?"

They scattered like baby chicks at the first sound of thunder.

"Twins!" Karlee shouted as she darted one direction, then another, not knowing which girl to chase first.

The bell tolled again.

"Come here, girls." Karlee tried not to panic, but the children were like rabbits rushing just out of her reach. "Don't be afraid to go to church." She reasoned.

Laughing, they used the long table as an escape tunnel. They weren't afraid. They were playing a game with her. A game she had no idea how to win.

Ten minutes later, she struggled out of the house with a firm grip on two little hands. Forget combing their hair or washing off jelly. She had to find the church before the bell stopped ringing.

The twin on her left was crying, begging to be turned loose with the earnestness of a condemned man being led to the gallows. The girl on her right pulled at Karlee's fingers one at a time, hoping to work free.

"We don't want to go!" the child shouted. "You can't make us. You're not our dad. You're just a cousin. We don't have to go with you!"

Karlee kept moving.

Since the day she settled in with her old maid aunts, she'd seen very little of children. The aunts made a point of never inviting anyone to tea who brought a child too young to hold a cup properly and sit quietly. All her knowledge of children lay deep in memory when she had been too young to do a full day's work and was assigned to watch younger cousins as she traveled from place to place.

She thought about the alternatives available. She could stop and have a talk with the girls, only what would she say? Or she could turn back and allow them to win, only what would the preacher say if his own daughters weren't in church? If she spanked them, Daniel might not believe in hitting his children. If she didn't, they most likely would out-yell the church bell at any moment.

Karlee stopped in the middle of the walk. She twisted the girls in front of her and knelt to their level. The mirrored angel had been replaced by tiny creatures with red runny noses and open hatred in their eyes.

"Stop crying and yelling!" she ordered.

The twins didn't seem to be listening.

"Stop this right now, or I'll tell your father."

In one gulp of breath, both girls quieted.

"You'll really tell?"

"Tell him what?" the other added.

"I'll tell your father how you've acted from the time I mentioned going to church. I'll not leave out a detail of how you ran and cried and screamed."

One twin wiped her face with her sleeve while the other stared at Karlee and whispered, "Do you promise to tell?"

Karlee studied them closely, not understanding the game, but guessing the rules. "I promise only if you'll be quiet from here on."

Both tiny blonde heads nodded.

Karlee stood slowly and took their hands lightly in hers. Neither made a sound until they reached the church door. She must have done something right. They'd stopped screaming, but somehow it didn't feel like she'd won the battle.

"Promise to tell," one whispered.

Karlee nodded and stepped into church with a silent angel on either side.

The Jefferson Congregational Church was polished and shining. The windows had been washed, the pews dusted and the floors swept. The church was perfect as any Karlee had ever seen . . . and completely empty.

For a moment, she thought she'd made a mistake. Maybe it wasn't Sunday. Maybe she'd stepped into the wrong place. Maybe she was too late.

But the bell's welcome still lingered in the air, and the doors were wide open.

The twins started down the aisle.

"Wait," Karlee whispered. "No one's here."

One little angel glanced up at Karlee with her head tilted slightly in confusion. "No one is ever here," she answered and hurried to join her sister on the front pew.

Karlee followed slowly. Just as she sat down between the twins, Reverend Daniel McLain stepped from a side door to the pulpit. He looked very stern in his black coat and string tie. He stood tall, unsmiling as he faced the empty building. All hint of the shy, tongue-tied man she'd known last night had vanished. Here was a man in control, in full command. Even if his troops were missing.

He read from his notes in a clear, deep voice. Karlee thought, no welcome, no songs, no passed plate, no handshaking . . . no wonder the twins didn't want to come.

The only thing normal about the service was that within ten minutes Karlee caught herself nodding off to sleep. She jerked awake and twisted, fighting to keep her eyes open.

Daniel's rich voice continued to drift through the warm air. Karlee's wool jacket felt like a blanket wrapped around her. She jerked again as her chin touched her chest.

Stay awake! she screamed inside her head. But the hours of little sleep were catching up to her. She lost the battle.

• • •

Daniel tried not to look at Karlee as he read his carefully prepared speech. She'd combed her wild hair and tied it back into a respectable bun. Her dress, though faded, was quite proper for church, but something about her bothered him. Maybe it was the fact that, even properly dressed, he saw her as a woman.

Last night, all he'd wanted to do was comfort her when he'd found her crying, but the feel of her pressed against him had kept him awake most of the night. He was unprepared for how naturally she'd leaned against him to say "thank you" when they'd talked upstairs. He was unprepared for the effect her nearness had on him.

He pushed the thought from his mind as he jumped a few pages ahead in his sermon. Not that it mattered, no one would notice. A few minutes later when he closed his Bible, she jerked awake. His gaze met hers. She looked newborn, innocent, accepting, almost welcoming.

Frustrated, he turned away. He had no business noticing a woman, any woman so directly. He hurried down the center aisle to the open doors as though there were a hundred people he planned to greet as they left the church.

He watched her collect the twins and walk slowly toward him with a natural grace in her movements. She was too big, he thought. His May had been tiny, almost childlike and that's how he liked women. Karlee was taller than most men and rounded in places a woman should be rounded. She was no girl, but a woman fully matured.

"I'm sorry," she whispered as he shook her hand with a stranger's formality.

"We'll talk about it later," he answered as though there were crowds who might overhear now. "I promised the Buchanans I'd bring the twins to Sunday dinner if Willow didn't make it to the service."

He crossed behind her and closed the doors, locking

them carefully as though someone might try to break in the moment he was gone. "I'm sure you will be welcomed. They're good people who enjoy company. The twins and I lived with them when we first came to Jefferson."

Daniel didn't wait for an answer. He lifted the twins and carried them to the only wagon tied in front of the building. He sat the girls behind the bench seat in what looked to be an old iron cradle that had been attached to the bench. The topless cage was padded with a quilt offering the girls a comfortable, safe ride.

They'd also grown sleepy during the sermon and curled into the cradle as though it were a feather mattress.

"Interesting," Karlee studied the homemade compartment for the girls. "Very inventive and safe."

The preacher frowned at her praise. "After Willow married, I drove her home every night and I didn't want to leave the twins alone in the house. We could make it fine while the twins sit between Willow and me, but on the way back there was no place to make sure the girls were safe while I handled the horses."

He took a step toward her to assist her. She moved out of his reach.

"How far out is the Buchanan place?" Karlee moved to the front of the wagon.

He sensed an intelligence about her as well as a naiveté of life and men. He could almost hear her thinking, reasoning out what she should do. Maybe she was afraid of new places, new people, or maybe she didn't want to go where she wasn't wanted. "It's not far, a few miles."

"I don't know . . ." she mumbled. "Maybe I should just go back to the house. I've a thousand things to do."

Daniel cleared his throat trying to think of something to say that might make them more comfortable around one another. If the woman was going to live in his house, he had to be able to talk to her. "Come, you'll be welcome."

Without another word, Daniel closed his hands around her waist and helped her into the wagon. He told himself he was only being polite; after all, he'd touched her before. She was his wife's cousin, not some stranger. He'd lifted Willow in the wagon hundreds of times while she'd been the twins' nurse. This was no different.

Only he knew better. He wasn't sure how, or why, but it was. The awkwardness between them had nothing to do with his shyness or her inexperience.

She didn't say anything as he climbed up and sat beside her, which suited him fine, he decided. He was not a man who liked idle talk. They just needed time to get used to one another.

Half an hour later, he sat at one end of a long table at the Buchanans' Sunday dinner, finding himself constantly searching the crowd for Karlee. She'd remained silent for the ride out, but once he introduced her to the farmers, she blended in like family.

The Buchanans were hardworking folks with a house built to hold generations. Their men had served on the frontier as rangers and scouts during the war, refusing to fight for the North or the South. At first they'd been alienated by the townsfolk and some still crossed to the other side of the street when a Buchanan neared. But as their losses matched any family's around, most of the neighbors accepted them.

They'd been the first to welcome a Northern preacher, even though the entire lot of them had a problem making it to church regularly.

Deuteronomy Buchanan was the eldest man. At fifty he had half a dozen grown sons, but Deut still answered to his ma. She might be called Granny by all her children and grandchildren, but she ruled like a general.

At the Buchanan Sunday meal, talk and food were

plenty. Granny never turned help away and grinned when Karlee politely offered after the introductions. Karlee seemed to know what to do. She worked alongside the other women, talking and laughing as though she'd been to dinner a hundred times. Daniel couldn't help but notice she did what needed to be done, pitching in with the serving as well as the cleaning.

"My four oldest boys will be leaving at dawn tomorrow." Deut drew Daniel's attention back to the conversation. "There's real money to be made in the drives."

"I hate to see them go," Daniel injected, "with all the trouble around." He didn't have to say more, Daniel knew Deut kept up with the problems even if he rarely said anything.

"Me and the three youngest will still be here." Deut chewed as he talked. "But those who are married need to fill their pockets and settle into their own places. They figure four months on a drive will pay them enough to do just that. This land will have several more homes on it by planting time next year."

"You're probably right," Daniel answered as he watched Karlee circle the room with a tray of seconds.

"You say your cousin is single, Reverend?" Deut Buchanan asked, with his mouth still full of mashed potatoes. "Fine looking woman to be left on the vine." Except for his mother, Deut was the oldest and therefore given free range to state any opinions.

Daniel frowned. "Yes, she's single." All the men within hearing distance of Daniel's comment were staring in Karlee's direction. The entire clan seemed to be on a population frenzy, birthing and marrying as fast as they could. "She came to Jefferson to help me with the twins," Daniel added. "Not to marry any of you Buchanan boys."

Deut laughed, spitting a snow of potatoes. "Don't get riled up, Reverend. We only took Willow away from you 'cause Sammy loved her so. We know you have to have a woman to help out at your place. If I'd had a few daughters and not so many boys, I might could have saved you the trouble of sending for a woman."

"But Pa, she's got red hair and the greenest eyes I've ever seen." Ray sighed deeply, "and her hair. Did you ever see a woman with so much red hair?"

"Now you forget about courting her, Ray. The preacher's got no woman. He needs her more than you do. Besides, you got another year before you're twenty and at the hurry-up stage for marrying."

Daniel was thankful for all the people talking around him. He couldn't have said a word if his life depended on it. He wished he could scream that he had had a woman and wanted no other now, or ever. His grief had settled into anger over the years. Anger at the world and at himself for caring so deeply.

But Deut was right, Daniel needed Karlee. With all her imperfections and strangeness, he needed her. He couldn't raise his daughters alone. If he tried, he guessed Gerilyn would be knocking at his door demanding custody of the girls. She'd married a man with enough money and power to put up a fight if it came to that. They were just waiting for him to make a wrong move.

He stood so suddenly half the room turned his direction as though expecting a speech. But when he said nothing, they returned to their conversations and food.

Daniel walked the length of the long dining room and entered the kitchen. Like everything else in the Buchanan homestead, the room had been built for a large family. Karlee was cleaning the table where everyone under twelve ate while several women hurried the children, including the twins, outside to play.

Daniel stood in the doorway for a minute, unaware of anyone in the room except Karlee. She might not be a cook, but she knew her way around cleaning. He couldn't help but wonder if she, like himself, pushed herself to work harder than anyone else so she would be exhausted enough at night to sleep.

When she finally glanced up, he asked, "We need to talk, Miss Whitworth. Want to see the bayou?"

"Now?"

"Now." He walked outside, hoping she'd follow. There were plenty of women to finish and watch the twins. The Buchanans treated child rearing with the herd philosophy. Except for sleeping, the children all stayed together and the adults took turns sitting on the nest. They traveled in a pack, with older ones taking care of younger. His twins loved the attention.

Daniel marched past two huge live oaks and headed toward the bayou where old cypress trees tiptoed into the water's edge. He didn't bother to turn around. If she followed, she followed. He'd not beg for her attention.

When he reached shade so thick it seemed like twilight, he stared out across the bayou, listening for the sounds of passing boats. The air hung damp and warm for late February, but the wind off the water was cool. He could almost close his eyes and think he was back home in Indiana. As a boy, he'd loved rowing out to the center of the lake near their farm. When the day got hot, he'd lay down in the boat and let the sun warm him as he listened to water lap against the sides.

"I'm sorry." Karlee broke into his thoughts. "I didn't mean to fall asleep in church. I know you're probably mad at me, but not speaking to me won't solve any problem."

Daniel turned around to face her and was surprised to find her so close behind him. She still wore the tea towel she'd tucked into her waistband as an apron. "I'm not mad at you." He tried to think of how to put words together as he backed away from her a few steps. "I can't blame you. I'm not much of a preacher."

"Oh, no." She lied. "You're fine, just fine. I didn't
sleep last night. I was trying to think of some way to
say thank you for letting me stay. I want you to know
I'll try real hard to help out. I'll learn to cook and I'll
take good care of the twins and I'll . . ." She paused,
trying to remember a well-rehearsed speech.

"It's all right," he interrupted. "I said you could stay.
Fact is, I need you desperately." Daniel watched her
closely, sensing more than she was saying. "Is going
back really so bad?"

He thought he saw a tear in the corner of her eye
before she blinked it away.

She straightened slightly and looked directly at him.
"Yes," she said simply.

Daniel could see the truth in her eyes. A woman without money or family . . . where would she go? From the
way she worked for her meal, he guessed she'd been
working hard all her life, trying to pay back what she'd
probably been told she had no right to.

He forced out what had to be said. "Promise me you
won't leave, no matter what happens, no matter what
you see, or hear, or think you hear."

Surprise lifted her eyebrows. "All right."

"If you left I could lose the twins, and I couldn't live
with that. No matter what happens, the twins must stay."

"I think I understand. They're very lucky little girls
to be loved so much."

"They're all I have." His stance relaxed and he smiled.
"So promise you won't marry one of the Buchanans. At
least not for a year."

She tilted her head slightly in an action that reminded
him of his daughters. "I think I can promise that with
some ease. Granny's smart as a whip, but the intelligence seems to be watering down through the generations."

She'd expected him to laugh and agree, but Daniel

only stared out at the water. "I'll stay," she added wondering if he was even listening.

"Good." He let out a long breath. "I need you on my side, Karlee, no matter what."

He saw it in her eyes, a question, a doubt, a decision to trust. "I'll be there."

"Preacher!" Deut shouted from the house before Daniel could say more. "We got a rider who barely made it here. He's bleeding like a stuck pig and yelling your name."

Daniel glanced at Karlee. "It's started," he whispered. "Don't forget your promise. No matter what."

SIX

"KARLEE, GET THE TWINS!" DANIEL SHOUTED AS HE
carried a wounded man toward their wagon. "We need
to get out of here before the Buchanans share our trouble."

Questions jumped wildly across Karlee's mind, but
the stranger—covered in blood and dust—left no time
to talk. He couldn't have been more than a skeleton beneath his ragged Confederate jacket. His hair and beard
were long and unkempt. When exhausted blue eyes met
Karlee's gaze, she realized he wasn't as old as she. And
he was frightened, terrified.

"Get the twins!" Daniel snapped. "We've no time."

As she hurried the girls toward the wagon, Karlee
heard Deut Buchanan whisper to Daniel. "This is Cullen
Baker's doing, I'd bet on it. Most of the trouble blamed
on this boy weren't his fault. I'll take care of the animal.
You get Jesse dead and buried deep as soon as you can,
Reverend."

Karlee stared at the pale face of the wounded man.
Blood dripped from his chest, soaking into Daniel's
black coat. *He's not dead yet,* she wanted to shout at
Deut, but to her surprise, the man nodded a "thank you"
to the oldest Buchanan male.

Granny stood on the porch shaking her head as if she'd been predicting a storm and she could hear the thunder. "I ain't known nothing but trouble in this state since I come here twenty years ago. We got too many younguns around for there to be gunplay on my land." She gestured with her head toward her sons. "Saddle up, and make sure the preacher gets home safely."

Four Buchanan boys were on horseback before Daniel got the wounded man hidden in the back of his wagon. He tucked the twins just behind the seat and climbed up beside Karlee.

"What's happening?" She gripped the frame as he slapped the horses into action. The power in his movements frightened her. He was a big man, and strong, but until now she'd never thought of him as a warrior. Somehow, in a heartbeat's time, this quiet man of the cloth had donned invisible armor. She feared for anything or anyone who got in his way.

"We'll talk about it later," he mumbled, taking no polite care to allow the few inches between them as he had earlier.

His leg brushed hers as he braced his weight. Karlee tried not to notice. They had a wagon loaded with trouble; the space between them was of no importance. But each time his arm or leg moved against hers, she stiffened then reminded herself she was acting like a foolish old spinster.

They made it back to the house in half the time it had taken to ride out to the Buchanan farm. Daniel pulled the wagon around to the back door, but the location of the house allowed little privacy from homes surrounded it. The Buchanans stopped out front as though notifying anyone interested that the reverend had company. Karlee couldn't help but notice each man's rifle came with him into the house.

As Daniel lifted the wounded man, he called over his

shoulder. "Get the twins inside! Keep them in the kitchen no matter what you hear."

Karlee had no idea what was going on. All she could do was trust Daniel as she'd promised. And trusting a man whose favorite saying was "we'll talk about it later" wasn't an easy thing to do.

She followed behind Daniel and bolted the door. The girls clung to her skirts. Karlee fought to hide any worry and confusion, knowing the girls were already tired and cranky. They didn't need to be frightened as well. Tension hung in the air as thick as the smell of blood.

After trying everything she could think of to keep the twins busy, she finally gave up the battle and sat in a huge rocker pulled close to a cold fireplace. This corner of the kitchen caught the morning light but now lay in shadows. To her surprise, both girls crawled into her lap and wiggled their way to sleep.

She rocked them slowly, listening to voices somewhere beyond the kitchen door. Men were talking, but she couldn't understand what they were saying. She could hear footsteps but couldn't tell how many there were.

Daniel's words, "promise to stay no matter what you hear," filled her thoughts. Had he known this would happen, or had he only guessed?

Long shadows criss-crossed the room when she felt one of the twins being lifted from beneath her arm. Karlee looked up at Daniel's large frame hovering above her.

"I'll help you put them to bed," he whispered as he carefully settled one sleeping girl against a white spot of cotton on a shirt splattered with blood.

Karlee followed him upstairs with the other twin in her arms. The girls' room and hers were the only rooms on the second floor. She'd been here two days now and had no idea where he slept. In truth, she hadn't even had time to learn her way around the house, except for the kitchen and her plain, sparsely furnished room.

Once the girls were tucked in, she moved down the stairs, allowing Daniel a moment to say goodnight to his children.

In the parlor, the three youngest Buchanan men stood facing the windows, their guns drawn and ready. None looked old enough to need to shave regularly, but all held weapons with practiced ease.

One glanced in her direction, then turned back to his post without even bothering to nod a greeting. They might be poor farm folks to most eyes, but Karlee suspected they were men born to this land with an alertness for danger and a strength to act when needed.

Karlee kept her attention on the guards as she silently crossed the hall and slipped into the dining room. She navigated toward the kitchen in shadows. The smell of blood and dirt and dying filled her senses. She slowed, searching the darkness, letting her fingers guide her as her eyes adjusted.

Her hip bumped against the table a moment before her fingers trailed into warm, thick liquid.

Karlee froze as her eyes made out the dark forms before her.

Two men lay on the dining table. One was the wounded man they'd transported from the ranch. Deut Buchanan had called him Jesse. His wound had been treated, but crimson already colored the bandage and the table where he'd curled into a ball like an infant. The Confederate uniform he had worn was replaced by a rough homespun shirt and tattered trousers.

The other man on the table lay straight, as though at attention, and was dressed in Jesse's bloody uniform.

"Karlee, you shouldn't be in here." Daniel was close behind her. He reached around and lifted her hand from the blood pooled on the table.

The blood seemed to pull at her fingers, not wanting her to withdraw. Daniel's hand closed over hers, gently forcing her to form a fist.

"Karlee, we need to—"

She wasn't listening as she took a step closer to the table and gasped as she saw the second man's face. "He's dead," she whispered. The stranger's features were already drawn and white.

Daniel gripped her shoulder, guiding her backward against the hard wall of his chest for support. He leaned slightly to say against her ear. "Trust me, Cousin, you've seen nothing here tonight. Nothing!"

One of the men guarding the windows appeared in the doorway. "You better get cleaned up, Preacher. They'll be here any minute. We'll take care of Jesse."

Daniel nodded and hurried Karlee with him from the room. "I'll explain later." His hand moved over her shoulder and brushed her arm before he released her.

Karlee followed him into the kitchen light. "No, I think you'll—"

He tossed her his jacket. "See if you can get the blood off this," he ordered as though she hadn't spoken.

Karlee watched as he unbuttoned the first few buttons of his shirt, then jerked it over his head. A trim waist, then the molded muscles of his chest appeared before her, reminding her more of finely carved wood than of flesh.

When she gasped, his head snapped up. For a moment, his gaze searched the room, then he met her stare. A smile touched his lips. "Sorry," he said without giving any meaning to the word. "I guess you've never seen a man so undressed." He plunged the shirt into a pan of cold water, then used it for a rag to wash the blood from his chest. "But I've no time to be polite, Spinster Whitworth."

Karlee swallowed. She'd sound like an absolute fool

if she said she had never been so close to a man without a shirt. After all, she was twenty-three years old, not some child. "Of course I have," she lied. "Only they weren't as broad."

Daniel continued to wash. "When I first came to Texas, I worked as a blacksmith. I still work sometimes at night when I can't sleep."

Without asking, he reached for her hand still stained in blood and washed it in the dribble of water from the pump. There was nothing caring or caressing in his touch, only practical, but Karlee could feel her face warm from the way his rough fingers moved across her palm and threaded through her hand.

As he released her, he tossed the wet shirt toward her and turned away. "Is there blood on my back?"

Karlee accepted the shirt as he braced himself against the counter and waited.

"Hurry," he prompted. "I may have only minutes."

She couldn't breathe as she wiped the wet cotton across his muscular frame. Gently, she placed her free hand on his shoulder, as if she needed to balance herself. His flesh was hard and warm, unlike anything she'd ever touched.

He turned and took the garment from her hand. "I know I have no right to ask more of you, but I've no time to explain. A man's life depends on your trusting me."

He was so near she could feel the warmth of him.

"No matter what happens, follow my orders as close as you can and above all, protect the twins. I'll explain later."

She nodded.

"Thanks." He leaned the few inches between them and planted a light kiss on her cheek. "I don't know what I'd have done without you today. Despite all else happening, I knew my daughters were safe."

She watched him hurry from the room, grabbing a shirt off the stack of pressed laundry beside the pantry.

Without really thinking about what she was doing, she began washing the bloody clothes. Within minutes, the stains were gone, but the memory of his skin against her hand lingered.

Trying to ignore the sounds from the parlor, Karlee cleaned the kitchen. When she finally slipped up to bed, she glanced into the downstairs rooms as she tiptoed by. Only one body, the dead one, lay on the table.

She dressed for bed but couldn't sleep. Daniel's words, "I don't know what I'd have done without you," kept rolling around in her mind. She felt useful, truly useful. She couldn't remember a day while she lived with her aunts that she hadn't done something wrong. They were always watching, waiting until she made a mistake, then the aunts had their tale of the day to pass on.

At first light, she slipped silently into her clothes. After checking on the sleeping twins, she hurried downstairs. The Buchanan men and the body wearing Jesse's clothes were gone. In fact, except for Daniel's shirt in the kitchen there was no sign anything unusual had happened yesterday.

There was also no sign of the preacher.

It was time for her to explore. She'd learned early on, being passed from place to place, that the sooner she memorized every detail of a house, the better.

This house seemed a simple plan. Four rooms downstairs, a kitchen, parlor, dining room and small study. Since she knew the wall in the hallway slid open to reveal an arsenal, Karlee watched for other such doors. She took her time, running her hand along the walls as if it were a divining rod. She'd discovered long ago that houses, like people, hold secrets discovered only by the patient.

The study was packed with books and notebooks written in a clear hand. The room was large enough for a desk, one comfortable chair. A chest, like one her father used to have with latches on each drawer for travel, served as a table and footstool. The room was interesting, but held no secrets unless they lay within the pages of books. Karlee moved on.

The parlor was so sparsely furnished Karlee decided she'd seen hotel lobbies with more hominess. One short couch, one chair and a small round table.

Finally, in the dining room, she found what she'd been looking for. A slight pause in the wood. A secret passage, she guessed, or another panel to hide weapons. Or maybe only an imperfection in the building of the room.

Just as she pressed to open the hidden portal, a knock pounded at the kitchen door. Karlee jumped as if she'd been caught in the act of some great crime. She ran into the kitchen and had her hand on the bolt before she hesitated.

"Who is it?" she called, deciding she'd let no one in but Daniel. Frantically, her gaze searched the kitchen for a weapon.

"I'm Valerie, Miss," came a voice spiced with a hint of an accent. "My *madre* owns the bakery. She sends me every Monday and Thursday to deliver bread."

Karlee waited, afraid. She moved to the window and peered through the shutters. A young girl, almost ready to turn into a woman, stood alone. Her midnight hair hung long past her waist and a huge basket rested against her hip.

"Let me in, Miss. I promised I'd deliver bread to the preacher's house first."

Karlee took a deep breath and opened the door.

"Thank you." The young girl hurried in. "The basket was getting heavy." She sat it on the table and began unloading sacks. "I came over early because my *madre* said you'd be needing to know a few things. The reverend's already been by telling us you were here and you were now in charge of his house."

She smiled at Karlee without giving her time to say a word. "Milk and butter are delivered on Tuesday and Friday. *Madre* said she'll tell Jenson you want the same as usual 'til you tell him different. There's vegetables and fruit a block over sold out of wagons every Friday. Madre says to tell you to get there early or the pickings will be slim this time of year. She says she thinks the reverend buys his meat from the Buchanan's place."

"Thank you for all the information." Karlee finally managed to get a few words in.

"I'm Karlee Whitworth," Karlee rushed to say before the girl continued.

Valerie laughed. "Everyone says I never give folks a chance to get in a word edgewise. I figure it's because I speak so many languages. Around my house you had to if you wanted everyone to understand. My *madre* was born in Spain, my Papa's people were from France and my grandfather only spoke Apache from the time his mind started to go."

"Interesting," Karlee had never met anyone quite like Valerie. In a few years she would be a great beauty, but the most attractive thing about her wasn't her high cheekbones and warm sun-kissed skin. Her beauty was in her laughter.

"It's quite a story, how my folks met, but I've no time to tell you today. I've got tons to deliver. I'll come at the end of my rounds Thursday and we can visit."

"I'd like that." Karlee watched the girl pick up the huge basket.

"One more thing," Valerie whispered as she moved to the door. "Be very careful today. You're wise to keep the door locked. My *madre* says trouble is in the air so thick it almost caused the yeast not to rise."

Karlee smiled and nodded a thank you. She didn't put much stock in old cooks' warnings, but her Aunt Violet did, and so did this girl. "I'll be careful. I'll toss salt over my left shoulder and shake the flour flat before noon."

Valerie's face brightened again. "You stop by the bakery if you need anything, Miss Karlee. We're real glad you're here. The preacher is a good friend but he is lonely."

"I promise," Karlee said as she slowly closed the door and threw the bolt. "Thanks."

She returned to the dining room but Valerie's warning kept drifting across her thoughts. Instead of looking for any more secret panels, she went to the foyer and made sure she could slide the false wall open.

As before the rifles were displayed against what must have once been the real foyer wall. Why would a preacher have such a collection of weapons? Why would he need so many? Unless he wasn't exactly what he appeared to be.

Karlee careful closed the sliding panel. She noticed it latched just above her head.

A second pounding sounded from the kitchen. For a moment, she thought of reopening the wall and pulling out a weapon. Then she realized the caller was probably no more dangerous that Valerie.

She ran to answer it before the pounding awoke the twins.

"Who is it?" she called with her hand already on the bolt.

"It's Wolf, Carrot Top!"

His booming voice made her jump.

"Let me in."

Karlee didn't move.

"Hurry up, Cousin! I've got a lady with me who needs to be off her feet."

Karlee closed her eyes, trying to decide what was right. If he were someone Daniel trusted, surely she could do the same. But letting in a half-grown girl was a far cry different than letting in a man, even one she'd met.

She unlocked the door.

A woman, rounded with child, fell into Karlee's arms as the light rushed into the kitchen. The sudden weight of her caught Karlee off balance, and she melted to the floor with the mother-to-be cradled in her embrace.

Wolf stood above them, his hands moving in and out of his pockets as though he'd just been asked to pick up raw eggs with his fingers. He had no idea where to take hold of the puddle of females at his feet.

"Who is she?" Karlee brushed loose strands of dark blonde hair away from the visitor's face. She looked young, maybe a year into her twenties.

"She's Jesse Blair's widow, AmyAnn Blair," Wolf answered in his best effort to whisper. "She wants to make it through her husband's funeral before she delivers. I told her she should take to her bed, but come hell or high water she says she's going to the cemetery."

Karlee looked up at the helpless giant. "What time is the funeral?"

"Daniel's at the cemetery now. The body's probably already in the ground." He ran his huge hand over his face, brushing his beard in every direction. "I ain't no good with women this close to mothering. You got to do something, Cousin, and fast."

Jesse's wife moaned and sat up slowly. "I'm all right," she mumbled. "I have to be at the burial." Tears ran in a steady stream down her pale face. "You have to help me!"

Karlee gently pulled away from the woman, patting

her hand as she moved. "Don't worry, I'll get you there. You just sit here and rest a minute." She looked up. "Hitch the wagon, Wolf. I'll get the twins. We're all going to a funeral."

SEVEN

Daniel watched in disbelief as wolf maneu-vered a wagon around the church and alongside the cem-etery. Cold fear pounded through his veins though he stood in the cool morning air of late February. He'd sent Wolf after Jesse's wife, but somehow the hairy giant had managed to pick up Karlee and the twins along the way.

He wanted his daughters as far away from the cem-etery as possible. If there was to be a fight this morning, blood would be spilled over the graves.

A sparkle of silver blinked off the barrel of a rifle hidden in the trees. In the clear of dawn, it seemed no more harmful than an imaginary daylight firefly. But to the three men lowering the casket, it was a signal that all was ready. The war might be over, but in Texas, under the Union's Reconstruction, defeated men still had to fight to survive. And somehow, with his sense of right and wrong, he'd gotten involved far deeper than he'd planned.

Daniel watched as Karlee climbed down from the wagon and helped AmyAnn Blair. Wolf swung the twins to the ground and eased his Springfield from beneath the bench seat. The girls followed him like baby ducks as he wove toward Daniel and the open grave. They were too young to know of death and would only see the flowers and grass between the headstones.

When Wolf stood within a few feet of Daniel, he whispered, "Best get the burying over fast, Danny boy. I think the widow is already in labor."

Daniel nodded. He knew why she had to be present. No one would believe they were burying Jesse Blair if his wife wasn't standing over the grave. He stared at Karlee as she helped the widow maneuver across the uneven ground. AmyAnn Blair reminded Daniel of his wife when she'd been pregnant. She'd probably been a tiny woman until pregnancy had rounded her into a ball.

Karlee glanced up and met his gaze. For a moment, he glared at her, fighting the urge to order her back to the wagon with the girls. She had no idea what she had just walked into. He had his hands full and now he added worrying about her.

"Why'd you bring her?" Daniel mumbled to Wolf without taking his attention from Karlee.

"When she saw the shape the widow was in, she insisted. There wasn't much I could do without telling her more than she needed to know."

"Let's get started." Daniel frowned and opened his Bible. The three gravediggers acting as pallbearers lined up with heads bowed. "Dearly beloved, we . . ."

The pounding of hooves echoed through the cemetery and Daniel raised his voice slightly. ". . . to bury a husband and a hero of the South."

Federal troops, outfitted in new blue uniforms, raced down the dusty road to the church and galloped straight for the burial sight with total disregard for the graves they thundered across.

The widow began to cry in fear. Karlee placed her arm around the little woman, holding her upright. The twins ran to Karlee's skirt and wiggled into its folds.

"Hold up, Reverend!" a young lieutenant shouted.

"We've got a few questions before you Rebs try to pull your Dixie wool over our eyes."

Daniel slowly closed his Bible and drew himself to full military stance. All he had to do was speak to prove his side of the Mason-Dixon line, but Daniel let the officer have more rope. He'd heard about Lieutenant Logan for a month now. The man must have missed his ration of fighting during the war and was looking for it in Jefferson.

"Bunch of lying traitors, the lot of you," the lieutenant mumbled. He dismounted without noticing he'd stepped on newly planted flowers. "You all should have had the sense to run to Mexico in sixty-five like your governor Murrah."

Daniel waited. The widow's cries were more of pain than sorrow, but the Union officer didn't notice. Karlee pulled both girls against her sides and tried to move the widow backward.

Logan unfolded a paper from his pocket with great ceremony. "I've got orders to arrest Jesse Blair, and this fake funeral isn't going to stop me." He signaled. His troops lifted their rifles. "No one will stop me. Jesse Blair is no hero but only a common criminal."

Daniel stepped away from the open grave but didn't lower his gaze.

The lieutenant glared at him for a moment, resenting Daniel's lack of respect but unsure what to do about it. He motioned two of his men to pull up the coffin. "If this box is empty, as I suspect, I swear it will be full before sundown."

AmyAnn Blair cried out in pain and gripped her middle, but the lieutenant paid no heed. As the coffin reached ground level, he raised his Colt and fired three shots through the center of the pine. "Just in case Blair's playing possum." Logan laughed.

The officer looked disappointed when no one around

the grave reacted except one of the twins, who started crying at the sudden sound.

Karlee lifted the girl to her hip and covered the child's ear with her hand.

Soldiers pried the case open and stepped back quickly, turning their faces away to gulp fresh air.

The Yankee officer moved to see inside the box. But as he leaned close, he gagged and turned away. The smell of death drifted across the morning air. With a handkerchief over his nose and mouth, he moved close again, examining the dead man inside.

"Is this man your husband, Madam?" Logan turned for the first time to the widow.

She cried softly and straightened slightly. "He was wearing that very uniform the last time I saw him."

The lieutenant turned to Daniel. "Something is not right here. There's more that stinks than the corpse. Why wasn't he buried sooner?"

Wolf moved beside the preacher, his rifle riding unseen along the back of his leg. "We decided to wait as long as we could in case you boys wanted to see the body. Figured you'd never believe Jesse was dead unless you seen it with your own eyes."

"He's dead. With that smell he could be nothing else. But something's not right here. I can feel it." The officer stared at Daniel. "I'll be watching you."

Daniel raised his chin slightly but didn't say a word. If the man were corrupt, Daniel would learn the truth faster by letting him believe there were only Southerners present.

"Fall out!" the Yankee yelled as he climbed on his horse. "There's nothing here. Jesse Blair is nothing but worm meat now."

No one moved as the troops rode from sight. Daniel knew what he'd just done would amount to treason if he were caught. When he'd first landed in Jefferson, he went to what the Union Army called the stockade. The locals called it Sandtown. Week after week, he watched innocent men die of fever and exposure. Men who served their state well in the Confederacy. Men who fought beside their neighbors and family, not for slavery, but for the right of free choice as they saw it.

Texas entered the Union as an independent country. Texans figured they had the right to leave. Daniel's greatest revelation had been to learn that the war he and his brothers fought over slavery wasn't about that at all, to the Southerners' way of thinking.

Jesse Blair was just into his twenties and far too poor to have owned a slave. He'd turned from a boy to a man in the middle of battle. He came home wanting to forget the war and start a family. But pride in a dead cause branded him as a troublemaker. Wolf told Daniel most of the things that got blamed on Jesse couldn't have been done by the kid and were probably done by an outlaw named Cullen Baker.

The way Wolf figured it, the only crime Jesse committed was refusing to stop wearing a uniform he'd been told to wear with honor.

Daniel glanced at the grave. The uniform would be buried today and, maybe, so would the problem.

"Danny!" Wolf broke into his thoughts. "We got trouble."

For a moment Daniel glanced back to the road, expecting to see the lieutenant ordering a full charge across the graveyard. But he saw nothing and only heard the clenched whisper of a cry of pain.

Karlee tried desperately to hold up the widow as Daniel ran toward them.

"The baby's coming," Karlee called as she lowered AmyAnn Blair to the ground.

Wolf took two steps toward the women, then two steps back. "What'll we do?" he asked Daniel.

The woman's sudden scream of pain clawed across Daniel's mind. How many hours had he listened to his wife scream with labor? How many times had he wished it had been him who died and not her?

"We got to do something." Wolf paced. "Water! Where'll I find water? I know there has to be water at a birthing."

Daniel didn't move. He couldn't. Her agony held him like granite inside the hell of his memory.

"We have to get her to the doctor," Wolf finally decided. "That's it. There's bound to be a doctor a few streets over on Main."

"No!" AmyAnn begged. "Don't move me. Please. I can't move."

"It's too late to take her anywhere," Karlee mumbled holding her breath with each contraction while encouraging the woman to breathe. She pointed at the three gravediggers who'd been quietly watching. "One of you run for the doctor and tell him to hurry. And you . . ." She raised her head toward the second man. "Go inside the church and bring me any clean rags or cloth you can find." To the third undertaker she shouted. "Get that man buried!"

Her sharp tone brought order to the men. Daniel looked at her, really seeing her for the first time. "Can you handle this?" he asked in a voice that hid his own fear.

"I haven't got much choice." She loosened the woman's jacket. "I've been doing what I had to all my life."

"How can I help?" Daniel asked, marveling at this woman who couldn't make a pancake but thought she could deliver a baby.

"Take care of the twins."

Daniel nodded. She'd given him something he could do.

"What about me?" Wolf roared. The hairy giant looked like he'd gladly be sent on a mission to kill a dozen men rather than have to stand around waiting for the next contraction.

"Get the blankets from the wagon and see if you can wall us in. We don't need a shelter, only a little privacy. And clean that knife sticking out of your boot as best you can. If the doctor doesn't make it fast, I'll be needing something to cut the cord with."

The widow gripped Karlee's arm with bruising force. "It's coming. It's coming. Dear God, I'm so afraid. Jesse! Where's Jesse?"

Karlee worked faster, removing the woman's under-garments, keeping the outer skirt covering her like a blanket. "Now don't you worry, Ma'am. I've helped with many a baby coming into this world," she lied. "This one's just in a hurry."

As Wolf stabbed two shovels into the ground and raised the first wall, the woman's screams shattered the peaceful morning. Karlee noticed birds flutter and fly from the line of trees and thought she saw the flash of sparkle off of metal. If someone was hidden in the trees he would have a front row seat to the birthing.

Karlee stroked the woman's damp hair as she rode the contraction down. "With the next pain, you got to push if you feel the need. This little fellow's knocking at the door, and we have to let him come on out."

The widow nodded in understanding, but her eyes were wild with fear.

"Grip the earth," Karlee ordered near her ear. "The next time you feel the pain take a big handful of Mother Earth and hold on."

AmyAnn's nails dug into the grassy ground.

Karlee accepted a handful of clean clothes from a man already running backward as she reached out. She was vaguely aware of another side of their shelter going up.

Now the women were hidden from all but the distant trees bordering the cemetery.

Karlee raised AmyAnn's hem and watched in wonder. The baby's head slowly appeared. Within what seemed seconds, a tiny body lay in her hands. He was wet and blue and so slippery she could hardly cradle him. She tried several ways to hold him, then decided on lifting him by the feet out of all the blood and water.

The widow relaxed back into the grass. "Is he breathing?" she whispered.

Karlee stared at the liquid dripping from the baby's mouth and nose. "No," she answered. Sorrow choked her own breathing.

She held him in one hand and patted his back, trying to force the fluid from him. "Breathe!" she demanded. "Breathe!" The pace became harder. There was nothing else to do.

After only a few more pats, the baby jerked and breathed, then let out a cry. His jelly-like body took shape as air filled his lungs.

"Yes!" Karlee shouted. "Yes, he's breathing."

She looked up smiling and saw the woman's body contract once more. Warm, sticky liquid and blood seemed everywhere. About three feet above the woman's head a hand poked through the blankets. Nervous fingers held a long Bowie knife.

Karlee giggled. She didn't have to ask who was on the other side of the wool wall. "Thank you, Wolf."

She took the knife and cut the cord binding baby and mother, then tied each end as the baby wiggled atop the pile of rags.

"Where's the woman in labor?" a voice shouted from near the church. "I'm the doctor."

"Over here!" Wolf's gruff holler answered. "Only she ain't a woman in labor no more. She's a mother!"

The doctor stepped between the blankets, glancing

first at the baby then the mother. "Take care of the babe, Nurse," he ordered. "I'll make sure the mother isn't hemorrhaging."

Karlee wanted to scream that she didn't know what to do, but then she smiled, realizing she must have done it right if he thought she was a nurse.

She wiped the baby off and wrapped it in a square of cotton that looked very much like the covering for the church altar. The infant was wiggling and making all kinds of noises with his mouth wide open, just like a newborn bird's.

She crawled up to the new mother and lay the infant at her side. "He's beautiful," Karlee explained. "Prettiest baby I've ever seen."

"Thank you."

Karlee shrugged. "I didn't do anything. You did all the work. I just watched the miracle."

"You're an angel God sent in my darkest hour," the widow announced. "I will be forever in your debt."

AmyAnn's pale hand covered Karlee's bloody one. "Forever your friend," she whispered and closed her eyes. "Forever."

"Doctor?" Karlee fought panic.

"She's fine," he answered quickly, understanding Karlee's fear. "Lost a lot of blood, she has. Best to let her rest for a spell, then we'll see about getting her home and putting her in a proper bed." He lifted the baby. "And this little fellow is grand, just grand. I think I'll nickname him Rip."

"Rip?" Karlee questioned.

"Yeah, Rest In Peace like the headstone here says. He'll be one brave man, I figure. For anyone born in a cemetery ought to have no fear of dying."

He slowly stood, building his height one joint at a time. "Stay with her and little Rip for a while." Without a word, he slipped a small derringer beneath the stack of clothes. "This won't hit nothing more then three feet away, but it should make enough noise to attract attention. I'll tell the men you'll fire if you need help."

Karlee started to shake her head and tell the doctor how much she hated firearms, but then she remembered the Union officer. She didn't want him to return and find her and AmyAnn alone. She could fire a round to call for help.

The doctor looked at her and smiled. "You did a fine job today, but stay alert. The trouble may not be over. I'll be back soon."

EIGHT

KARLEE STAYED WITH AMYANN UNTIL HER NEIGH-
bors came to take the new mother home. The women
might have been afraid to come to the cemetery during
the funeral, but they promised to stay with AmyAnn and
the baby until she was able to get around by herself.

To Karlee's surprise they all took turns hugging her
as if she were a long time member of their circle. Several
promised to come by and visit. She'd never felt so welcomed in her life.

Karlee hugged the new mother and kissed the baby,
then walked home alone in the late afternoon sun. She'd
stuffed the derringer in the pocket of her skirt. "Forget
about it," she told herself, but the thumping of metal
against her leg kept reminding her that she carried a
weapon.

All the day's stress pressed over her body, tiring muscles and making her step heavy. Blood and dirt splattered the front of her dress. Her hair ribbon had
disappeared. She knew she looked a fright, but she'd
never felt so satisfied.

She'd done something right! All day, as AmyAnn
slept in the grass and Karlee cradled the baby, she'd felt
a pride in herself unlike she'd ever known. The doctor

left them in her care, trusting her to do what was right. He'd ordered Karlee not to move the little widow until he finished his rounds and came back to make sure she was strong enough to travel.

When he returned, he told Karlee that if she ever needed a position as a nurse, she had one with him.

Karlee opened the kitchen door, thinking how odd life was. A week ago she had no way of supporting herself, and today she'd been offered her second job. Maybe when Daniel didn't need her to watch the twins any longer, she could visit with the doctor. She was sure nurses didn't make much, but she didn't need much. She could rent a room and live alone.

"About time you got home, Cousin," Wolf boomed in welcome. "I'm worn out playing with these two. Danny left an hour ago, saying he'd be back before dark. I don't think I'll stay alive if I don't get some relief."

Karlee looked past Wolf to the kitchen. Forty field hands could have done no more damage. Pots and pans were everywhere on the floor. Dirty dishes filled the sink.

"Wish I could stay and help you clean up." Wolf stood slowly and moved toward the door as she walked around the room. "But I got to go. A bar fight looks down right restful at this point."

He broke into a run as if he feared she might catch him and make him help. Karlee laughed at the sight of such a cowardly uncle. The twins joined her by dancing around and giggling.

"What have you two and Uncle Wolf been doing?" Karlee brushed their hair with her hand.

One of the girls proudly showed off a paper chain necklace. "We made paper chains. Uncle Wolf didn't know how to make the paste, so he tried lots of ways."

"And he made us jelly sandwiches with eggs inside," the other twin added. "And we drank coffee with cream

from the tea cups. And he said we didn't have to take a
nap, just because."

The first twin nodded.

They didn't need to list their activities for the day,
Karlee could read it on their clothes. Jelly, flour, dried
paste, coffee stains.

"Well, I've got one last treat for you." Karlee reached
for the tub leaning in the corner.

Ten minutes later, she had both twins playing in a
bath of warm water while she washed the dishes a few
feet away at the sink.

By the time she toweled them off, their skin was all
wrinkly, and they were too sleepy to dress themselves.
She gave each a cup of buttermilk with cornbread pieces
crumbled up in it.

They ate their supper, then didn't complain as she
carried them up to bed. Karlee was a little surprised
when both hugged and kissed her cheek goodnight.
Somehow the sleepy little hugs and the buttermilk kisses
made it all worthwhile.

Karlee crossed to her bedroom and changed into
Rosy's huge hand-me-down nightgown. She placed the
tiny derringer the doctor gave her in the top of the chest
of drawers, knowing there was no way the twins could
find or reach the weapon. It would probably be better to
unload the thing, but Karlee wasn't sure she knew how.
Tomorrow, she'd return it.

The house was in shadows when she went back downstairs. Instead of going to the kitchen, she walked across
the entry hall and out the front door, needing the cool
night air. When she was a child she used to pretend the
wind was her mother's fingers brushing her hair at night.

The long porch on the front of the house had been
built with thin slats from the railing to the roof. The
slats let air onto the porch but blocked most of the view
of anyone passing. In the twilight, the area shone like a

dream come to life, with slivers of silver slicing across the night every few inches. At this hour, anyone on the porch could never be fully in darkness, or in day.

Karlee closed her eyes, enjoying the cool breeze and the sounds of evening. Far away crickets and frogs whispered to one another. Somewhere out of sight, horses shuffled and whinnied. She could almost hear the sound of dishes clanking against tables and children being called to supper. A hundred sounds blended together until none were known but all seemed familiar.

A movement in the darkness of the porch startled her. She froze, wishing she'd slipped the derringer into the pocket of her robe.

"Who's there?" She inched toward the door and safety.

"Don't be frightened." Daniel's voice drifted across the night.

Karlee straightened, angry at herself for panicking at the first sound. "I wasn't. I was only alarmed. I thought the porch empty."

"I didn't mean to startle you."

Something sounded different in his voice, a sadness, a longing, a sorrow too great to speak. He could be no more than ten feet from her, but his words echoed as though they crossed ages of time and space.

She moved toward him, unsure of what to do to help. He was a man who wore his sorrow silently without expecting condolence, but the very air around him was humid with unshed tears. She guessed if she tried to penetrate his invisible barriers with sympathy, he'd block her efforts and resent her attempt to trespass into his private hell.

An empty whiskey bottle toppled at her foot and rolled lazily toward the steps.

"You've been drinking," she said the obvious.

"Not enough," he answered.

"I never thought you'd be a drinking man." She could only be honest, for no lies would fit between them in this perfect time separating day and night.

"I'm not." He slipped into the deeper shadows near the house, covering his mood as effectively as he concealed his body. "Maybe I would be if it helped, but it doesn't. How's Jesse's wife?"

"She's fine. The doctor made her rest in the cemetery for a while. With the blanket walls as shade, it wasn't so bad."

"And the boy?"

"He's wonderful. AmyAnn wants me to bring the twins and come out to see her in a week or so. If you have no objection."

He didn't answer.

Karlee moved closer. "I kind of lied about my experience with birthing. In truth, I have been near several times. But all I did was fetch water and carry out soiled linens to wash. I lived with a cousin of my father's once who was a midwife. She'd wake me up to go and tote for her."

She could feel him watching her in the half-light, but he didn't speak.

"It was hard some days. I'd be up with her all night, and her husband would still expect me to work a full day come dawn. He always said I was lazy. Once when he caught me asleep in the field, he refused to let anyone feed me for two days."

"Why didn't you run away?" Daniel sounded as if he didn't quite believe her story.

"I couldn't have been more than eight. I'm not sure. My folks drowned when I was six. There were no birthdays after that. Aunt Rosy figures my age by the number of years since my parents died plus six. Since they died in the fall, I turn a year older just as it starts to get cold."

"Did you live with those cousins long?"

"No, I never lived any place long. I stayed with Aunt Rosy and Aunt Violet almost three years. That's the longest I've ever been anywhere." Karlee stiffened, re-alizing she'd told him too much. "Don't go feeling sorry for me. I don't want roots. I'm not some orphan looking for a home."

He didn't answer. She could just make out his outline leaning against the house in a place where shadows dou-bled over him.

She changed the subject. "I figured out what happened today. You were—"

"Don't speak of it," Daniel snapped. "Don't ever speak a word of what you think happened. We buried Jesse Blair today, and his wife gave birth to a child. That's all that happened."

"Not saying something doesn't make it not happen," she answered, resenting being snapped at. If she didn't know better she would think she talked to a child trying to pick a fight. "You can't just—"

Daniel moved so suddenly she didn't have time to react before he closed his arm around her waist and pulled her to him. One hand covered her mouth while the other held her in an iron grip.

His rough jaw rubbed along her cheek as he whis-pered very low in her ear. "Speaking of what happened could get us all killed, Miss Whitworth. I've been to the stockade where the overflow of prisoners are held. Jesse's brother is scheduled to die in less than a week. If Jesse wasn't dead, he'd be swinging beside his brother."

"But . . ."

He didn't allow her to ask. "Lieutenant Logan wanted Jesse but now it seems his brother will do. Logan saw Jesse as trouble. I think he thought if he could hang Jesse, he'd stop all this undercurrent of hate. Since Jesse was buried, someone has to take his place in Logan's plan and the brother seems to be the best choice although there doesn't seem to be any proof the man had committed any crime."

For a moment, he continued to hold her, pressing her close. She couldn't tell if he wanted to frighten her or needed the nearness of another human, if only in this stiff, forced hug. His heart pounded against hers. His face moved slightly next to her hair. His fingers trailed from her mouth and rested along her throat.

She didn't pull away, but raised her hands to his shoulders and stood on tiptoes to whisper. "Jesse's still alive, isn't he?"

"Yes," Daniel answered finally, in a voice so low she barely heard. "But if anyone besides us knows, he'll be hunted down and truly buried."

"What about his wife and the baby?" She leaned closer to his ear, making sure no one hiding in the shadows could overhear. Someone passing who caught a glimpse of them would only think they were lovers in an embrace. But this nearness was far from an embrace. They were trapped together in the need to keep another man's secret.

Daniel took his time answering her as he brushed her hair away from her cheek. "When she's able, she'll go further west. Past Fort Worth no one thinks about Reconstruction. They've got too many other problems. She'll meet up with him there and start over."

"And the brother?"

"I'll do what I can." He hesitated a moment before adding, "I'll do what I have to."

She had a feeling that this preacher might cross the law if he had to.

"But, thanks to you, Jesse and AmyAnn have a son to raise."

Karlee lowered her head. "I didn't do anything," she

mumbled against his chest, but she couldn't help smiling.

"You did a great deal." He brushed his cheek against
her hair. "And you know it."

She felt his laughter more than heard it.

"Of course, according to the story Wolf is telling in
town, he did most of the work." Daniel's hold around
her relaxed, but he didn't step away. "He delivered that
baby all by himself while Union troops threatened to
charge and shoot. He held his knife in one hand to cut
the cord and a rifle in the other while the undertakers
put poor Jesse in the ground."

Karlee joined in the laughter. All the day had been
like a dream, part nightmare, part fantasy. Now, with
Daniel's arms around her, she could almost believe it
wouldn't end. She felt a part of something . . . or someone.

Hoping she could truly be a part of this world she'd
stumbled into, she whispered, "Do you do this kind of
thing often?"

He lowered his head a little, touching her cheek with
his words. "Would it bother you if I did, Spinster Whitworth? Would you leave and run back to the aunts if all
days were like today?"

Karlee closed her eyes and breathed deeply of the
scent of him. All her life, she'd wished for an ounce of
adventure, and today she'd had a gallon. Hundreds,
maybe thousands of days while she'd worked in the garden, or done laundry, or cleaned, she'd dreamed of living a life on the edge of danger. What Daniel had done
today was good and right, even if it had been against
the law. She could ask for no greater cause than to help
someone. She knew she'd live this day hundreds of
times in her mind. She'd had a taste and would always
long for more.

"No," she answered. "I'll not leave you and run back

to the aunts, if you'll promise to follow one rule."

Daniel stiffened and moved an inch away. "What rule?"

"You'll tell me the truth about the dangers you face. I'll gladly stay home with the twins and keep them safe, if you'll promise to tell me everything that happens. If I know what's going on I can make wiser choices."

Daniel hesitated. "I'm not used to telling anyone. I thought you'd ask to be kept in the dark; it would be safer. Then if you're ever questioned, you'll know nothing. Knowing too much in this part of the country can be as dangerous as not knowing enough."

"The truth, the day it happens, if I'm to stay. That's my price."

"But it's late sometimes before I get in."

"Wake me," she answered. "The truth, the day."

Daniel shook his head. "I'm no good at talking."

"You'll have to learn if you want me to stay." She knew she was pushing him, but she'd live an adventure even if it came secondhand through him.

"All right. No matter what, if there is trouble, I'll let you know. You've proven your bravery today. If I trust you with my children, I can trust you with my life."

"And you'll let me help if I can?"

Daniel smiled. "I'll let you help if you can. But don't expect to live a highwayman's life judging from today. Most of what I do is just paperwork, trying to help people find their footing after being knocked down by the war. Most days here are no more adventurous than back home in Indiana."

"Does Aunt Rosy know about what you're doing here in Texas?"

"No. And I hadn't planned on you knowing about it. We're just a few men trying to prevent a handful of sour Union officers from being harder than they need to be and a few Rebs from taking the law in their own hands."

"A small group of men and one woman," she corrected.

Daniel laughed and moved several inches away. "Shall we seal our bargain with a handshake?"

"No." Karlee felt like she'd just stepped to the edge of a cliff, and it was time to jump. "With a kiss," she blurted out, taking the plunge.

He wasn't touching her, but she could sense his body tighten. She'd gone too far, she knew it. But there was no turning back now.

"Karlee," he finally found his voice. "I can't feel anything . . . there can never been anything between . . . I'm dead inside since . . ."

"I don't care," she hardened herself against the rejection. Her hands balled in fists. If she were changing her life to one of adventure, she might as well start now. "You don't have to feel anything and neither do I, but I've made it to the ripe old age of spinsterhood without ever having a man kiss me. I'd like you to correct that problem, and I'll never ask again for such a favor."

Daniel remained stone.

"I know I'm not one of those pretty, petite, young girls every man longs to embrace, but I'd still like to at least understand what the act's all about."

He didn't answer, making her feel dead-toad ugly. She tried to shrink a few inches shorter and wondered if she'd combed her hair at all today.

"You do know how, don't you?" she asked, more angry at herself for proposing such a thing than him for hesitating. But there was no way to back down now.

"Of course I know how," Daniel answered, equally as angry.

He probably didn't want to kiss her any more than anyone else ever had, but she was twenty-three, and since no man had made a move, it was time she did the asking. He didn't seem to find her all that repulsive—

after all, he'd pecked her on the cheek. That almost counted, she reasoned.

"Then kiss me and seal the bargain between us. Once, just once, but it has to be real."

He didn't respond, and she realized her "good idea" was crumbling like an overbaked corncake. Embarrassment rose, firing into her face. She'd probably burn him if he did touch her. He must be so shocked by her request, he couldn't speak.

"Oh, forget it!"

Karlee ran into the house, welcoming the cool darkness that closed around her. Tears blurred her vision as she hurried toward the stairs. When was she ever going to learn to keep her mouth shut? The aunts were right. She was an idiot destined to make a fool of herself at every opportunity. If the aunts were here, this story would keep them laughing for a month.

Her hand touched the railing a moment before Daniel caught up with her. He closed his grip over her shoulder so suddenly the force pulled her backward against him.

She cried in surprise when he twisted her around and flattened her back against the wall. Fear danced in her blood as he held her upright and leaned toward her.

"We seal the bargain. Once and for all, you'll be able to say you've been kissed, Spinster Whitworth." Angry words brushed against her cheek as the weight of his body pressed against her.

His mouth closed over hers, hard and strong. His body pushed her to the wall.

Karlee fought to free herself. This wasn't what she wanted, not at all. She'd seen couples kiss at weddings and a few times when they thought no one was watching. A kiss was soft and petal-light on the lips, not bruising hard. He wasn't supposed to press her mouth against her teeth. He must know even less than she did. Or maybe he'd forgotten? Or maybe he wanted to hurt her?

As she struggled against his hold, Daniel's fingers moved down her arms, pinning her limbs with the length of his body. She jerked her head away, but his followed. When she tried to cry out, he invaded the inside of her mouth, taking her breath away.

Tears of anger bubbled in her eyes as she tried to kick at his legs and jab at his chest.

After a while, she stopped struggling, exhausted at the wasted effort for the force of his advance never lessened.

When she went limp in his arms, he loosened his hold on her and moved his fingers into her hair. With her head held still, the kiss changed, softened. He no longer demanded her response. He silently asked.

Karlee closed her eyes and let the wave of sensations wash over her. The pounding of his heart against hers. The feel of his strength all along her body. The warmth of his hands on her face. The demands of a kiss unlike she'd ever dreamed existed.

She relaxed in his arms, letting him guide her. He was not taking, but giving her what she'd requested. A kiss, a real kiss. It was so much more than she thought it might be. She'd never be able to forget. She'd been kissed, fully and completely kissed.

His hands turned gentle, almost hesitant, as he touched her face and brushed her hair back. She joined in the embrace doing as he did, letting his lips teach her with tender patterns. He brushed her arms, catching her hands and bringing them to rest on his shoulders. When she raised her arms to circle his neck, he sighed and leaned into her body, pressing her gently along the length of him.

The kiss changed once more. A fire seemed to build between them. A fire that might consume them both. He wove his fingers in her hair and closed his hand into a fist as though he needed to hold on while the kiss raged through them both. The taste of him was a part of her now. The feel of him, a need growing as he pressed against her. Even her breathing matched his as though they would forever be the same now they'd found the same rhythm.

Just when she thought she'd surely died and floated up to heaven, the kiss ended as suddenly as it began. He shoved away from her with such force she felt the wall creak.

"There." He was out of breath as if he'd been running for miles. "You've been kissed."

Karlee waited. It couldn't be over! It couldn't be. Surely he wanted to continue as desperately as she did.

She opened her eyes.

He was gone.

NINE

Daniel stormed from the house and circled it twice before he figured out where he was going. He couldn't believe what he'd just done. He kissed Spinster Whitworth! And not a polite, formal peck, either. He'd really . . . fully . . . completely kissed her.

He walked to the barn calling himself every kind of fool. How could he have done such a thing? It was crazy. He must be insane to allow it to happen.

Sliding the railing that concealed a room, Daniel vanished into a hidden corner of the barn he called his own. Since he'd been a boy, he'd always needed a place to disappear away from the world. It wasn't much, little more then a shack. Sometimes, he practiced his sermons here, sometimes he drank. Here he could drop his guard and be himself, or better yet, be nothing for a time. Not preacher, or father, or widower . . . just a man.

He pulled a velvet blue hair ribbon from the folds of a book and told himself he still loved May. He loved and missed her with every ounce of his being, just as he had the day she died. She'd been his private angel, his reason for living, his Heaven on earth.

He twisted the ribbon around his finger, but it didn't seemed to hold as tightly as it had in the past.

How could he have kissed Spinster . . . Daniel's frown deepened. Maybe since he'd had his tongue in her mouth, he should call her Karlee.

In the three years since May died, he'd never looked at another woman. He didn't want to care about another and run the chance of losing again. All he wanted to do was live with May's daughters and May's memory. That was enough for this lifetime.

He'd never asked anyone out, or hinted that he would. He'd never even danced with a saloon girl, or flirted at a social.

But he'd kissed Karlee!

He had to be honest with her. She had a right to know he'd never marry her. He never wanted a wife or any more children to have to raise alone. His life and his bed were too full of memories to allow another woman in.

Daniel slipped the velvet ribbon back in between the folds of a book.

If he had to be honest with Karlee, he had to be honest with himself as well. He'd never kissed a woman the way he'd just kissed Karlee. Never!

When he'd decided to kiss her, it had just been something he planned to get over with and go on. He could understand how a woman who'd never been kissed might want to know what it was like. He'd thought to deliver a hard, cold, impersonal kiss and be done with it.

But before he'd gotten up enough nerve to do it, she demanded he forget the request and ran away. And he'd snapped. First she told him what to do, then she told him not to do it.

Daniel paced around the dark room wishing he could shove the walls away. Everything in the barn was too small. Everything in the house was too small. Suddenly this town, this state, this planet was too small.

Without looking back, he left the barn and headed toward the edge of town. He'd walk out his frustration, then he would come back and work in his shop until his eyes refused to stay open. Then, maybe, he'd be able to get a few hours of sleep before he apologized to Karlee.

He almost ran until he reached Big Cypress Creek. As always, the ancient trees welcomed him. Their shadows invited him to disappear into the folds. The sounds of the night were not slight and recognizable as they had been when he was a boy in Corydon, Indiana. Here, the calls of the night were a hundred low cries beating together in a rhythm dark and forbidding. The water along the shore didn't lap in welcome, but ebbed and flowed as if wanting to pull all life into its depths.

"May," he called, knowing he'd see her face in the water. "May."

He stared harder. The wind whistled through ancient branches, calling her name to Heaven.

"May!"

For the first time, he couldn't summon the face of his sweet, young wife. She'd been his life, the reason he did everything. He forced his eyes closed and tried to picture her in his mind, but tonight the image wasn't clear. She was only a shadow moving through his memories. He remembered their long talks, but the subjects escaped him. He thought of the times they'd laughed, but couldn't think of the reason. The nights of lovemaking drifted thought his mind, but the feel of passion no longer throbbed his body with need.

She'd been tiny with dark hair and eyes. He'd called her angel. Daniel could think the thoughts in his mind, but the image of her wouldn't appear. She had a smile just for him that no one else ever saw. She never raised her voice. She made his world complete.

"May," he whispered, but the water remained dark.

Daniel sat on the edge of the water and lowered his head in his hands. He'd lost her all over again.

Karlee didn't know whether to be happy or sad. She'd been kissed, that was for sure. Only the man who'd done the deed ran.

She looked at herself in the tiny mirror over her chest of drawers. In truth, she could find nothing pretty or particularly ugly about her. Her nose was straight but definitely no button. Her chin was strong but not pointed. Her eyes seemed the right size. And her hair, when she kept it combed down, looked almost brown.

But something must be very, very wrong with her, she thought. Daniel was a strong man, seasoned in war and widowed in love, yet he ran like a rabbit at the first round being fired. He'd done his duty and kissed her. Maybe all her relatives should give him a medal for that. After all, it was the first time she'd gotten a kiss since her parents died. A few times kinfolk had almost kissed her, but the affection had been lost in the air a few inches from her cheek.

But Daniel had really kissed her. Once on the cheek when they'd been in the kitchen and once fully. In her life, these few days in Texas could be classified as a regular epidemic of affection.

Karlee crawled into bed. She couldn't wait for tomorrow to come. Good or bad, it was bound to be interesting.

Her prayers had been answered. Adventure had found her at last.

Deep into the night, Daniel raised his head. Strong winds circled across the creek and harassed branches above him. The far away smell of a campfire danced in the wind, and the creek rustled with tiny ripples as if irritated by a change in nature.

Daniel stood, sensing trouble. He glanced toward the quiet town like a knight of old would have watched a sleeping dragon.

At first, all looked well, the outline of buildings along the water. Jefferson was a small village with wide streets and gas lights on every corner, just like a real city.

Then he saw it. A flame too great to be lamplight. A flame that lit the midnight sky to early dawn.

"Fire!" he yelled as if there were someone to hear.

He broke into a dead run toward the flames that seemed to grow as he identified them. Orange and gold flickers danced along a two-story structure and jumped to other buildings as though escaping the blaze. By the time he reached the outskirts of Dallas Street, the flicker had grown to a monster.

The dragon had awakened.

Several buildings were ablaze. People ran everywhere, some saving their property, some in fear, some looting warehouses in the dawn-like light of chaos. In this town of wealth and trade, no one had thought to organize any kind of fire department. Panic spread faster than flames.

Daniel watched a whirl of ashes climb toward Heaven like a mini-tornado. The twister caught in the wind and funneled high in the sky. Ashes, still red with life, scattered across rooftops like crimson rain. The fire was spreading. In a few blocks it would reach his church. Another block his house. Daniel turned and ran.

He plowed through his kitchen door without slowing down. "Karlee! Get the twins. You've got to get out of here."

He was halfway up the stairs before she opened her door. "Will it spread?" She was buttoning her blouse, telling Daniel the fire had already awakened her. "How long do we have?"

"I'm not sure. It looks like at least a block of downtown is already burning. I'll hitch the wagon. Can you drive to the Buchanans' place? Most of the men are gone, but Deut and his younger sons are still home. You'll be safe there."

"I can," Karlee answered as she ran for the twins' room.

He hoped she wasn't lying. There was no time for discussion. He hitched the team and pulled it to the back of the house. She hurried out with a twin in each arm. A large bundle hung over one shoulder like a cotton picking sack.

"I threw what I could of clothes in a sheet." She surprised him with her calm. "We're ready."

Daniel helped them into the wagon. The fires pushed midnight away. The air was summer hot even though it was only early March. As he kissed each child, he thanked Heaven for the cradle he'd attached to the back of the wagon's bench. The twins would be safe as Karlee gave her full attention to driving.

"Aren't you coming?" She lifted the reins with skill.

"I have to do what I can here," he answered. "I'll be all right." He closed his hand around hers in reassurance. "Take care of the girls, Karlee. Don't worry about me."

Before she could answer, a rider pounded into the small yard on a horse that looked half-mad from the flames. The horseman reined with expert skill, fighting the animal's desire to remain at full gallop.

Wolf yelled for Karlee to wait as he climbed off his mount and slung a body he carried over his shoulder. "Hold up," he stormed toward them. "I got something you need to get out of town."

He slammed the figure wrapped in a saddle blanket into the back of the wagon. "You're going to Deut's, right?"

Karlee nodded, speechlessly watching the blanket wiggle.

"Tell Deut to watch him close, and whatever he does,

don't untie him." Wolf stepped back and wiped his brow. "And if he can, be gentle with the man. Don't hurt him."

Daniel raised an eyebrow as a bare leg kicked free of the blanket, but asked no questions of his friend.

"Tell Deut I'll explain more later. He already knows some." Wolf slapped the wagon team into action and yelled, "Remind him if the fellow gets free, it'll take ten men to hold him back down."

Karlee had her hands full fighting the reins. The horses smelled the fire now and were edgy. She glanced back at the twins riding in their box. They were both watching the blanket tossing in the back of the wagon with a mixture of curiosity and fear.

Another bare leg kicked free.

She drove the team faster than she'd ever driven horses. Luckily, the road was clear and smooth. The girls were safe. She didn't want to even think about what might happen if whoever was under the blanket managed to get uncovered.

She tried to ignore the noise from the back of the wagon. Finally, she slowed and dared a glance.

Standing in the center of the wagon bed, balancing as best he could was a full-grown, mostly-naked Indian. He fought wildly against the ropes binding him.

Karlee let out a cry and slowed more. She knew what he was. She'd heard of Plains Indians and how they were wild cold-blooded killers. This must be one. His hair was long and black, his eyes fiery coals, his body, all that she could see, which was most of him, was the warm brown of the earth.

"I'm going to be killed," she mumbled even though the man's hands were tied behind his back and his mouth gagged. "We'll be murdered right here on the road and no one will find us because of the fire and we'll be buzzard meat. I've read the dime novels, I know," she said to herself. "The wild savages have to kill a few people and the women and children are always the first to go."

She glanced again. He'd taken a step toward her and the twins. One arm was almost free of the ropes.

"Sit down!" she yelled the order as if she expected to be obeyed.

He looked like he could beat them all to death even with his hands tied.

"I got a gun!" She tried to make her words a growl.

He didn't show any sign of understanding, or caring. His eyes blazed through her with such hatred the stare might kill her. His chest heaved up and down like a bull preparing to charge.

Her grip of the reins tightened. She stared back at him and tried not to look frightened out of her skin.

The twins began to cry.

He had no right to scare the children. Anger mixed with the fear in her blood. "Stop frightening the children!" she screamed at him.

The twins cried louder.

Wolf had told her to be gentle with the monster he'd so carelessly thrown into her wagon. She'd not have the girls frightened out of a year's growth by any man, monster or not.

"I said sit down!" She slapped at the horses. Maybe she could make it to the Buchanans before he killed her. She'd never win in a fight, but she could drive.

A sudden jolt shook the wagon, but Karlee didn't slow down. She slapped the horses again and glanced back to see how near death hovered.

The man was gone!

Karlee pulled the leather so hard she felt it cut into her palms. "He must have jumped out," she said aloud. "I'll tell Wolf that's what happened and we'll be done with the wild man."

She looked at the girls, who were both shaking their heads as though they'd come loose during the ride.

"He didn't jump out?" Karlee shook her head at the same rate.

"He bounced up," one said with a sniffle.

"And over," the other finished.

Karlee turned the team and headed back. After a few yards, she stopped and tied the reins. "Stay still, girls," she ordered as she climbed down from the bench. "I'd better go the rest of the way back alone."

Clinching her fingers around the derringer in her pocket, she ventured forward. If he wasn't already dead, she might just shoot him for being such a bother.

She hadn't gone twenty feet behind the wagon when she saw the prisoner lying in the center of the road. The moon shone off his bare skin. He lay flat with his arms and legs outstretched, his ropes circling his body loosely.

"I've killed him! Wolf said be gentle, so I killed him." She ran to the man and lifted his mud-covered head. "First, I almost kill Wolf. Now, I murder his blood-thirsty savage."

"No one in their right mind jumps out of a traveling wagon on their head," she reprimanded, as if he'd had a choice. "I didn't kill you. You killed yourself. I told you to sit down."

She leaned down into his face and felt his slow breathing against her cheek. He was still alive!

Karlee gripped his arm and dragged him back to the wagon. He didn't seem to weigh all that much. He must be her height, but he was thinner than a lean crop scarecrow. Now that he was limp as a rag doll, he didn't seem nearly so frightening.

When she reached the wagon, she dropped his arm and tried to think how to get him in the flat bed. It didn't seem right to put her arms around his bare body. He wasn't a child she could just pick up. But there was no help. Unless she planned to be on this road all night, she had to do something.

Reaching for him, Karlee encircled his chest with her arms. He smelled of rancid bacon grease and mud and the sad end of a cow.

She let go, dropping him back into the dirt with a thud.

The twins laughed. They thought she was playing a trick on the near-dead blood-thirsty savage.

Karlee grabbed the blanket Wolf brought him in and repackaged the strange man inside. Then she tied a rope around and around the middle. If the stranger got loose again, he'd be taking the saddle blanket with him.

Slowly, she lifted him once more, trying not to breathe as she rolled him into the wagon bed.

"I said, sit down!" she repeated. "A man should really listen to a woman."

He fell into the wagon with a thump.

"Now stay there," she ordered. "I'll have no more trouble out of you."

Karlee circled the wagon and climbed back on the bench. "Sit down, girls," she ordered, slapping the horses with the reins.

Both girls plopped down in their box.

No one said a word until they reached the Buchanan farm. By the time Karlee stopped the wagon and climbed down, lamps were being lit inside the main house and one of the younger men came running from the barn.

Deut was the first on the porch. He seemed lost in trying to straighten his suspenders for a moment before he spoke. "Is that you, Miss Karlee?"

"It's me," Karlee answered, thinking she'd had enough excitement for one day. She lifted one twin to the porch. "The town is on fire. Daniel sent me here. Can we stay the night?" She was too tired to say more than was necessary.

Deut just stood there fiddling with his suspenders as though his brain hadn't awakened yet. He needed time to understand her words.

"Of course you can," Granny answered from just behind her aging son. She slapped Deut on the back with her cane, priming him to act.

Karlee handed Granny the other twin.

The woman added, "I'll take the girls to Willow's room. Sammy's away on the drive, and she'll enjoy you all as company. We'll put a cot in with her for you to sleep on."

"Thanks." Karlee let out a long breath and started to follow, then remembered her captive.

"Before I go in," she backed toward the wagon with Deut finally awake enough to join her. "I think you better have a look at who else I brought, Mr. Buchanan."

Deut picked up the lantern and peered over the wagon's side, as did three of his sons who'd joined them on the porch. One of the men scooted the roll of blanket to the edge and untied it carefully.

The blanket slipped away from the Indian's face as Karlee repeated Wolf's instructions.

To her surprise, none of the Buchanan men looked shocked at the near-dead, near-naked, blood-thirsty savage she'd brought.

"I almost killed him," Karlee whispered. "He fell out of the wagon."

She watched as Deut tenderly brushed the black hair away from the sleeping man's face then ran a hand over his scalp checking for cuts or bumps.

She saw the prisoner's features for the first time in the lantern light. He was little more than a boy. Out cold, he wasn't near as frightening. Several days growth of beard outlined his deeply tanned and dirty face.

"I didn't mean to," she added, trying to remember if she'd ever seen a picture of a Plains Indian with a beard.

Deut pushed the dirt from the savage's face. "Lift him up carefully, boys, and take him to the cellar. Tie him three times what you would a normal man before you doctor him. Then bolt the door. One of you stand watch all night. No one opens the door unless we're all standing there."

Karlee watched the sons followed their father's orders. One cradled the young man in his arms and walked toward the cellar while another grabbed a bucket of water from the well. The third passed Karlee, mumbling something about getting bandages and food.

"Is he a friend?" she asked. The caring was there, but they planned to tie him. Maybe he was a madman they all knew who only thought he was an Indian. She'd heard of families keeping insane relatives tied and locked in cellars.

"No," Deut answered. "I never seen him before. Wolf told me a few days ago that he was holding him in one of the warehouses down by the waterfront until the other McLains arrived. My guess is the building was burning, or Wolf wouldn't have taken the chance of moving him. I'm surprised he let the boy out of his sight."

"The chance? What chance?"

"If that young man gets free, he'll do whatever he needs to do to escape, including kill anyone who might try to get in his way. And knowing the McLains like I do, I'd bet anything Wolf and Daniel would be right in his way. They plan to keep him here until Daniel's brothers arrive."

"But who is he?"

"Did you ever meet Daniel's older brother, Wes?"

"No," Karlee answered.

"Or his sweet little wife, Allie, who'd been captured as a child by the Apache?"

"No."

"Well, you just met her brother."

TEN

By the time Daniel returned to the fire, men were organizing, but they were ants fighting a raging wall of destruction. Building after building fell. One block of downtown was already ashes, and three more burned in a frenzied rush. Men fought, then pulled back again and again to make a stand farther out.

The smoke stung his eyes. The heat slowly toasted his skin, but still Daniel struggled alongside businessmen and dock workers trying to save a fraction of their world.

When the blaze reached his church, Daniel doubled his efforts, moving to the front of the bucket line. A yellow glow behind the glass in the door warned it was already too late. The frame might be standing, but fire had reached the core of the building through the roof.

With a sudden anger, cast in frustration, he charged, ramming the glass with an empty bucket.

Glass shattered an instant before he felt wind rush past him toward the fire. The flame seemed to draw a breath just moments before an inferno roared out of the building at full charge. The building shuddered in death and crumbled, feeding the fire below.

Daniel felt a blast like an iron-fisted blow, lifting him off the ground with heat and glass and smoke. Pain was everywhere as his vision flashed to white light. Fire washed over him in a crushing tidal wave of crimson. Darkness followed, blanketing the white crystal brightness before him. All went black. Only the pain—agonizing, gut-wrenching pain—remained.

He rolled with the blow, vaguely aware of Wolf yelling his name. Then there was no pain, no fire, nothing.

Dawn spread across the sky in shades of violet and white-blues. Karlee leaned on the railing of the Buchanans' porch and drank her third cup of coffee. She'd been up over an hour. In a house so packed with people, everyone awoke with the first person and only slept when all slept.

She'd tried to busy herself by helping with breakfast. She made a great effort to learn to make biscuits. But Karlee doubted she fooled anyone. Worry over Daniel filled her thoughts, making simple conversation difficult.

The Buchanan women were a grand lot. They carried each topic on without her when she faltered. They understood. Daniel might be off fighting a fire, but most of their men were working the spring cattle drives. None mentioned the fire in town, or why Karlee had spent the night, just as none spoke of the dangers of a drive.

Granny treated Karlee's inability to cook as a personal gift Karlee gave to her. The old woman rambled on about all her secret recipes.

The house was bursting at the seams with people. Three Buchanans had married within the past few years, bringing wives beneath the roof. The four remaining single Buchanan boys had been delegated to sleeping in the barn. Most of the morning talk was about how several couples would build houses as soon as the men got back from the cattle drives to the west. The Buchanans might be rich in children and land, but they needed money to build.

Finally, Karlee escaped onto the porch. She drank her coffee and watched the black cloud rising from the direction of town. Daniel was somewhere in the ruin, and she could do nothing but follow his orders.

The twins ran onto the porch, laughing as Willow waddled through the door.

"Don't you girls giggle at me," Willow yelled, "or I swear I'll have a boy to pester you both."

The girls circled around Willow, patting her tummy gently.

"Now, none of that." Willow plopped down in the only chair on the porch. "Don't go waking up the baby." She spread her hand over her abdomen and cooed, "I don't have long before I'll have a little one to hold. Another month Granny guesses."

Karlee liked the woman with her childlike mind and open smile. For her, the world was a simple place with no fear or doubt. She was loved and cared for here.

The pregnant girl's gaze met Karlee's. "Thanks for bringing the twins out. I love playing with them. I came to live with Mr. McLain the day his wife died on account of my still having milk from a baby I lost. He took me away from a pa who beat me regular. Mr. McLain was never nothing but good to me. I'm mighty pleased to see he found you."

"He's a good man." Karlee didn't know what else to say. Daniel had made it plain she was here to just look after the girls. Willow was guessing wrong if she thought there was anything between the preacher and Karlee.

"He's a measure better than good. He told me that if my Sammy don't treat me right, I can come back with him and the twins any time." She blinked away a tear and smiled. "That sounds like somethin' a real papa would say."

"Does Sammy treat you well?"

"Yes, Ma'am." Willow giggled. "He says I can have as many babies as I want. He'll see they're all loved and fed. A man don't get no better than that, I figure."

"No better," Karlee answered.

A wagon's rattle sounded up the road. Both women moved to the steps. In the dawn light it took a few minutes to make out the forms.

Karlee spotted Wolf. His clothes were covered in black, and he was alone. He looked out of place atop the newly painted army supply wagon he drove. The struts bowed up over the wagon's bed, rounding the top, but the canvas had been rolled a foot above the bed to allow both shade and ventilation. Dread hit the bottom of Karlee's stomach.

"Willow, would you mind taking the twins out back to play?" Karlee said the words, but her voice sounded strange even to her own ears.

Willow nodded and took the girls' hands. She didn't look back or question the request. "When a caller comes this early, it ain't nothing but bad news," she mumbled as she passed. "I'd just as soon not know."

When Willow was out of sight, Karlee gave her full attention to Wolf's approach. Why wasn't Daniel with him? Why wasn't Wolf on his horse? Each question added fuel to her worry.

The smell of burned flesh reached her before the wagon pulled to a stop. Karlee was off the porch in two steps. She took a glance at Wolf's sad expression and rushed to the back of the wagon.

Something was wrong. Very wrong.

A wet army blanket spread over the outline of a man's body resting in the shadows of the tarp covering.

Karlee couldn't stop the cry that escaped her lips. She reached for the blanket. "Is he dead?" she whispered.

"No." Wolf eased his way down from the bench. "He's not burned as bad as some. We fought most of the night. A few hours ago, the fire seemed to lash out from nowhere. Daniel couldn't have gotten out of the way. He took a raging blow of fire straight on."

"But why . . ."

Wolf waved her question away, knowing what she'd ask. "I stopped by the hospital and they didn't have room for him. Told me to take care of him as best as I can myself."

Karlee slowly lifted the blanket. Daniel lay out as straight as the dead man she'd seen in the dining room a few nights ago. His eyes were closed. His face the red of a deep sunburn with tiny cuts along his cheek and forehead.

She lifted the blanket further. His hands rested across his chest. They were burned and bleeding, and his fingers were so swollen they didn't look quite human.

"Doc gave him something to help him sleep. He said keep him out of light as much as possible, and keep him quiet. When he comes to, he'll be in a great deal of pain." Wolf rubbed the tired muscles of his arm. "I wasn't sure what to do with him. He needs care, and I got my hands full. I can't leave the wild boy here much longer, not with most of the men gone. There's no telling what he might do if he managed to get free. But Daniel . . . he . . ."

Karlee stood very still. She knew there was more. "What else?" she demanded.

"He's blind." Wolf choked on the words. "The doc ain't sure if it's permanent or not. He made me swear to keep him in shadows. And there's a deep cut in his leg. It's been treated and wrapped."

Karlee watched her hand shake as she replaced the blanket over Daniel's face. Several Buchanans were on the porch waiting for orders. There weren't enough beds now for everyone at the farm. Daniel would need a room and quiet to recover. Here she'd have help, but he'd get little rest.

Karlee glanced at the porch crowded with caring people. They'd take Daniel in, but he might keep them awake.

"Is our house still standing?" She looked back at Wolf hoping for the right answer.

He nodded. "But the town's a mess. It'll be days before there's any order."

"Then we take him home."

Wolf frowned. "But you can't take care of him and the twins all by yourself. I'm not sure I can help much. I've got my hands full until Daniel's brothers get here. They should be well on their way. I wired them two days ago about the wild boy the Rangers brought in. Until they arrive, I've a prisoner to watch. I've got to keep him from killing me while I try not to kill him."

From the porch, Granny shook her head in disapproval. "You can't take care of the preacher and the twins, Child. Leave the girls here until he recovers."

Karlee looked at Daniel's sleeping form. "He'd want his daughters with him," she voiced her thoughts. "Thank you for the offer, but I'll manage. You've got your hands full here."

Granny nodded. "Then I'll get you medicine for his burns. And as for his eyes, put a cool cloth on them three times a day and leave it for a spell. Don't let no bright light reach him for at least a week. If the day gets warm, wet sheets and hang them across the windows. It'll help the breeze be cool. Any heat or light will bother him."

Karlee listened carefully as she hurriedly gathered her things.

An hour later, Wolf set up a bed in the sparsely furnished parlor and carried Daniel in from the warming sun. The preacher still hadn't opened his eyes, but he thrashed restlessly in his sleep.

"I have to go." Wolf shook his head as though hating to say the words. "I don't want to leave Danny, but it's not fair to have old Deut watching the wild kid. There ain't enough menfolk left at the farm to hold him down if he gets untied."

"I understand. We'll be fine here."

"While I've got the wagon, I'll smuggle him back into town and keep him in the barn loft. It ain't the best place, but don't you worry, I'll tie him good. There are some folks around, if they knew he was here, who would kill him on sight."

"But why?"

Wolf shook his head. "I've lived most of my life with half the world hating the other half. During the war it was Rebs and Yanks. Men who looked just alike except for the color of their uniform. That didn't make no more sense then this does. Spilling blood over land when there's plenty to share."

Karlee knelt beside Daniel's bed. "I know Daniel would help you if he could."

"You're right, Cousin. But now, you got to help him. There ain't no one else. You'll be lucky if the doctor makes it by once a day. Do what you have to do, but keep Danny alive."

Karlee promised bravely, but as Wolf left the weight of her task almost overwhelmed her.

She fed the twins quickly and left them playing with their tent-table in the kitchen. It was time to see what she could do for Daniel.

"We'll be fine." She lifted his burned hands. "I can do what needs to be done."

Slowly, with great care, she lowered one hand into the pan of cool water beside the bed. Daniel jerked in pain, but she held the hand fast.

"Granny gave me some salve," she whispered not really caring what she said, only wanting to calm him. She washed Daniel's charred flesh in cool water. At first she was reluctant to touch him, but slowly she grew accustomed to the feel of him.

"She says she made it from elderberry bark, lard, rosin and beeswax. She made me repeat the mixture twice so I could make it if I had to."

Daniel moaned as she worked. Carefully she placed his hand atop her apron and patted it dry with a clean cloth. Then, feather light she began rubbing the salve over his hands.

His eyes never opened, but she knew he was awake. At first he stiffened when she brushed her fingers over the tender flesh, but slowly his hand moved in rhythm to her caring touch.

"Wolf said four blocks of the town burned, with damage to the blocks all around. Some of the cotton on the dock is still burning but everything is under control."

She circled to the other hand still talking. Karlee didn't want to think too much about what she was doing, she only wanted to help him and then leave him in peace.

"He says some folks are blaming the fire on a man who came here right after the war, presuming to control the former slaves. He was quoted as saying the whole town would have to burn before the freed men got their rights."

Daniel seemed to relax as she talked on about every detail she could remember of what Wolf said and all about her adventure last night. The fire might have been wild and crazy, but sleeping in a room with an eight-month pregnant woman and two three-year-olds was no picnic.

He made no comment when she wrapped his hands

in cotton strips. She hesitated only a moment before starting on his face.

With two fingers wrapped in damp cotton she began to clean. At first he froze at her touch just as he had with his hands, then relaxed, allowing her to pull slivers of glass away from cuts and brush his hair free of ashes with her fingers.

When she brushed her finger over his lips, now swollen, he opened his mouth slightly and she remembered their kiss.

"That was some kiss," she said. "I'll probably never be kissed like that in my whole life ahead. I wished I could have told you thanks. You needn't worry about me asking again. If there's one thing I am it's true to my word. I said I'd only ask once. But I got to tell you preacher, you sure don't do nothing halfway. I always figured preachers to be the milk toast on the banquet of life where passion was concerned. You proved me wrong."

He didn't answer. She wasn't sure he was awake but she had to keep talking if only to calm herself. She was so close to him she could feel his breath on her throat as she worked. In another time, another place, what she was doing, running her fingers through his hair, might be considered a very forward act.

"Would you like me to help you pull your shirt off?"

He didn't respond.

"Well," Karlee reached for her sewing basket. "I guess I could cut it off. I'd probably hurt you if I tried to take it off any other way. Plus there's not enough cotton left to patch the thing."

She placed the scissors at his throat and began cutting away the material. There were red splotches on his arms and chest, but no more burns or open cuts. She washed him as best she could. His skin felt warmer than hers, as though a bit of the fire remained.

"When I finish, I'll get you something to eat. I brought back stew and biscuits from Granny."

His bandaged hand covered hers as she ran a dry towel over his chest. She froze. He *was* awake.

"How long 'til dawn?" he whispered in a low voice.

Karlee blinked away tears as she glanced at the bright afternoon sun coming in from the parlor windows.

"I don't know," she answered as calmly as she could. "But I'll be right beside you until then."

"Good." He relaxed against the white sheets, his blond hair reflecting the sun's rays. His breathing grew slow, and he drifted into sleep.

Even with the cuts and burns, she couldn't help thinking he was one of the handsomest men she'd ever seen. When he was awake, there was something in his manner that held folks at arm's length. But asleep, she could see a young man who must have once dreamed and laughed, and loved.

Karlee leaned close, resting her head lightly against his chest. The solid rhythm of his heart welcomed her while he was asleep as his arms never would when he was awake.

"All right, Lord," Karlee whispered. "I got about all the adventure I can handle right now."

ELEVEN

THE NEXT FEW DAYS PASSED WITHOUT SLEEP FOR Karlee. She took care of the twins, doctored Daniel as best she could during the day and cleaned at night. Long after midnight, when all the work was done, she curled into the chair beside Daniel's bed and tried to rest a few hours before starting over.

On the second evening, Valerie passed by on her way home from her last delivery of bread. The girl stopped to talk and noticed Karlee was doing laundry by the firelight. Without a word, she began to help, cutting the chore in half.

After that Valerie was a constant and greatly appreciated guest. She'd drop off fresh baked goods each morning. Then she'd usually stop by to play with the girls for an hour while Karlee changed Daniel's bandages in the afternoon. Since Valerie said her grandfather had been Apache, Karlee trusted her with the secret of the man being held in the barn loft.

From that moment on, the young girl gave Wolf no peace. She wanted to see the savage. He finally conceded to allow her to take the boy water at noon, nothing more. She might hate the idea that he was tied up; but Wolf convinced her that if he were free, the boy would be dead within the hour. There were people in town who would shoot him on sight.

"I promise." She jumped around the kitchen in delight. "Nothing more. But, I have to know you're not hurting him. I'll never sleep another second until I know."

Wolf growled at Karlee. "The only reason I'm agreeing to this is because Adam and Wes are bound to be here tomorrow. If her mother knew I was letting Valerie near the savage, she'd slice me up and serve me between two pieces of fresh bread. But Adam and Wes will take him off my hands for good when they ride in. I've only had the kid a few days and I've already done a month's worth of worrying."

"What harm can come?" Karlee reasoned. "He's tied up, and you're usually within shouting distance."

While Wolf issued a final warning to Valerie, Karlee slipped into the parlor to check on Daniel.

It bothered her that he lay so still. She'd expected to have to fight to keep him resting quietly. But since the doctor bandaged his eyes, he didn't even respond most of the time when she checked on him. He swallowed a little water from time to time, but he wouldn't allow her to feed him and he made no effort to feed himself. She felt as if all his senses had been wrapped with the blindfold.

Each time the doctor came by to rebandage his leg, Karlee watched silently from the shadows. The cut would leave a long scar across a leg that already bore the marks from a bullet he'd taken in the war. Wolf said Daniel had worked for over a year after the shooting until he could walk without a limp.

She knew Daniel had asked the doctor to do the bandaging because he didn't want her to see his scars. Though he was a full-grown man now, she suspected he must have been in his teens when he was injured and not far out of them when May left him with two daughters to raise.

No wonder the darkness seemed so complete around him. It wasn't as if he'd given up, but more like he'd made a stand in his midnight world. He was a proud man who resented his helplessness.

As she watched him from the parlor door the next dawn, she made up her mind to somehow break through the wall he'd built around his private hell.

"I brought you some coffee." She knelt by the bed so that she could be closer to his level. "I didn't even burn it this time. Wolf says it's near drinkable."

Daniel didn't respond.

"Would you like me to hold your head up and give you some?" She touched his shoulder. He turned his head away. It was going to be another day without communicating.

"Fine." She sat the cup down beside him and began unwrapping his hand. Each day there was less blood on the bandages. The salve was working. Even the swelling had gone down.

"You don't have to talk to me," she said as she worked. "You don't ever have to talk to me again for as long as you live, but you do have to see the twins. They've been asking about you every few minutes. I'll not go another day keeping them away from the parlor."

She wasn't sure he was listening. It seemed he'd hidden deep into the caves of his mind and never planned to come out.

"I don't need your conversation. I'm used to being all by myself. I've gotten where I like it that way, so don't feel the need to be chatty with me around. Most folks just rattle on with nothing to say, anyway."

Karlee bit her tongue realizing she was doing the same thing. But talking kept her from thinking about the feel of his hand beneath hers and wondering what it would be like to touch him when there were no wounds to treat. She couldn't help but wonder whether his caress would be gentle if he ever chose to touch her.

When she finished with the bandages, she hurried back to the kitchen to make the girls' breakfast, calling herself a fool for even thinking about something that would never happen.

The twins loved Valerie's warm fresh bread with butter and cinnamon piled on top. When they were both around her, there seemed a pleasant chaos that drew her full attention.

"After we eat." Karlee laughed as they tried to help prepare the bread. "We'll go in and have a quiet-as-a-mouse visit with your father."

One twin looked interested in seeing her father while the other sprinkled more cinnamon in her hair than on the bread.

"We'll be quiet," the first one promised. "We'll use our go-to-church voices."

"If you do, I'll work on your dolls."

Ten minutes later, the girls sat beside Daniel's bed playing with the scraps of material Karlee had cut for rag dolls. They asked about their father's bandaged eyes but didn't seem overly concerned. All they needed to know was that he was near.

One stood by his bed and kissed his blindfold to make all the hurt better. When she moved away, he whispered, "Cinnamon."

Karlee braided rag strips together in a bracelet of red and blue and tied it around the girl's wrist. Then she made another of yellow and green for her sister. Both loved their bracelets.

Karlee knew she now had a way of telling them apart.

They chattered and talked as she worked on the dolls. When they talked to one another, Karlee couldn't understand them clearly. It was as though they had their own language, secret from the world. Every few minutes, one would stand and pat her father, reassuring herself he was there.

Daniel didn't speak, but turned his head toward them, listening to their voices. His strong features never moved a fraction to smile, but she knew they brought him peace.

Near noon, Karlee collected the scraps and the half-completed dolls. "Say good-bye to your father. It's time for lunch. He needs to sleep a while."

The twin with the red and blue bracelet stood and kissed Daniel while the other said good-bye.

To Karlee's surprise, he leaned into the golden curls of his daughter. "Good-bye, my little cinnamon angel," he said.

All day, Karlee watched the two girls. Now that she knew them apart, she noticed how very different they were. The one with the smell of cinnamon in her hair was quieter, letting her sister take the lead every time. She was also the most loving in her manner.

The other twin, with the yellow and green bracelet, was far more questioning. Her words came faster and more clearly. As night fell and they ate their supper on the back porch with Valerie and Wolf, this twin asked one question after another about the stars. She said that when she grew up she wanted to be a star.

By the time she dressed them for bed, Karlee had began calling one Starlett and the other Cinnamon. Though they were asleep, she knew she'd never think of them as twin again. Even without the bracelets, she'd know which one was which. They were so different, she found it surprising she hadn't noticed.

When she tucked them in and went back downstairs, Wolf was sitting beside Daniel's bed. The huge, hairy man twisted his hat in his beefy hands as if determined to strangle the covering before it could get away.

"We've got to do something," Wolf's gravel voice filled the hallway. "Gerilyn heard about the fire and wired the sheriff as to your and the twins' condition. Old Hank didn't know no better than to wire back the truth. Like a snake smelling spring, she's on her way."

When Daniel didn't answer, Wolf added, "If Gerilyn sees you like this, she'll insist on taking the twins back to New Orleans. She may say it's just for a while, until your eyes heal. Once she has them, there will be hell to cross to get them back."

Daniel didn't respond. Karlee couldn't help but wonder if he was awake enough to care. She moved to the foot of the bed and watched his face carefully for some clue. Wolf swore under his breath, telling the world how he felt about the woman's arrival.

"Do you know May's sister?" Karlee asked Wolf.

The big man shook his head. "I've just heard about her. She got all upset when he brought the twins, as newborns, to Texas. Swore she'd find a way to take them from him. She's visited a few times, but I've managed to be several hundred miles away. I figure if she don't like the McLains, finest men I know north or south, there isn't much chance she'll like me."

"I've met her." Karlee let out a long breath. "She was three years older than May and, as far as I know, she's always gotten everything she ever wanted. When I met her, she considered May . . . and me . . . nothing more than pests."

"What else do you know about her?" Wolf had given up trying to talk to Daniel.

"I know she married a well-to-do man, so if she had the girls, she could take good care of them. She has no children of her own that I've heard about. Aunt Rosy corresponded with her from time to time." Karlee frowned. "From what I remember when I visited, Gerilyn wouldn't talk to May most days. And I was invisible.

It's surprising that she'd want to raise her sister's children. I'd never thought of her as a nurturing woman."

"If you ask me, she doesn't," Wolf grumbled. "Gerilyn just can't stand Daniel, that's all. Seems he married May, the youngest girl, before she was eighteen, leaving Gerilyn to have to bear the social shame of being the old maid in the family. I heard Daniel talk about how she tried to stop the wedding."

Karlee wasn't surprised at Gerilyn's hatred. She remembered being given some of the girl's hand-me-downs when she was leaving their house. Gerilyn's mother had insisted on packing the dresses, now too small for her daughter, in Karlee's box. All the time she packed, she apologized that they couldn't keep Karlee as long as planned, but "things come up, you know."

Gerilyn resented having her dresses passed on to someone else. Two days later when Karlee opened the box, the dresses had been cut to shreds. The book May gave her had been ripped in half.

The memory frightened Karlee, but never so much as it did now. For now it wasn't a few dresses at stake, but two little girls.

"What can we do?" Karlee fretted.

Wolf shook his head. "If Daniel's brothers get here, they might can stall Gerilyn. After all, they've as much right to the girls as she has, since Danny has no wife."

"But he'll never give up his girls. Not to anyone." She brushed her hand across the bandage covering Daniel's arm. Maybe he was using all of his energy trying to think of something. Maybe he was too wounded to know there was a problem.

But one thing she knew, if there was an ounce of life left in him, Daniel McLain still cared about his daughters. Even blind and hurt, he wouldn't give them up.

"We have to think of something." She understood why he held on so tightly. They were all he had. She saw him as far richer than her, and knew she'd fight dearly if the twins belonged to her.

"He could let Gerilyn have them now and then go after the twins when he recovers. I'd ride by his side." Wolf's tone was dull. They all knew he voiced no option, only a fear of the inevitable.

"No." Karlee patted Daniel's hand lightly. If she hadn't met Gerilyn as a child, she would never believe a woman would do such a thing. Even at eleven, her eyes had been the crystal blue of one without a heart. "He can't let her take them away."

Wolf stood, wanting action. "I'll go check on the boy out yonder. Maybe if I walk, my brain will work better and I can think of something." He stormed out without another word.

Karlee knelt beside Daniel's bed. She knew he was awake. She told herself she didn't blame him for not talking. There was nothing to say. A blind man was no match for Gerilyn.

Leaning her head against the mattress, Karlee fought back the tears. She knew what it was like to grow up in a home where no one wanted her . . . where no part of the house belonged to her . . . where love and caring were things she watched but never felt.

Silently, she cried, wishing she could reach out and comfort Daniel but unsure what he'd do if she tried. She pushed her tears onto the sheet and swallowed any sobs.

A rattle sounded beyond the kitchen and Wolf was back wrinkling his beard with a huge smile. He slapped his leg with such force Karlee jumped.

"I got it," he boomed. "You could marry Danny."

"I don't think so." She wiped her eyes and tried to guess if the man could have gotten drunk in the time it took him to walk to the barn and back.

"Of course you can. You're not married, he's not married. That's the way it works. If Danny had a wife, there'd be no question about the twins staying."

"No." Karlee began shaking her head and moving away. "I don't plan ever to marry. We'll have to think of something else. He wouldn't want to be married to me anyway." Daniel had run when he kissed her. There was no telling what he'd do if he had to marry her.

"You care about him and the twins, don't you?" Wolf paced beside the bed with a finger in the air, obviously his vision of a great orator.

"Well, yes, but I'm not the kind of woman he'd want in a wife." Karlee had to put an end to this idea before Daniel did. Better that she said no, than hear it from him.

"Do you care about the man?" Wolf frowned like an angry father and brought his finger down to point at Daniel. "You must know. You've been living under the same roof for near a week now."

"Well, yes, I care about him. He's a fine man."

"You figure some better man will ask you? Some man with no children to raise that ain't your own? Some man with more to offer?"

"No!" Karlee resented his statement. "I love the girls. I want to help raise them. No better man would ever ask me, but don't you see . . . he deserves better than me." There, she said it. That should put an end to Wolf's idea.

She didn't want to have to list all her shortcomings; she'd heard others list them all her life. Daniel was an intelligent, brave man who could have his pick of women. He didn't need to be saddled with her. She was too big, too clumsy, too . . .

As she pulled away, a bandaged hand caught hers.

He didn't try to argue or reason. He only held her hand and pulled her slowly back to the side of the bed. She tugged, trying to break free. Then she saw the bloodstains along the cotton covering his knuckles. The effort to hold her was costing him dearly.

She stopped struggling and moved close, allowing him to guide her.

"You said," he took his time with each word. "You said you'd stay with me until the dawn."

Karlee straightened, her pride keeping her silent. She didn't have to tell him what a poor wife she'd make. He could probably guess. To marry him with no love between them was crazy, by far the most half-baked scheme she'd ever been part of.

"You don't have to worry about better or worse, it can't get much worse than this," Wolf mumbled. "He hasn't got much money so the poorer is a sure bet. And in sickness has already fallen."

"Shut up, Wolf, I can talk her into it without your help." Daniel's voice sounded forced, drawing all his energy. "Marry me, Spinster Whitworth."

Talk her into it—she almost laughed. Never would she have guessed that anyone would try to talk her into getting married. She never thought the question would come up, but now and then she'd allowed herself to dream. And in her dreams the only answer was yes.

Daniel cleared his throat. "But one thing. I'll have no make-believe marriage, even to keep my girls. If you say yes, you'll stay by my side until death separates us. A real marriage, a forever marriage or no marriage at all."

"Until death separates us," she repeated his words. What a fine way to end a promise.

An hour later they were married by the Methodist preacher from a church across town. The bride wore her best faded dress. The groom slept through most of the service. There were no rings, no flowers and no wedding night in one another's arms.

. . . but there was forever.

TWELVE

IF KARLEE HAD EXPECTED A HUSBAND TO BE MORE talkative than an employer, she was greatly disappointed. Daniel didn't say a word when she brought breakfast on the first morning of their marriage. She made no attempt to feed him, but when she returned an hour later with the twins, the food had disappeared.

She sat beside the bed, her sewing spread across her lap while the girls played on the floor between Daniel and the windows. As she'd expected, one twin, the one she'd sprinkled with cinnamon at breakfast, leaned close and kissed Daniel.

"Ah, cinnamon," Daniel whispered.

"Yes, Papa," she answered. "That's me."

The chubby hand of the other daughter patted his arm. "Karlee says I'm Starlett, Papa. 'Cause I ask too many questions to count, like the stars. When you going to take that thing off your eyes?"

"Starlett," Daniel nodded. "It fits you. I couldn't have chosen better names myself."

He cleared his throat. "Girls, I married Karlee last night."

"We married Karlee?" they both squealed.

"Does that mean she's going to stay?"

"Will she get big and fat and have a baby inside her like Willow?"

"Yes, she'll stay, and no, she won't have a baby." Daniel said the words as if they were final, telling Karlee just what kind of marriage they would have. He wanted no more children.

She tried to keep her hands moving across the material though she knew he couldn't see her. What had she expected? That he suddenly loved her just because he married her? That he'd take her in his arms and to his bed?

Only a fool would think such a thing. She told him she didn't want a husband when she'd arrived, and he made it plain he didn't want a wife. What they'd done last night had been for the twins' sake. The forever part had just been said because he was a man of honor. They both knew, no matter the reason, there would be no turning back. A divorced preacher would never lead a church, and a divorced woman would be looked down on in any community.

Like it or not, they were tied together until death. Without love.

About mid-morning, Valerie arrived and offered to take the twins to the porch for a picnic. As soon as the girls were gone, Karlee collected all she needed to redo the bandages on Daniel's hands. She thought of asking if she could care for his leg as well, for the wrappings needed cleaning, but she decide to wait at least until they'd been married a full day. Changing bandages on his hands was one thing, on his leg would be quite another.

He didn't say a word as she soaked the stained bandage and slowly pulled the cotton away from dried blood along his knuckles.

"I'm sorry." Newly hardened scabs came away with the cloth. "I'm trying not to hurt you."

"It doesn't matter," he answered blandly.

He didn't move as she washed his wounds and spread salve over his fingers. The strength of his hands fascinated her. She gently rubbed the soothing medicine in far longer than was necessary.

After she'd wrapped the wounds with clean cloth, she hurried to the kitchen and returned with a pan of hot water and a razor she'd found in a drawer.

"I thought I'd shave you, Daniel." She called him by name for the first time. "In case we have company. I'll be careful of the cuts."

A brow lifted above his bandaged eyes, but he didn't comment.

Karlee had seen men shave a few times. She'd even watched the barber shave a man while she was waiting for him to pull one of her teeth. He did a fine job of shaving the customer, but she felt sure he pulled the wrong tooth in her mouth. And to add to the injustice, he'd charged her two bits for the crime.

From that day on, she brushed her teeth religiously with baking soda and elm twigs gnawed on one end. She never planned to have another barber put his hand in her mouth, again, and any teeth she lost would have to fall out on their own.

Karlee lathered up Daniel's strong jawline with the flare she remembered the barber used.

The first swipe of the blade was perfect. The second disastrous. Blood dotted his chin as if he had a bad case of the measles.

Daniel jerked away. "Did you ever shave a man before?" he snapped.

"No," she admitted. "I never had a man to shave, before you."

"Well, I won't be around long if you keep spilling my blood so freely."

His voice was hard, but she thought she saw a hint of
a smile beneath the lather.

"I'll try again."

Two strokes later, he jerked and grumbled again. "My
jaw curves, the blade doesn't. Please leave some hide,
Madam."

"Your skin is sensitive from the fire's heat." She
leaned close to work on his throat. For a man of few
words he spared none in criticism. "I'm not cutting you
that deeply. I've no wish to make myself a widow after
one day of marriage, but you are starting to look like
you're related to Wolf."

He didn't answer. She couldn't be certain he was
breathing. Surely she wasn't frightening him with her
shaving.

"What is it?" she asked.

His Adam's apple moved up and down slowly, but he
didn't move.

"Don't worry, I won't slit your throat. I think I may
be getting the knack of this shaving."

He didn't move.

"You've nothing to fear," she reassured.

"Spinster . . . I mean, Mrs. McLain." His words were
almost thick enough to be liquid. "Would you mind not
pressing against my chest?"

For a second, she wanted to laugh. She wasn't hurting
this big man by pressing on his chest. She'd seen the
wall beneath his shirt, touched it. He was solid as stone
with muscles.

Then, she noticed *what* was pressing on his chest. Her
breasts. She'd leaned too close.

"Oh." She was thankful he couldn't see her embarrassment, for her cheeks were on fire. "I'm sorry. I didn't
notice."

"I may be blind," he explained. "But I can still feel

what is pressed against me." He seemed almost as embarrassed as she.

Her hands shook so badly she couldn't hold the blade level. How could she have done such a thing? She wasn't used to being around men and certainly not this close to one. Her breasts had always been too large, getting in her way since she was twelve. Usually, she wrapped them tighter within a bodice, but this morning she'd worn her loosest dress.

His hand covered hers, steadying her strokes even though he couldn't see where she aimed. He was in as much of a hurry to get the shaving done as she now was.

It seemed hours before she finished and wiped the last of the lather from his chin.

"I'll be more careful next time. Both with the shaving and the other," she said with determination. "You do look a sight more presentable."

"I'll wait until I get this bandage off, and shave myself next time," he answered coldly. "Or I'll grow a beard."

Wolf bellowed through the door before she could apologize again. When he rounded the corner and took one look at Daniel he yelled, "Did the savage get loose and try to kill you, Danny me boy?"

"No." Daniel didn't seem to appreciate the humor. "Karlee shaved me."

Wolf shook his head. "Your face is the best reason I've seen yet for staying single and keeping a full beard. If she'd cut any closer, you'd be missing a nose."

Karlee picked up the pan and razor. "It's not that bad," she defended.

"That bad! I've seen scalped men left with more skin." Wolf watched her hand holding the pan carefully.

She thought of tossing the pan of soapy water at him but decided against it. After all, she'd be the one to have to clean up the mess. "Want any lunch? I was about to bring Daniel some."

"Sure." Wolf sat down by the bed. "One thing I will say, Danny boy. Your wife is a better cook than she is a barber."

Daniel pressed the towel to a trail of blood running down his chin. "That's not saying much. But I'll give her one thing, she tries. She's not a woman who lets not knowing stop her from trying."

Karlee closed the kitchen door and tried to figure out if Daniel's last statement had been a compliment or a complaint.

Thirty minutes later, when she returned with a tray of food that could be eaten easily with one's hands, Daniel's bleeding had stopped. She thought of reminding Wolf that several of the cuts on her husband's face had been made by flying glass and not her razor but decided the subject was best left forgotten.

She had no doubt whenever Daniel thought of her shaving him, he'd also think of the way she so boldly leaned against his chest. He probably thought her some scarlet woman pretending to be naive. After all, she'd acted shamelessly so many times in the past few days, he must think her the dumbest woman he'd ever met. Or worse, a flirt.

No. Hugging him that first night could be considered flirting. Maybe even the kiss she asked for. But what she'd done while she shaved him could only mark her as a brazen harlot. Karlee wasn't sure exactly what that encompassed, but she felt certain she fit the criteria. The first morning after he'd married her, Daniel must be sure she was a fallen woman with countless sins to account for.

She set the tray down and planned to exit as soon as possible when their conversation drew her.

Wolf was explaining how he'd wired Adam and Wes,

Daniel's brothers, for a second time and again had no reply. They were either on their way, or there was too much trouble for them to come. Adam was a doctor in Fort Worth with a wife and new baby to worry about. Wes lived in the middle of nowhere on a ranch that took the better part of a day to ride across. They might not be the easiest men to get a hold of, but Wolf knew they'd come as fast as they could once they got word.

Gerilyn Whitworth Landau was another story. She and her husband had a winter place in New Orleans. They might already be in town looking for Daniel. It wouldn't be long until she found him. And once she did, Wolf was convinced, trouble would rain aplenty.

"I thought I'd bed down in the barn tonight. The boy is getting tired of my hospitality. I don't think he knows why I'm keeping him captive. Probably thinks I plan to fatten him up for a winter kill." Wolf shook his head as he bit off a chunk of apple. "It's just a matter of time before he figures out some way to get free. When he does, there's going to be the devil to pay, I'm afraid."

"It wouldn't do to have Allie on her way and me have to kill her brother before she gets here," he added as he finished off the apple.

"He knows why you have him tied." Valerie's voice came from the kitchen doorway. The young girl stood with her arms folded as she leaned against the frame.

"You think so, little lady?" Wolf laughed. He obviously irritated Valerie by treating her like a child and not the woman she thought she already was.

"I know so," she replied calmly. The girl knew Wolf well enough to have no fear of the man. "I told your Apache why he was here when I took him water yesterday."

Wolf knocked his chair over as he stood. "He speaks English?"

"No." She smiled. "I speak Apache. Or at least

enough to communicate. My grandfather made sure I could, just as my father insisted I know a little French."

"And what does our friend have to say?" Wolf looked doubtful.

"He says he has no white sister." She glanced to see if the twins were listening, then lowered her voice. "And he says he will kill you all and sprinkle the ground with your blood before the next full moon."

"Did he tell you his name?" Wolf was starting to believe her story.

"Niccohoma," she replied. "It means 'without fear.' "

"I don't want you going near him again," Wolf ordered as he realized just how dangerous the boy, still a year short of being a man, could be to all of them. "He might just kill you, little lady."

"He said he wouldn't harm me. The blood of his people flows in me." Valerie held her head high.

"But the blood of the Apache doesn't flow in that kid. He was captured during a raid on a settlement northwest of here. I talked to an Apache who remembered the day they dug him, half dead, out of a plowed field and took him home with them like a war prize."

"But how can you be so sure he is the brother of Allie all these years later?" Karlee interrupted.

"The Apache described the same scene Wes's wife did of seeing the bodies of her family and others piled in front of the settlement. Then everything was burned. The old Apache that told me about John, not Niccohoma, also said another warrior carried a little girl about the same size over his saddle. Only he went to another village and by the time the two warriors met again to hunt, the little girl had been traded. Like I've heard of them doing, they adopted the boy as a son and traded the girl as a slave."

"I told him you thought him a captive," Valerie answered. "He said you lie. He is Apache. He has no memory of any other world. Of any other people. His mother is the wife of a chief and she has no sons but him."

"He can say anything he wants, Valerie, but that doesn't make it true." Wolf didn't like to be called a liar, even in another language.

The kitchen door popped suddenly as if the wind caught it and threw it open in a wood-splitting snap.

A cry, not quiet human, shattered the air, frosting the stillness with fear. In one heartbeat, everyone turned toward the sounds from the kitchen and cried one thing.

"The twins!"

THIRTEEN

Karlee bumped into the back of Valerie, and Wolf ran into them both as they bolted into the kitchen. The twins were nowhere to be seen, but the wild savage Wolf had called John stood next to the pump with a knife in each hand.

His body glistened with sweat. His eyes were wild with fear and hate. Bloodred rope burns circled his wrists, and dirt covered his body almost to his shoulders.

"Now, hold on there!" Wolf ordered. "Put down those knives, son."

The boy raised the blades, preparing to fight.

Karlee held Valerie's shoulders, pulling her back a few inches to the relative safety of the doorway.

"No!" The girl jerked free and ran deeper into the room. "I can talk to him. He'll listen to me."

Niccohoma glared past her to the others crowded at the door. He obviously considered the girl little threat. But she drew his attention when she spoke Apache.

Wolf inched his way along the wall. A knife would never stop a man like Wolf Hayward. Judging from the boy's gaze darting from Wolf to Valerie, he guessed as much.

Someone from behind Karlee gripped her shoulder

suddenly, causing her to jump and cry out almost as loudly as the captive had when he burst into the kitchen.

The intruder hardly appeared to hear her. He backed against the counter and prepared to make a stand.

"Help me," Daniel commanded, pulling himself beside her.

His hands were wrapped and the blindfold covered his eyes. He didn't seem to be able to put any weight on his injured leg, but still he moved forward.

Karlee slid her arm around his waist and donated her strength to his useless quest.

"What's happening?" he whispered. "Are the twins all right?"

Karlee glanced around the room and noticed the blanket tent wall move slightly. "They're safe in the tent for now. Valerie is talking to the boy, moving closer as she speaks. He stands at the pump."

Karlee tried to keep her voice low so the Apache wouldn't turn his anger toward her. She wanted to argue that Daniel should be back in bed, but she knew it would be wasted time. "What can I do to help?" she asked.

"Get us between him and the twins." Daniel's powerful arm pulled her against him for strength.

"Can you move with me?"

"Yes!" The word came between clenched teeth.

Guiding Daniel slowly forward, Karlee tried to remember to breathe. The table waited only five feet away. When they reached it, he leaned on it, allowing the wood to take as much of his weight as he dared.

"He'll come toward me," Daniel predicted. "When he does, it will be your one chance. Grab the twins and run to the front door. Don't look back, just run."

"He has a knife in both hands."

"Good." Daniel almost smiled. "I can take several blows and still fight. With a weapon in each hand, he'll have no way to guard. I might get in a few swings. It'll give you more time. If he's been trained for battle, he's been trained to kill the men first. Even wounded I must be killed if I stand to fight."

The savage spit words angrily at Valerie in Apache, arguing with her.

"Valerie, be careful!" Karlee cried. If she could have turned loose of Daniel, she would have run to the girl and pulled her back. Valerie was getting far too close. Her youth made her unable to see the danger of death so near.

She took no heed of Karlee's cry. For her, there was only the boy, almost man, almost warrior. But for now, only a boy.

She waved her hands in front of him as if erasing what she heard him say. To the girl's credit, she faced the man with no sign of fear. In fact, she placed her fists on her hips and raised her voice in argument. Her boldness might be the only thing keeping him from attacking.

"Where's Wolf?" Daniel leaned closer to Karlee depending more on her strength.

"He's moving along the wall. He's near the pie safe now, halfway."

Karlee watched as Valerie took a step closer and pointed her finger at the savage's bare chest. She'd been raised in this wild country with generations of pioneers in her blood. "One savage with two kitchen knives isn't going to kill my friends!" Valerie screamed, more angry than frightened. Rapidly, she translated her own words into Apache. "And I'm not going to let you commit suicide by rushing Wolf."

The words of several languages blended as she spoke, drawing the boy's full attention.

Karlee's low voice told Daniel of each movement. They stood at the end of the table, protecting the twins. He held his head high, listening. If the savage sprang toward them, he would not be taken unaware.

"Talk to the twins." He fought to maintain his balance. "Tell them not to be afraid and to be ready if you call them."

Karlee nodded. She knew if Daniel spoke above a whisper, he would draw the boy's attention. Yet the youth paid no more notice of Karlee than if her voice had been a gnat's buzz around the room.

The savage seemed fascinated with Valerie. Karlee wasn't sure if he thought the girl brave or crazy. The beauty of several cultures flowed in her along with the fire.

"Where's Wolf?" Daniel brushed Karlee's ear with his words.

"Six feet away, on the left," she answered. "He's ready to move."

"When I yell, step back and dive under the table with the twins." He touched her hair with his cheek. "And stay there."

Karlee opened her mouth to argue, but there was no time.

Daniel braced himself against her and shoved hard, almost knocking her off her feet. In one step, he covered a third of the distance between the table and the sink.

"Move away, Valerie!" Daniel yelled stumbling toward the well-armed intruder. "Move away now!"

The sight of a blind man with wrapped hands charging across the room caused the boy to hesitate. Karlee had no doubt he would have fought another. But he was like everyone else in the room. All he could do was stare as Daniel made his way across the floor like a raging bull.

All were frozen except Wolf, who jumped from his corner like a mountain lion. Before Daniel was within a knife's blow of the savage, Wolf slammed against the kid at full force from the side. The two tumbled, knives spilling across the floor.

Karlee ran to Daniel's side, helping him out of the

way while Wolf and the boy wrestled. Arms and legs thrashed across the kitchen in a wide path of destruction. Valerie screamed for them to stop. No one listened.

In all the madness, fear, and panic, Karlee heard the front doorbell chime ... a touch of normality in the midst of insanity.

It rang again.

The thought flashed that she should answer it. "Excuse me," she'd say. "We can't entertain company right now. We're in the middle of being scalped and murdered in the kitchen."

"Don't hurt him!" Valerie shouted as she tried to hit Wolf on the back. "Don't kill him. Oh, please, Mr. Wolf, don't kill him."

Wolf wrestled his way on top of the savage. "I'm not trying to kill him, girl. I'm trying to keep him from killing me! Maybe you should tell him a few things. Like, stop trying to kill poor old Wolf."

Suddenly, Daniel's weight slid against Karlee's side. He'd used all his energy. Blood from his leg pooled at her feet. His effort to distract the savage had cost him.

Karlee fought to hold him upright but his weight made it difficult. He grew heavier as consciousness left him.

As they crumpled to the floor, she twisted, trying to take the fall first so that his injured body would land atop hers.

Without warning, the kitchen door flew open. The crackling pop of wood splitting was becoming a familiar sound in the room.

Two men covered in dust and leather charged into the room, their Colts drawn.

Daniel's unconscious body made it hard for Karlee to breathe or see all that was happening. She twisted, but couldn't free herself. The world began to spin as a man with a long scar across his face knelt above her.

The stranger smiled as if he'd simply come to dinner.

"Howdy, ma'am." He touched the tip of the barrel of his Colt to his hat. "Mind if I have a word with my brother here?"

He rolled Daniel off Karlee as a tiny woman stepped timidly through the door. She had golden brown hair and huge blue eyes that reflected her fear. Though her riding clothes were as dusty as the men's, she looked far too fragile to ever belong to the scarred man.

Karlee scooted to a sitting position and stared at the three strangers who invaded her home. Not a one said he was sorry, or seemed to feel the need to introduce themselves.

"Adam!" The scarred one cradled Daniel in his arms. "Over here!"

The other man, now kneeling beside Wolf and the savage, stood. "Hold him down a minute, Wolf. I'll check on Daniel and be right back."

Wolf grunted loudly and slung sweat off his hair. "Oh, sure. No problem." The youth fought against Wolf with all his strength. "Never mind that he's bitten me twice. I'm starting to feel like supper."

The second dust-covered man, who'd been called Adam, squatted beside Karlee. His gaze leveled to Daniel even though he spoke to her. "What happened to him, Miss?" Strong caring hands moved along Daniel's frame.

"He was burned several days ago in a fire and cut by flying glass on the leg." She didn't have to ask. She knew the man called Adam was a doctor. His every movement told her so. "I think he reopened the leg wound when he tried to charge the savage."

Adam examined Daniel's leg, pulling away useless bandages covered in blood. "Is there somewhere I can work? This needs care immediately."

Karlee scrambled to her knees. "We've got a bed for him in the parlor. I'll help."

"Allie, will you get my bag," Adam requested of the woman still standing in the doorway. "Wes, help me carry Danny into the parlor." Adam glanced at the girl crying in a corner.

"Valerie?" He tested his memory from times past when he'd visited. "Can you help?"

She wiped her eyes. "Yes, sir." The woman in her had disappeared. Only the child remained.

"Can you bring hot water to the parlor? Lots of water."

"Yes, sir." She straightened, gaining control of herself now that she had a mission.

"We can help, Uncle Adam." Starlett's head appeared from beneath the blanket. "Is Papa all right? Is Wolf hurting our savage? Can I have a drink of water?"

"Your papa will be all right with your help." Adam smiled at the twins while he and Wes lifted Daniel off the floor. "Stay close to Valerie, girls. She'll get you a drink then let you help. And no, Uncle Wolf is only playing with your savage."

No one paid any attention to Wolf's snort.

Karlee hurried to ready the bed. The two dust-covered men moved through the house with their patient, bumping into walls and doors on their way.

"When did the kid get so big?" the one called Wes mumbled to no one. "He weighs a ton."

"Can you take the sight of blood, Miss?" Adam glanced up at Karlee as they lowered Daniel to the sheets.

"Yes," she answered. "I've been changing his bandages for days." Karlee knew she should have added, "except for his leg," but that didn't seem important.

Adam removed his jacket and hat while Wes returned to the kitchen. The woman Adam had called Allie brought a black bag, then ran to follow Wes.

A moment later, when Valerie brought in the first

bucket of water, Karlee couldn't help but smile. She watched the doctor roll up his sleeves and wash his hands at the washstand. It was something she'd never seen any other doctor do. With this one gesture, he marked himself as outstanding.

"Cut away the rest of the bandages, will you, Miss?" Adam tied a clean sheet around his middle like an apron and pulled supplies from his bag.

Karlee did as instructed, using her sewing scissors left beside the bed. Valerie brought more water and asked if she should take the twins over to her mom's bakery for a while.

Both Karlee and Adam said "yes" at the same time.

When the girl had gone, Adam cleaned Daniel's wound. "I forgot to introduce myself." He didn't stop working. "I'm Dr. Adam McLain, Danny's brother."

"I guessed." Karlee stood on the other side of the bed helping him. The doctor she'd seen from town was good but nothing compared to the skilled surgeon before her. "I'm Karlee McLain." She couldn't help saying the last word slowly, putting it on for the first time. "Daniel's wife."

Adam's hands hesitated only a moment before continuing working. "Oh."

Karlee didn't know what else to say. Should she tell Adam the reason for the marriage, or would that somehow be betraying Daniel?

Her husband solved the problem by moaning loudly and thrashing.

"We'd better get to work, Karlee." Adam glanced up and smiled at her. "Welcome to the family."

She nodded and gave her full attention to doing what had to be done. While Adam treated the leg wound, Karlee cut away the remainder of Daniel's clothes and went about bathing him as if it were the most natural thing for her to do in the world.

If Daniel wanted his brothers to know the marriage was in name only, he'd have to be the one who did the telling. As for now, she'd be the wife.

She tried to allow Daniel as much modesty as possible. But by the time her task was complete, she'd soaped and washed every part of him that wasn't bandaged. A sense of pride grew inside her. Karlee did what any wife would have done. They might not have the kind of marriage most couples did, but she'd play her part well.

When Adam finished with the leg, he unwrapped Daniel's hands and commented on what a fine job she'd done. He helped her cover the windows with blankets and turned the light low before he cut the bandages away from his brother's eyes.

Carefully, he opened first one, then the other.

Daniel didn't respond.

"Bring the light closer very slowly," Adam ordered.

Karlee lifted the lamp and walked toward the bed. When she was within three feet of Daniel's head, he turned away, moaning in pain.

Adam smiled.

"Can he see?" Karlee fought to keep her hand from shaking and moving the lamp.

"Only a little, but it's a start." Adam rewrapped the blindfold. "In time his eyes may heal. If he hadn't reacted at all to the lamp, he wouldn't have any hope. Now at least we know he does. A slim one, but a chance."

Adam stood and offered her his hand. "Come on along now and let him sleep. It's time you met the rest of the family, Mrs. McLain."

Karlee wanted to scream "no" and run. She knew they'd judge her and find her lacking. They'd wonder how Daniel, such a handsome man, could have married someone as ordinary as her. Wolf would probably tell them she was Daniel's only hope to fight against Gerilyn. They'd shake their heads and marvel at how Daniel could have made such a sacrifice.

"I don't know . . ." She stared at his hand. "I should stay here with Daniel. Or go after the twins. Or . . ."

"He'll be fine." Adam didn't lower his hand. "Don't worry. Wolf is the only one who bites, and you've already met him. Wes only looks like he does. He hasn't bitten anyone in years."

There was nothing to do but accept his offered hand. As they neared the kitchen, the sounds of an argument allowed Karlee to hope she wouldn't have to be paraded for inspection.

FOURTEEN

"UNTIE HIM!" THE LITTLE LADY ORDERED. ALL THE meekness of when she'd first entered the kitchen had disappeared along with most of the trail dust. "Untie him right now, Wes McLain."

Karlee glanced at the savage, now tied to a chair with Wes standing on one side and Wolf on the other. Both men looked like they'd fought a tornado and lost.

"I'm not going to untie him, Allie," the scarred man grumbled. "He'll kill me. It seems he's not too happy at the thought of my being his brother-in-law."

The woman glared at Wolf as though she expected him to follow orders even if the scarred man did not.

"Don't look at me." Wolf held his hands in the air in surrender. "I ain't even kin, and he don't like me. I'm not untying him without four Rangers to back me up. I'm also not getting in the middle of an argument between a husband and wife."

Allie glared at them both then knelt in front of the wild boy. She placed her hands on his knees and spoke to him softly, in a language no one else in the room understood.

The boy shook his head and pulled at his ropes. He

gave no hint of understanding what she was trying to tell him.

Adam walked behind the chair. "You're going to have to untie him soon and let me doctor those wrists or he'll have an infection."

"He's so wild," Wolf mumbled. "I'm surprised he didn't gnaw his own arm off to escape. He bit me so many times I probably got hydrophobia."

Wes pulled Allie gently to her feet. "I know it hurts you to see him tied, darling, but it's the only way. He'd kill us all if he had the chance."

Allie tried once more speaking to him in Apache, but he wouldn't answer. His eyes spoke volumes though. He hated her and everyone in the room. All he wanted was to be as far away from them as possible.

"I could take him down and put him in one of the cells at the jail downtown," Wolf offered. "Then at least he wouldn't be tied."

Allie's eyes filled with tears. "You can't put him in a cage. You can't."

"Then he stays tied," Wolf insisted. "I'm too old to fight him again tonight. One of us will have to stay up to keep an eye on him. If he gets free, he'll murder us in our sleep."

Allie tried again to speak to the boy. He didn't answer but held his chin proudly as though daring them to kill him.

"All right." Allie reached to touch his face, but he jerked his head back. "I'm too tired to argue. He stays tied tonight, and I'll try again tomorrow. I should make coffee and we'll take shifts watching him."

"No." Wolf winked at Karlee standing in the doorway with Adam by her side. "Let Karlee make the coffee. She makes it so strong, it stands up beside a man all night and keeps him awake."

"Karlee?" Allie turned and noticed her for the first time.

"Karlee McLain," Adam corrected. "It seems Daniel married again while we weren't looking."

All at once everyone started hugging Karlee. Allie patted her face and welcomed her. Wes swung her around and planted a kiss on her cheek. Adam's warm hug was too long and tight to be anything but sincere.

"We're mighty glad to have you in the family." Adam smiled. "We've all be hoping our little brother would find love again."

Wes shoved Wolf. "Tell us all about it, Wolf. I have a feeling you know the details of this secret marriage."

Wolf scrubbed his face with cold water. " 'Course I do," he mumbled beneath the towel. "I was the best man."

Karlee held her breath. Now the charade would be over. Wolf would tell them why they married, and the family would no longer have to act happy. She'd been just a means to an end and nothing more. She wasn't part of their family, only a necessary tool to hold it together.

"It was a simple wedding." Wolf lowered the towel and stared at Karlee. "And, to my recollection, it was the most normal wedding any of you McLains ever had."

Wolf didn't say another word.

Wes began telling the details of how he and Allie married in the middle of a near gunfight, with Allie holding a knife in her hand. Adam laughed about Daniel marrying him and his wife while they were tied up in a cellar waiting for Wes to be hung as a horse thief.

Karlee found the stories unbelievable and wonderfully distracting. She asked questions, and the men talked first of their lives now and then of Daniel as a boy. They were his big brothers, so they thought they had a right to tell everything, good and bad, that ever happened to Danny.

They talked of May, for she could not be separated from their brother's past. They told of how she followed him home from school when he was six and how they all loved her, and how he'd chopped the barn down the night she died giving birth to the twins.

Karlee didn't mind the stories. Somehow it felt warm inside to know that the man who was now her husband had been capable of such love once.

Allie warmed the stew. While the others ate, she tried to feed the young man she believed to be her brother. Over and over she called him John, but he never even looked up when she said the name.

He refused to eat. When she addressed him in Apache, he lost some of the fire in his eyes, but nothing more.

Karlee did the dishes. Just after dark, Valerie and her mother brought home sleeping girls with powdered-sugar smiles.

Wes excused himself to care for the horses while Adam checked on Daniel. Wolf spread his bedroll beside the boy's chair and stretched out, listening to Allie talk to her brother. No one knew what she said, but Karlee guessed Allie was reliving every detail of her and John's life in the settlement and describing the day of the raid.

When the twins had been put to bed, Karlee returned to ask Allie and Wes to take her room for the night. She wanted to be near Daniel, she told them.

Wes put his arm around Allie's small shoulder and pulled her to her feet. "We'll try again tomorrow," he said in a voice kinder than Karlee would have thought the hard man would ever use. "We both need rest."

Allie nodded, her body leaning into him for support.

"But if he doesn't respond," Wes led his wife toward the door, "we may have to face the possibility that he's not your brother. The Rangers recover many former captives every year."

"His hair is darker than I remember," Allie admitted. "The eyes are the same color, but they are filled with such hate. And there's a scar on his chest about where I remember he'd been wounded."

"There are scars all over his body," Wolf added.

"He doesn't look Apache." Wes tried to comfort her. "Even if he's not your brother, he's not full-blood Apache like he claims."

Karlee studied the boy more closely. The savage looked Apache to her, but then she wasn't sure she'd ever seen one. Maybe she was looking more at his actions and dress, or lack of it. In truth, if his hair was cut and he wore regular clothes, he would appear like most young men his age. Only, most young men his age didn't look at everyone as if they planned to slice them up for stew meat.

Wes pulled Allie into a hug. "We've come a long way. Let's get some rest."

They moved upstairs leaving Wolf and Karlee alone in the kitchen with the boy, who appeared to have fallen asleep in his chair.

Karlee lowered the wick on the table lamp. "You didn't tell them why Daniel and I married." She straightened the tablecloth so she didn't have to gaze directly at Wolf. "I was wondering why."

"I didn't figure it was anyone's business. A marriage is a marriage."

"But don't you think they'll know we're not in love when Daniel recovers?"

Wolf huffed. "I don't know. Half the couples I see don't look like they're in love. I figure love's something you make up your mind to be in, not something you fall into. That probably explains why I'll always be single.

There ain't never going to be a woman who makes up her mind on loving me."

Karlee moved to the door. She'd always felt the same way about herself. Now, she'd found a man who wanted to be married even if he didn't want her.

Crossing into the parlor, she curled up in the chair next to Daniel's bed. He was resting quietly, his bandages clean and free of blood. His sandy blond hair curtained the white blindfold over his left eye.

She blushed, remembering how she'd washed him so completely. Aunt Rosy would have one of her fainting spells if she knew how boldly Karlee had touched this man.

Laughing to herself, she leaned over him until her cheek rested lightly on his chest. The strong rhythm of his heartbeat seemed to welcome her again.

"Good night, husband," she whispered as she stretched and kissed his lips. He might never be a full husband in every way to her, but she could pretend tonight. There were a house full of relatives who called her Daniel's wife and somehow it made her feel like she belonged.

Deep into the night, Karlee awoke to the sound of Daniel's moaning. He clawed at the blindfold with bandaged hands as he twisted in his sleep.

She slipped off her chair and knelt by his side, pulling his hands from his face.

"Daniel," she whispered, "Daniel, don't pull the blindfold off."

He batted her away, but she returned, sitting on the edge of the bed as she held each arm just above his hands. "Please don't."

He stopped fighting and leaned back, awake enough now to escape from the dream. He seemed to be forcing himself to take deep breaths.

"I'm tired of the darkness," he finally said in a voice

that told Karlee he was fully awake. "I can take the pain in my leg and the constant need to scratch my hands, but I can't stand the darkness. It's like I'm standing on the edge of a cliff with only blackness below. I know eventually I'll have to step off, but will I fall one foot or a hundred?"

Karlee didn't know what to say. It would be cruel to give him false hope and crueler still to give him no hope at all.

"I'll wait with you until the dawn," she finally said. "No matter how long."

Daniel sneered. "And what if it never comes?" He almost choked on the words.

"Then you're stuck with me." She tried to laugh though tears rolled down her cheeks.

Daniel smiled. "Hell of a deal."

Karlee patted his arm. "Preachers aren't suppose to swear."

"And if I wasn't a preacher, Mrs. McLain, would you stay married to me?"

"I married the man, not the profession." Could he really think that just because he was blind he could no longer be a minister?

He was silent for a long moment. "Would you mind rubbing some more salve on my hands?"

She began unwrapping his hand in answer. As she rubbed in the greasy medicine, his fingers moved with hers. When she spread the salve, he caressed her hand until she had as much on her as now covered his burns. If hands could dance, she thought, they were dancing.

"Is that better?" She wrapped his fingers with fresh bandages.

"It helps. The darkness doesn't seem so complete when I'm touching someone. In those first few days, I think your touch was the only thing that kept me sane.

Even when I didn't say anything, the feel of your hands pulled me back to earth again and again."

"I'm glad I could help." Karlee wiped her fingers on a towel and moved back to her chair. He had a way about him, a way of making her feel needed without making himself seem helpless. "Maybe you can sleep now. Do you need anything else?"

He lifted his hand. "Come here."

As she had when he asked her to marry him, Karlee put her hand in his and allowed him to pull her close.

When her legs bumped the edge of the bed, he tugged again.

She crawled onto the bed, not knowing what he wanted.

"Lie down next to me," he whispered. "I don't want to be alone."

Very carefully, she stretched out at his side, leaving only an inch between them.

He opened his arm, and she used his chest as a pillow.

"Are you cold?" He placed his hand at the back of her waist and pulled her against him. She was surprised how easily she fit next to his side, almost as if they were a match.

"No," she managed to say while she tried to breathe. They were doing nothing improper. Nothing wrong. Yet the room seemed to have grown summer warm.

"Do you mind keeping me company, Mrs. McLain? I don't want to be alone tonight."

"No." She swallowed hard. "I don't mind."

He kissed the top of her head. "Thank you."

"You're welcome."

With her tucked securely against his side, Daniel drifted into a peaceful sleep.

Karlee had never been more awake in her life. Each time she breathed, the smell of him filled her lungs. His heart pounded in her ear like a drum. His hand moved slowly from her back to the fullness of her hip where it rested peacefully.

She told herself he was asleep, that he didn't know, or feel anything with the bandages and her layers of clothes. After all, he was a preacher.

She twisted until she pulled his hand back to her waist.

After a few minutes, he slid his fingers back to the fullness of her hip.

He can't feel anything, she reminded herself.

But an hour later, when she was finally almost asleep she could have sworn he patted her bottom lightly and spread his fingers over the curve of her hip.

Tomorrow, wild savage, company and all, she'd have a few words about what the preacher wasn't feeling between the clothes and bandages.

FIFTEEN

Daniel awoke slowly, one pain at a time. The cool of the night had passed. He heard the first sounds of stirring in the kitchen. It was morning. He'd always liked the smell of a fire starting and coffee flavoring the air at daybreak. But today, his body ached. His head pounded and it tasted like something had died inside his mouth.

Karlee was no longer at his side, if she ever had been. He remembered a dream of her lying next to him, all soft and warm. Her head, resting atop his heart, had been more real than dream in the quiet of night. She'd pressed her ample breasts against the side of his chest as though she had no idea how much the feel of her made his whole body aware. In the dream, he'd felt the firmness of her hip in his hand and she hadn't protested.

In his dream, Daniel reminded himself. It could be nothing more. He wasn't attracted to Karlee. Not a woman like her. Not any woman. He'd seen her type. She was destined to be an old maid, taking care of others all her life. There was something about her that would make any man run in the opposite direction. A craziness, an impulsiveness, a freedom. His grandfather would have said she was a person not comfortable in her own skin.

A man might never know what she would do next. That's not the kind of woman who made a good wife. Not the kind who would be a trusted friend . . . a partner . . . a lover.

No, he told himself. He shouldn't even be dreaming about a woman like Karlee. Or thinking about her in the way he was.

She was the type of woman who shipped herself in a trunk, or flattened a huge stranger with a frying pan . . . or married a blind man.

"Morning." Karlee's voice came from a few feet away.

Daniel frowned. He should have heard her approaching. The dream had crossed into reality. "Morning," he grumbled. "Is the coffee ready yet?" He was in no mood to wake up, much less face anyone.

"I brought you a cup." Her words grew nearer as she spoke.

He reached out, but she was closer than he guessed. His bandaged hand swung against the hot cup. She squealed as coffee splashed over her hand and onto the sheets.

"Oh, I'm sorry!" She backed away. "I filled it so full. I was watching the coffee and didn't see you reach up."

He heard the clank of the cup on the bedside table a moment before she returned to his side. She wiped up the spill and patted the sheet that covered him.

"I've made such a mess." She continued rubbing the stains, totally unaware his body lay beneath the depth of cotton.

The coffee's warmth hardly registered, but the touch of her hand burned his flesh. The woman treated him with the same careless handling she must treat the rag dolls she made. Any moment, he half-expected her to be sewing new button eyes onto his head.

He caught the tea towel she dabbed with and pulled it from her. "I can clean up myself." He knew his voice was harsh, but she seemed to have a complete disregard for his modesty. "Watch where you're patting. And, while we're on the subject, I can bathe myself from now on. There's no need for you to do it."

He knew she was still in the room. He could hear her breathing. She must be standing next to the bed like a statue.

"But . . ."

"But what, Mrs. McLain?"

"But, last night . . ."

"There was no last night." He knew he was being harsh, but she'd better understand once and for all that there could never be anything between them. They might be married for the rest of their lives, but he didn't want her harboring any hope that he'd love her. He'd loved once and that was enough for a lifetime. "And in the future, I'd like to drink my coffee, not bathe in it."

He heard a tiny little sound that seemed to come from deep in her throat. Words so jumbled they blocked all speech.

Then, without warning, hot coffee splashed across his chest.

Daniel yelped and lunged forward, reaching for her, almost toppling off the bed in his haste. Growling like a wounded bear, he wiped the brew from his face with one bandaged hand. The other swung wide, trying to catch her in his net.

It didn't matter that he had no idea what he'd do with her if he caught her. No one had ever dared do what she'd done.

He might not have heard her enter, but he heard her stomp out of the room. No apology, no explanation.

"Unpredictable," he mumbled. "Temperamental old maid!" He dragged his injured leg to the edge of the bed. The pain fought its way through his anger. If he tried to follow her, he'd only hurt the wound more. She wasn't worth it. He didn't even like the woman. She was one level worse than the plagues of Job.

"Morning, Danny boy. Wearing your coffee these days?" Wolf chuckled. "The politeness of the honeymoon doesn't last as long as it used to."

A dry towel hit Daniel's chest as he heard the chair beside him groan under Wolf's weight. The huge man seemed to think every chair in the house was a rocker.

"I wanted to allow you two newlyweds some time alone before the house wakes up, but Karlee just stormed into the kitchen and told me she'd guard the savage while she fixed breakfast. From the look in her fiery green eyes, I'd feel sorry for the boy if he picked her watch to try and break free."

Daniel wiped off his chest, feeling the coffee grounds against his skin. "She still hasn't learned to make a decent cup of coffee," he mumbled. "And the woman has no gentle spirit, I can testify to that. She also has no patience or understanding about a man getting up on the wrong side of the bed."

"Maybe you'd better learn which side is the right side, Danny, if you plan on waking up at all. Trust me, next time the cup could be a frying pan."

Daniel didn't get Wolf's humor. "Why couldn't I have found a kind soul to marry, with soft ways and a sweet heart? Why'd I have to pick the one woman I've ever met who might truly be insane? She's cursed, double-odd, from a family too imbalanced to notice. She's more than twenty and can't make coffee. There's something seriously wrong with a woman who can't cook. It's not natural."

Wolf seemed to have gone deaf.

"I'm an even-tempered man." Daniel tossed the towel so hard it hit the opposite wall with a thud. He'd resigned himself to coffee grounds in his chest hair. "I never do a thing or say words to anger anyone. Why would the woman throw a cup at me?"

"Maybe you'd better ask her. If you've calmed down enough," Wolf reasoned.

"I'm calm enough. I'm always calm enough." He heard movement on the other side of the bed. "She's back, isn't she?"

"I'm here," Karlee answered, "with your breakfast. And I'll thank you to address me directly."

"I would if you'd make enough noise when you enter. I can hear everyone in this house walking from room to room, but you manage to sneak up on me again and again."

The front two feet of Wolf's chair bumped to the floor. "I need to be getting back to the kitchen." He scrambled away.

Daniel sat very still, his muscles tight, anticipating another blow. "If you're expecting me to say I'm sorry, you'll have a long wait." He wasn't in the habit of apologizing when he couldn't see he'd done anything wrong.

"So will you," she answered.

"Then I suspect, Mrs. McLain, we will have very little to say to one another in the future."

"I suspect so," she snapped. "Would you like to eat your breakfast or wear it?"

A smile fought its way through Daniel's anger, despite his efforts to keep it down. "I'll eat it. And I'll have another cup of coffee. My cup's around here somewhere, or at least the dent of it is still here."

He sat up in the bed, pulling the sheet around him. "I've night shirts in a trunk in my study, if you don't mind bringing me one. I might look more presentable dressed in it than bare-chested."

She sat a tray beside him. "I don't mind."

Unsure how she meant the words, he heard her cross to his little study and open the old trunk he used for a footstool when reading. Her step was so light he couldn't help but wonder if she'd practiced it since childhood. If so, he imagined she surprised a great many people in private conversations. That might explain why she was passed from place to place so often.

But of late, he could think of a few other reasons as well. The idea of shoving her in a trunk and shipping her back crossed his mind.

She returned before he managed to swallow the first bite of a flour-crusted biscuit. The half left in his fingers crumbled. He could smell the eggs and wondered if they were encased in a crispy layer, burned beyond taste as usual.

"Would you like me to help you put on the shirt?" Her voice could have frozen the Mississippi.

"No, thank you. If you'll just lay it on the bed, I can manage from here on." The coffee actually tasted good as it softened the biscuit in his throat. "If you'll close the door, I think I can bathe without help."

"All right."

That was it then. They'd settle into the politeness of strangers.

The moment he heard the door click, he set the tray aside and stood, letting the sheet fall away from his bare body. Careful not to put any weight on his leg, he hopped the few steps to where he'd heard her get water. As he'd expected, a bucket stood beside the washstand.

He felt for the washcloth and soap. The scissors, he guessed, might be near, for he'd heard her lay them again and again on the night stand while she sewed. His fingers patted the corner of the table. Her scissors were exactly where he'd thought she left them.

Carefully, he cut the bandages from his hands. The

burns felt healed enough to take the air. It was time to let his skin breathe.

Ignoring the pain, he dipped the rag into the cold water and began to wash. Jefferson was warm enough to swim in the river most of the year. He'd give a great deal to float in the water now, for hard as he scrubbed, he couldn't feel clean with cold water and hard soap. The smell of the fire still lingered on his skin.

The cool morning breeze dried his flesh as he worked down his body, rubbing away coffee grounds.

When he finished, he hopped back to the bed and felt for his nightshirt. He'd never liked the things, but since the twins needed him in the middle of the night, he'd taken to wearing one. That way he didn't have to search the darkness for clothes while one or both of them cried upstairs.

The sheets were twisted and damp with cold coffee, but he couldn't locate the shirt. His large hands spread out, searching.

He straightened slightly, planning to hop further along the length of the bed. As his hand moved in the air, he touched cotton. The night shirt seemed to be floating in front of him.

Daniel stiffened and took the shirt from her hand. "Thank you," he managed to say. Every ounce of his being wanted to turn around and run. But he was just as bare from the backside and, with his leg, all he could have managed was a hop. He figured a hopping nude man might look fairly ridiculous.

"You're welcome," she answered as formally as if she'd just handed him a songbook in church.

He knew she was grinning. He could feel it.

Daniel squared his shoulders and mustered enough dignity to put on his shirt. She'd watched the whole time he'd bathed. Watched him boldly, like no woman would watch a man. He'd heard his mother say once that she'd never seen his father completely nude. Even when he'd bathed and she washed his back, he had the decency to cover his private parts.

He pulled the shirt down. He had no private parts. She'd seen all of him. And from the time he took bathing, she'd stared for quite a while.

"If you can stand on that leg a few seconds more, I'll change the sheets." The polite coldness was back in her voice.

He didn't trust words, all he could do was nod. There were a few hundred things he thought about saying to her. She was no lady to stand silently in a room and watch him. A respectable woman would have made her presence known.

Maybe she wasn't insane, but she'd surely drive him over the edge at this rate. What kind of wife watches her husband?

Then it hit him . . . probably every one with the exception of his mother. What Karlee had done was a normal act. She'd stood near while her wounded husband bathed after he'd told her he needed no help.

"I'm finished." She touched his arm lightly. "The bed is ready."

She was close, very close.

"Would you like me to help you?"

He brushed the edge of the mattress. "I can manage." He sank down, slowly moving his leg into place. "In truth, I think I'll go back to sleep. I feel as though I've walked miles."

He didn't protest when she helped him straighten up and tucked him in. Then she was gone, as silently as she'd appeared.

Daniel closed his eyes and decided the dreams of the night were not nearly as frightening as the reality of waking up.

SIXTEEN

THE NEXT FEW DAYS PASSED IN A HAZE FOR KARLEE.
Since the savage now lived in the kitchen, and Adam
had set up a cot in the dining room, she spent most of
her time in Daniel's parlor room with the twins. The
little house seemed to shrink smaller with each tick of
the clock.

When Daniel drifted into sleep, she'd move the twins
upstairs to play in their room, or to the porch. But the
days were cloudy, and it rained off and on all week. The
girls seemed happiest near their father. So the area
around Daniel's bed became their play area and her sewing room.

She'd always loved playing with fabric, making dolls
from scraps of material. When she'd been with the aunts
they'd made fun of her pastime so she'd only been able
to work early in the morning or late at night after they'd
gone to bed. Now, she could work as the twins played
without anyone criticizing her.

Her only time alone seemed to be late at night when
she slipped onto the porch for a few minutes. One evening, she saw an old woman in rags standing across the
street just out of the lamp light's glow.

Karlee watched her for a while, but the old woman

didn't move. From her clothes Karlee guessed she must be one of the many Germans who lived by the lake. Wolf told her most of them were good people who'd paid all they had for land in Texas only to discover they'd been swindled and left in the port towns with no money and no way home.

On impulse, Karlee walked across the street and joined the old woman. For a while they just stood, side by side. Finally, Karlee asked, "It looks like rain tonight."

"Yes, it does," the woman answered in a thick accent.

"Have you a place to stay."

The woman shook her head.

Karlee felt as though she were wealthy for the first time in her life. She smiled. "I'm the preacher's wife and I have been greatly blessed. Too much, I think. So much so, I waste some of what I have. And I think that is a sin."

"A sin," the woman agreed.

"Would you please help me, dear lady? I have guests so my house is full, but the barn is empty. Would you be willing to stay there? It's clean and dry and I know of a room hidden away."

The old woman thought about it. "Me and mine?" she finally asked.

"You and yours," Karlee answered. "Thank you. You do me a great favor, Madam."

"Ida," the woman answered. "My name is Ida. And you are welcome, Mrs. McLain."

Karlee went back into the house knowing what she'd done was right. She curled into the chair in Daniel's room and fell asleep.

Daniel managed to keep his bad moods to himself since the morning he wore his coffee. The polite coldness that somehow developed between them grew into a constant. Much as he seemed to hate it, he was dependent on her. But he allowed her to do nothing for him that he could do for himself.

She no longer wrapped his hands but continued to change the bandage on his leg. Thanks to Adam's expert care, the wound was healing fast. Each time she touched his leg she felt his muscles tighten, but he didn't say a word. The knowledge that she embarrassed him made her hands linger longer. She told herself that it was for the best. The more she touched him the more comfortable he'd become with her near. He couldn't jump every time she came close for the next thirty or forty years.

Wes's wife, Allie, spent the greater part of most days trying to talk to John. Finally, he stopped fighting the ropes and allowed her to feed him. But he still showed no sign of listening to a word she said. Her determination that he was her brother, John, seemed equaled only by his desire to be full Apache.

Adam took his turn guarding the savage at night but spent most of his days in town. Several people had been hurt in the fire, and an extra doctor was much appreciated. The churches left standing had been transformed into hospitals.

Karlee tried to sleep in the girls' room but found she woke Wes up each time she moved downstairs to check on Daniel. He'd spent four long years in the war aware of every sound. Even her slight movements brought him to the bedroom door with gun in hand.

After a few nights of being frightened out of a year's life by Wes jumping onto the landing, Karlee moved permanently to the chair in the parlor for sleep. Thanks to the wide windows, this room was by far the warmest in the day and the coldest at night.

Daniel had been asleep the first night she moved her things in, but on the second, she sensed he was still awake. Trying to be as quiet as possible, she deposited her belongings on the small couch that had been pushed beneath the windows to allow room for Daniel's bed.

"What are you doing still up?" He showed no sign of having been asleep.

"I thought I'd curl up in the chair by your bed."

"I don't need a nurse. I'm fine."

"I know. I just don't want to sleep upstairs. I wake Wes up when the stairs creak. He runs out expecting to find John and frightens me to death." She pulled off her dress. "You don't mind my being here, do you?"

"No. It doesn't matter. I don't know when you're in the room half the time anyway," he answered coldly. "What are you doing now?"

"I'm putting on my nightgown." Her petticoats joined her dress in a pile.

"In front of me?"

Karlee laughed. "Rather bold of me undressing in front of a man. Aunt Rosy would be shocked. Except you can't see me."

"But I can hear you." Daniel's voice lowered slightly.

Karlee stopped her progress and stared at him for a minute. If the bandages were removed, he would have been looking right at her. And she stood with her nightgown unbuttoned all the way to her waist.

"What do you hear?"

"I feel you staring at me." He smiled as if he saw her before him. "I heard your dress fall and the ruffle of cotton when you pulled your nightgown over your head. If I were guessing, I'd say you haven't buttoned it yet or tied the bow at the throat."

"It has no bow at the throat." She relaxed a little. He'd almost convinced her he could see through the bandages.

Daniel frowned. "I'm not that familiar with ladies' nightgowns."

Karlee enjoyed talking with him when the coldness between them wasn't so strong, even if it was about nightgowns. "Well, this gown is very grand. I only wear it on special occasions, like nighttime. It's a hand-me-down from my aunt. I'm afraid it's embarrassingly short, just past my knees, but two of me could easily fit into it."

"Aunt Rosy's gown?"

"You remember her?"

"I met her once, just before May and I married."

Karlee sat on the edge of the bed and buttoned her gown. "She's a woman who prides herself on first impressions. What do you remember about her?"

"Wet kisses." He wiped his face as if more than the memory remained of a slobbery smack. "I felt like a wide-mouth bass sucked on my cheek when she stood on her toes and greeted me. Other than that, I thought her a tug boat."

Karlee couldn't hold back a giggle.

"You don't believe me?" Daniel frowned as if offended. "Why would I lie?"

"Oh, no." She tried to control her laughter. "I can just picture Aunt Rosy puckering up for her famous kiss. You should feel very honored. She only bestows it on men she thinks highly of. I've watched her preacher bob in and out of crowds to avoid her wet greeting."

Daniel laughed. "I'm glad she thought so well of me. Aunt Violet certainly didn't share her view. She told me I was too young to know my mind and was robbing the cradle with May. She said I had no means to support a wife and . . . she's probably still adding more ands as we speak."

"Oh, no! She told me how wonderful you were. They collect the articles you write, you know. They think you've a great mind." Karlee argued with a laugh as she began unbraiding her hair. "In fact, Aunt Violet was still telling me of your perfection when I waved good-bye to the two old women."

Daniel leaned closer. "Do you miss them?"

"You must be joking."

"Don't tell me you're happier here with all the trouble and bother."

Karlee stared at him a long moment before she answered. "I'm happier here," she whispered. The tension between her and Daniel was nothing compared to living under the constant eye of the aunts. Here she felt equal. There, she would always be a charity case, no matter how much work she did.

"But all the chores?" he added. "Not to mention people dropping in and out all the time. I've heard you out doing the wash long after everyone else is in bed. You're the first one up every morning and the last to go to sleep."

"I'm happier here," she insisted. She placed her hand over his. How could she tell him that, even if it were ten times the work, she'd still stay? For here, amid all the people and trouble, she felt needed.

Daniel turned his palm up and caught her fingers. His hand was rough with scabs, but his strong grip felt good.

Before either could say more, a tapping sounded at the door. A moment later, Wolf's hairy head poked inside.

"Hate to interrupt you two when you're not yelling." He moved into the room as though he'd been invited. "Thought I'd tell someone that I have to leave for a few hours. There's a meeting in town. Trouble's about to boil over and there's rumors the outlaw Baker is planning a visit. I'd like to meet up with the man if he's there tonight before the fighting starts. I swear there ain't two people in Jefferson who get along."

Karlee quickly stood and pulled on her robe.

He winked at her. "Except maybe the two of you. You seem to be getting along just fine."

"We've always got along," Daniel corrected.

He couldn't see both Wolf and Karlee turn toward him in surprise, but neither called his lie.

"Be careful, Wolf." She tightened the belt on her robe. "The storm's getting worse." She'd felt the temperature dropping steadily since sunset and heard the wind howling.

"It's not the rainstorm I'm worried about." Wolf rubbed his forehead. "It's the storm between town folks. The only good thing about it is we might be able to get Jesse's brother out if the soldiers are distracted by what might develop into riots."

"Did you find where he is?" Daniel seemed to be giving Wolf his full attention.

The hairy man glanced at Karlee. She read what he was thinking in his face. Daniel's question, asked in front of her, meant that Daniel trusted her. Wolf nodded slowly toward Karlee. He planned to follow suit. From this point on there would be no talking behind her back of problems he and Daniel faced.

"No." Wolf turned back to Daniel. "Without a man in the stockade we don't get much news. The fire did delay his hanging a week though, so we've got some time. Last we heard he's somewhere amid the sick."

"Fill me in on the details in the morning. I don't want to be lost about what's going on when I get out of this bed."

"Will do." Wolf saluted. "I won't be out too long. I have to relieve Adam from guarding the boy."

Karlee followed Wolf and closed the parlor door when he left. Maybe the room wouldn't be so drafty with the door closed. She crossed to the chair and shook a blanket out.

"Goodnight, Karlee." Daniel turned on his side without another word.

Karlee twisted the lamp low and tried to get comfortable in the chair. After ten minutes of wiggling, she stood and dragged her blanket to the little couch. But the armrest made a hard pillow, and her legs hung off the end. With the draft from the windows, she could feel damp wind whirling around her. It could be no colder on the porch, she decided, huddling close to the cushions.

After another ten minutes of wiggling, trying to get comfortable and, at the same time, be covered with the thin blanket, Karlee heard Daniel roll on his back and let out a long breath.

"Enough," he hissed in anger. "If either of us is going to get any sleep, you'd better find another blanket."

"There are no more," she answered just as sharply. "We're using every one we have in the house with all the company."

"There's more on the shelves in the girls' room."

"They've disappeared." Now was not a good time to tell him where.

"Well, then come over here. There's enough room for two in this bed tonight. Tomorrow you can buy a few new quilts. I think my account can stand the blow easier than I can do without sleep."

Karlee opened her mouth to protest, but her legs were freezing and she knew she'd never get comfortable.

"All right." She stood, telling herself it was the only practical solution. "I've spent my life sharing a bed. Once, with a cousin's family in Indiana, we had to sleep six to one bed. It wasn't so bad. At least I was warm that winter, as long as everyone remembered to use the chamber pot."

"Goodnight," Daniel mumbled, as if her story was keeping him awake.

As she slipped in beside him, Daniel jerked when her cold feet touched his leg. "I know the couch is short, but did you have to stick your feet out the window?"

Karlee giggled. "Stop complaining, or I'll fish kiss

you." She touched her toes to his leg once more to test his patience.

He didn't jerk again. A sudden intake of air was his only reaction. As he had before, he pulled her against his side. "You'll be warm in a minute."

But when she'd lain next to him several nights ago, she'd been fully clothed with undergarments beneath her dress. Now there was only a worn cotton nightgown and his nightshirt between them. She tried desperately to hold herself a fraction away, close enough to feel the heat from his body, but far enough away so she wasn't touching him.

He didn't seem to notice. "When you go to the mercantile in the morning?"

Karlee relaxed a little. His mind must be on other things. "Yes? Do you need something besides blankets?"

"Definitely," he answered formally. "Buy yourself a few nightgowns that reach the floor. If not, you'll have pneumonia and I'll probably get frostbite."

"And should I send this one back to Aunt Rosy?"

"Great idea." Daniel chuckled. "Tell the old dear that you've given up wearing them. That should shock her mouth closed."

Karlee laughed. "And me, a minister's wife."

"You're shameless, Mrs. McLain." Daniel tried to hold in the laughter.

Karlee lay her icy fingers on his chest.

"And freezing." He covered her hand with his own. "I feel the cold through my shirt."

He raised her hand close to his lips and blew on her fingers.

Karlee's hands might be cold, but she felt the warmth of his breath throughout her body. She fought the urge to pull away. He was being kind, but the feelings he stirred in her were far more than kindness.

He kissed her open palm lightly. "There. Better?"

"Better." She pulled her hand free.

"Good. Now go to sleep." He straightened away from her.

"Daniel?" she whispered after several minutes of lying wide awake beside him.

"Yes?" He sounded sleepy.

"I need to know how it is between us." Since their marriage, they'd had so little time alone. "I don't know the rules."

"Neither do I," he answered with a sigh. "I guess we didn't have much time to think about what we wanted out of this marriage. Only that we wanted the twins safe."

Karlee rolled onto her stomach and propped her head on her elbows. "When I was a kid, moving from house to house, I always tried to figure out the rules as quickly as possible. Then I could stay out of trouble."

"I find that hard to believe," he mumbled.

"That each house had different rules?"

"No, that you stayed out of trouble." He leaned to his side and rested his hand on the small of her back as naturally as though he'd done it a thousand times. "All right. What are the rules we live this marriage by?"

"We need to be honest with one another." Karlee thought she'd start with one she knew they'd both agree on. "I always hated families where folks kept secrets."

"That sounds like a good rule." He didn't seem as interested in her bedtime game as she was.

"I'll be your wife. Take care of the children, try to run the house. That's my main job."

"Fair enough," he answered. "I'll try to provide for you and keep you safe."

"What else?" she asked.

"If I had a church, I'd probably expect you to go to service with me."

"That's fair. A minister's wife should go to church. What else?"

"That's about it." Daniel sounded half asleep. "Anything else you'd add?"

She hesitated, then seemed to jump in. "I know you want no intimacy, no children, but could I sleep in your bed when the nights are cold?"

"Karlee, men and women don't sleep together who aren't intimate. As soon as the company leaves, I think it would be better if we sleep apart."

"But we've already slept next to one another. We are now. There are only two bedrooms in the house, and I'm willing to share."

"Karlee, I'm a preacher, not some kind of saint." He let out a long-held breath. "What if I touch you while we sleep?"

"What if you do?"

"I mean in places . . ."

"I know what you mean," she snapped. He was making her feel like a child who knew nothing. Even if he was right, she wouldn't admit it. "You're my husband. I guess if you touched me it would be all right."

He moved his hand low, over her hip. "You'd settle for this? Touching you with no love between us?" He took his hand away quickly as though his action had disgusted him.

She thought about how, all her life, she'd wished someone would touch her. She'd watched mothers hug their children at night and pass by her bed without stopping. She'd visited churches where everyone seemed to embrace each other, but they all stayed away from her . . . the outsider.

"I'd settle." She thought even without love it was so much more than she'd ever had. "If we're going to spend the rest of our lives together in the same house, we don't need to be jumping every time we brush."

"You don't understand." Daniel rubbed his forehead as if she'd given him a headache. "Men and women don't just go around touching one another."

"Do you have a headache?" She reached to brush his temples.

Daniel seemed to turn to stone as her breasts moved atop his chest.

Karlee glanced down feeling her cheeks warm as she realized what she'd done. "Sorry," she whispered. "I know that bothers you." Now was the time to start being honest. "I swear I'm not doing it on purpose." She leaned away from him. "I've never talked to anyone about it, but I've always been too big. Violet used to say I should strap in tight or I'd look like a nursing cow."

Karlee knew she shouldn't be talking about such things with a man, but her mouth seemed to have sprung a leak. "I don't mean to brush you, I swear I . . ."

She forgot what she was about to say as his hand trailed along her arm and then covered her breast.

Only the thin cotton blocked the warmth of his fingers. He felt her fullness carefully. His palm flattened over her peak as his fingers encompassed her, molding her within his gentle grip.

Karlee didn't breathe as he felt her fullness completely.

"You're not too big," he said moving his hand to the other breast to continue his examination. "You're a tall woman and well-rounded in the right places. I think you're about the right size for your body. But then I'm no expert on such things."

"Thank you," she managed to say as he removed his hand. If he was trying to shock her by proving his point about touching, he certainly had.

"Now go to sleep, Karlee." He rolled away from her, his voice low and angry.

"All right," she whispered. "I'm not cold anymore."

He didn't answer.

Daniel lay awake most of the night, knowing that she was doing the same. About dawn, when her breathing finally grew slow and he knew she was asleep, he decided he must be possessed.

Why else would he have reached over and touched her, almost a stranger, a woman he didn't even like most of the time? He didn't want her in his life or his bed, but here she was, implanted firmly in both for the simple reason to make his life a living hell. Why else would she be constantly around? Why else would he find it so hard to stay angry at her? Why else would she have the most perfect breasts God ever made?

He reminded himself she had red hair, and that she was jumpy as an overflowing nest of newborn squirrels. He should have sent her packing that first day in the same trunk in which she'd arrived. She was trouble, more trouble than the mob in town. At this rate, she'd destroy not only his mind, but his work here in Jefferson.

She could talk all she wanted to about honesty between them, but Daniel had no intention of telling her the full reason he was in town. As soon as he could walk, he'd be out of here. Then she'd only see him now and then and he'd make sure the twins were always around.

He'd be formal and polite, but he'd keep his distance. And he'd keep his hands off her.

But, as for now, he was trapped by his leg in a bed with a woman willing to play by the rules he set. She didn't ask for love, or even expect it, only a little kindness. That bothered him more than he wanted to admit.

SEVENTEEN

Daniel woke to a room already warm with morning. Karlee had gone from his side without a word. He lay silent for a long while thinking of what they'd talked about last night and what he'd done.

A question kept lurking in the back of his mind. Why hadn't she protested or said something when he'd felt of her breasts so completely? Was she simply enduring what she thought she had to in a loveless marriage? Dear God, he hoped not. Then, his touch would have been something dirty and cruel.

If she liked his exploration of her body, she'd shown no sign of it. Surely, if his touch affected her a fraction as much as it had him, she would have said something. He could still feel the fullness of her against his palm.

The only thing he knew for certain was that she must not have hated it or she'd have reacted. She wasn't a woman who kept her feelings to herself.

But, then, why hadn't she said anything? He'd lost a night's sleep thinking about what he had done, and she hadn't bothered to say a word. He wasn't sure he could ask her. He had a strong feeling he didn't want to know the answer.

Allie brought his breakfast. One bite told him Karlee hadn't been the cook.

"Where's my wife?" Daniel mumbled between bites of unburned eggs.

"She took the twins into town to shop," Allie answered in her usual shy little voice. "She said she'd be back by noon. We needed some supplies, and she mentioned something about buying a nightgown and more material."

"Material?"

"She makes the most wonderful dolls for the twins. She buys cotton for a dress and uses the scraps to fashion dolls like I've never seen."

"I've heard her working." Allie's praise surprised Daniel. She usually talked to everyone, except Wes, as little as possible.

"Adam's talked her into making one of her dolls for his daughter, and Valerie said she wants one to keep for her children someday."

"Where is Adam? He's usually in to check on me by now like a mother hen."

"One of the Buchanan boys came for him before dawn. Willow's time is coming a month early."

Daniel tried not to react. Willow would do fine. Women had babies all the time without dying. But the girl was a part of his family. "Is everything all right?"

Allie didn't answer for a moment too long. "I think so," she finally said as she hurried from the room. "I'll let you know if I hear anything."

Wolf's assurance a few minutes later was no more convincing. Daniel didn't have to ask for details. Something was wrong. Birthing at the Buchanan house was a normal occurrence, not something they'd send to town for a doctor to help with.

He tried to listen to Wolf's account of all the trouble brewing over who might be responsible for the fire, but

all Daniel could think about was poor little Willow. He'd
been through a night of labor with his wife and watched
her die in his arms. He didn't want to think about that
happening to another woman.

He spent the morning worrying and listening for Karlee's return. Finally, he heard her voice in the kitchen,
but she didn't bother to come into the parlor and check
on him.

Just before noon another Buchanan boy showed up at
the kitchen door asking Karlee if she could come directly. Without a word to Daniel, she loaded the twins
in the wagon and left. He could hear her asking Allie to
take care of him like he was a pet left behind on the
porch.

Daniel acted like a wounded bear for the rest of the
day. Willow must be having problems or Adam
wouldn't have sent for Karlee, and then she'd left without saying good-bye. Which pretty much told him, Daniel decided, how she felt about last night.

He shouldn't have touched her. But she practically
asked him to, talking about how big her breasts were
when she knew he couldn't see them. How else could
he judge?

Forcing himself to stand, Daniel welcomed the pain.
Anything to straighten out his mind. He'd always known
right from wrong. He had never done anything he didn't
consider right and fair. He was an honorable man.

But he'd touched Karlee boldly . . . Daniel made himself take a step.

She probably thought him a mad man or worse . . . he
forced another step.

After all, how many men go around touching their
wives so openly? Daniel almost tumbled with the third
step as he realized . . . all of them.

Grabbing hold of the chair, he smiled through the
pain. He'd touched his wife, not committed a crime.

He'd simply touched his wife. There was no doubt in his mind, he was twenty-three and getting dumber everyday.

Wolf's heavy-footed stomp came down the hall. "You're walking!" he yelled from the open doorway.

Daniel smiled. "I may be blind, but I am still aware of what I'm doing."

Wolf moved nearer. "Are you all right?"

"I'm fine. Is there any blood on the bandage?"

"Not a drop." Wolf rested his hand on Daniel's arm. "You want me to help you make it back to the bed?"

"No. I'll stand for a while." Daniel gripped the chair tightly and tried to appear relaxed. "Have you heard from Willow?"

"Not a word, and it's good'n dark outside." Wolf's voice moved across the room. "Karlee told me she'd be there as long as she's needed. There's plenty of women to help with the twins. One of the Buchanan women could have probably helped Adam, but he wanted someone he could trust not to overreact if problems came aplenty."

Daniel shook his head. He wouldn't exactly put Karlee in that category.

Wolf must have seen Daniel's doubt. "You don't know what a rock that woman of yours is. Behind that blindfold, in this room, the world must look pretty calm to you, but the town's in chaos. You wouldn't believe the folks knocking on your kitchen door. Some hurt, some needing food. She don't talk about it none, but she does what she can for them all. Adam's seen her, and so have I."

"I'm glad she can help." Daniel would have been disappointed if she'd done less.

Wolf cleared his throat. "I might as well tell you before you find out. You know that little room you keep out in the barn?"

Daniel wasn't aware anyone knew of his room framed into the corners of the barn. When Willow had been in the house, he slept there. It wasn't much more than a cot and desk, but it was his private hideaway from the world.

"Of course I know about the room." Daniel waited.

"Well, Karlee found it last week and cleaned it out. She stored all your books in a box and gave the room to an old woman who had nowhere to go with her kids."

Daniel didn't comment. He would have done the same thing.

Wolf paced. "Well, it seems the woman claims to have a brother, and he had a wife and three kids."

"Don't tell me they are all in that room."

"No." Wolf hesitated. "They moved into the barn. I put your horses in the corral. There's enough of an overhang from the barn roof that they'll stay dry if it rains."

"Good." Daniel knew Wolf had more to say. "Anything else?"

"Well, yeah. The brother's wife had parents who arrived from Germany three days ago along with her two brothers and their families."

"How many people are living in my barn?" Daniel interrupted.

"You don't want to know," Wolf answered. "But I'm telling you all this, because one of the reasons Karlee went to town this morning was to find a few of them jobs." Wolf laughed. "She talked two folks into hiring men they couldn't even communicate with. Then, after they gave the men jobs, Karlee argued for a higher wage." Wolf shrugged. "Which she got by the way."

Wolf sounded like he stood near the windows. "I don't know if you are aware of it or not, Danny boy, but you've got a woman who can handle crisis. In this part of the world, that's no small talent. No matter what

Adam's facing out at the Buchanan farm, you can bet Karlee's there to help."

Daniel forced himself to walk back to the edge of the bed. When he was seated once more, he asked, "Will you cut off the blindfold? I'd like to sleep without it tonight."

Wolf grumbled. "All right. But I'll be in to put it back on before first light."

He cut the bandages around Daniel's eyes and took the lamp with him as he left the room.

Daniel leaned back against the covers, pretending the night was the only reason he couldn't see. He knew Karlee wouldn't return this late, so he wouldn't have a chance to apologize. Not that he would anyway. After all, a man didn't say he was sorry for touching his wife. He opened his eyes and stared out at the cloudy grayness beyond the windows.

He told himself he could touch her anytime he wanted. After all, they were married. He could just say it was his right in the eyes of God and man. He could even make love to her.

Daniel swore at himself in the darkness. He couldn't take her, or force her. He couldn't demand anything of her. He wasn't that kind of man. He couldn't make love to her if he didn't love her, even if she said she didn't mind. It not only would make her less than she was, it would make him less of a man.

Karlee stood on the Buchanans' porch and watched rain wash night into charcoal gray. She studied the shadows as if she expected an answer to materialize before her eyes.

Willow had been in labor twelve hours, and there was no sign of it ending. Karlee felt like she'd explained everything to the woman a hundred times. Adam had assured her all was fine, but Willow still cried and worried and gripped Karlee's hand with each contraction.

"You holding up?" Adam moved behind Karlee and placed his arm on her shoulder. "We may have a long night ahead."

"I'm fine," Karlee answered, liking the way he accepted her as family. "The twins are tucked in between the other children. I can help as long as needed."

"Thanks." Adam patted her shoulder. "I'll try to get this baby born and you back to your husband as soon as possible."

Yelling Karlee's name, Willow drew them back into the house. Hours later, just after sunrise, the newest Buchanan entered the world. Samuel Adam. Exhausted, Mother Willow slept comfortably.

Granny offered Karlee a bed, but she refused, wanting to get back home. The old woman next offered to allow the twins to stay the day and play. Karlee knew she'd have to have at least a few hours sleep, so she agreed. She could easily come back out before dark and pick them up.

Driving home was the first time she'd had a minute to think of Daniel. If she hadn't been called away, she planned to say something to him about their night together.

She'd felt him trying to lie so still beside her. Known he was awake. Guessed he wrestled with himself and what he'd done. He said he didn't want her near, but he'd taken more time caressing her than had been necessary to determine size.

He might never want to love or care for her, or be near her. But she didn't feel the same way. She thought she'd never have a husband. Now that she did, she wanted a *real* husband.

Karlee closed her eyes, forcing back the tears as she realized her need to love was greater than her need to be loved. If he'd just let her love him. Like Wolf said, it was a decision people make. She felt like she had a lifetime of love stored up inside her. Daniel, despite his moodiness, was a good man. She could love him and the twins. It wouldn't matter that he would never love her. It might not be the romantic kind of love poems are written about but more a practical kind of love.

She wasn't some woman he could marry and forget about. Karlee planned to make sure he knew she was around and that she could help him. He was a kind man, with a body that stopped her heart from beating when she saw him fully bare. He might not want a wife, but she wanted a husband, and she planned to have one.

Karlee set her jaw. She had nothing to lose. She started without anything. If she ended up without him, she was no worse off than she'd been all her life. And she found it hard to believe he could like her any less than he did now. He seemed to have to force himself to talk to her most of the time. But she'd keep trying.

This was no half-baked scheme. This was a great idea, for sure, this time. This was her one shot. When the time was right she'd tell him she'd decided to love him and all she asked in return was to be allowed to do so.

When she reached the house, she was too busy to speak to Daniel. The boy everyone thought of as John— except the boy himself—had toppled his chair and cut a gash in his head only moments before Karlee entered the kitchen.

She watched an exhausted Adam square his shoulders and open his bag. Wolf and Wes held the boy still while Allie cried and the doctor worked. Karlee moved around Adam as she had all night at the Buchanan home, guessing what he needed before he asked.

When the stitches were finished, the three men went to wash off the blood in the horse trough out beside the barn. The kid had managed to splatter them all with what he believed to be his pure Apache blood. Wes was the last to leave, glancing first at his tiny wife and than at Karlee. His gaze seemed to ask Karlee to look over this fragile woman he loved so dearly.

Karlee nodded in answer to Wes's unspoken question, then turned her attention to Allie.

"I won't be ten minutes, Allie," Wes whispered. "I'll wash up and then help Adam with his horse." He closed the door, not expecting an answer.

Allie didn't seem to hear Wes as she cried softly and knelt beside her bound brother.

"I'm sorry." She brushed his hair back from the bandage. "This is all my fault. You shouldn't be tied and forced into a way of life you don't want."

For the first time, Karlee saw no hatred in the savage's eyes. Only a pleading flickered from his dark depths. He wanted to be free, and he would keep trying until it killed him.

Allie must have seen it also, for she stood slowly and walked to the sink.

When she reached for a paring knife, Karlee's hand covered Allie's. The small woman looked up at Karlee with her broken heart shimmering in her blue eyes.

"I know what I'm doing." She gripped the knife and pulled away. "I have to help him before the men get back. My brother won't fight us, but he might try to kill one of the men."

Karlee nodded. She wasn't sure what her sister-in-law planned, but she'd back her up. There was an intelligence, an understanding within her that Karlee didn't question. Somehow Allie and the boy were connected by more than just the hope of a bloodline. Somehow their souls blended.

Allie crossed to her brother, speaking in a mixture of Apache and English. "I'll cut you free," she whispered. "If you kill no one. You must go before they return."

The boy looked at her with the same blank stare he'd

always used, telling her all he'd ever communicated . . . he didn't understand.

Allie sawed at the rope tying him to the chair and repeated her bargain.

John's chest rose and fell as he breathed for the first time without the restraint of the rope over his chest. He didn't move as Allie knelt and slashed the rope binding his feet.

He'd always fought, he'd always struggled, but now he sat perfectly still as Allie moved behind him with the knife.

"I'll set you free," she repeated. "I've no right to force you. You told me to run for the trees when we were children. Now I tell you to do the same. Run for the water's edge where the trees grow thick in the shallow. No one will find you in the bayou."

She said the words again in another language. "You told me to have a plan. You told me to run even if you fell. But I was afraid. When you were hit, I curled next to you. Now you must run. Run, John!"

The blade slit the last rope free.

EIGHTEEN

Daniel heard a racket that sounded like a chair toppling in the kitchen and the shuffle of several pairs of feet. Moving as fast as he could, he shoved the covers aside and stood with far more ease than he had the day before. He managed to make it to the door of his study before Wes yelled that all was settled.

No explanation. Daniel felt like a child being left out of conversation. He could hear movement and voices. Something *had* happened.

Bracing himself against the frame of his prison, Daniel tried to make out voices. Wolf's was easy. And Allie's crying drifted to him. And Adam's authority.

Several minutes past. Daniel could hear Wes swearing a few times. Then only shuffling, movements with no one talking above a whisper.

If Adam were back, Karlee could be also. Willow's baby must have been born by now. Daniel frowned. Willow was like a little sister to him. Why hadn't someone bothered to let him know if she were all right?

Daniel gathered his strength and moved slowly along the shadowy hallway. He'd be kept in the dark no longer. He was tired of being pampered and ordered around. His leg had healed enough to take a little weight. Daniel could stand.

As he touched the kitchen door he heard Allie's soft crying and Wes promise to return in a few minutes as the back door closed.

Slowly, hesitantly, Daniel opened the door to the kitchen. A bright light from the window slashed through his skull. His eyes watered and closed. He almost wished for the blindfold back.

When he forced them open once more, three figures stood before him in fuzzy shades of shadow.

One, a tall woman, near the sink. Karlee. Another woman, smaller, stood at the table. The third, very near, was . . .

Daniel blinked and tried to focus. The third was a man with very little clothes.

He tried to pull the picture before him from the haze of fuzziness. The throbbing in his leg almost buckled him as he realized the form closest to him had to be the savage Wolf said was always tied in the kitchen.

The savage took a step forward, his movements almost as unsteady as Daniel's. The boy headed toward the tiny woman standing in the center of the room.

"No!" Daniel cried, realizing she was his sister-in-law, Allie, and fearing she would be harmed.

"Wait!" Karlee's order came from across the room. "Daniel, wait."

But it was too late. Daniel had already turned loose of the door frame and was moving at full momentum toward the savage.

Allie screamed and ran between the two. "No! John don't hurt him! He's blind, John. Don't hurt him."

John's movements were faster than Daniel's. As he swung to deliver a blow to the blind man, Allie grabbed his arm. She seemed to travel with the punch.

Daniel tried to steady himself. He knew he couldn't

see well enough to offer a defense. Offense was his only chance. With a mighty lunge, he shoved into the intruder.

Like marbles in collision, they struck and spun away from one another with equal force. Daniel slammed into the table, almost blacking out from the sudden pain in his leg. He opened his mouth, but it was Karlee's scream that filled his ears.

The savage entangled Allie in his flight. Together, they hit the floor with a thud and rolled, their arms and legs twisting together.

Daniel fought the blackness, willing himself to stand.

Suddenly, Karlee's arms were about his waist, holding him up as she cried his name. Her strength kept him from falling.

Wolf's footsteps pounded across the porch like rapid gunfire.

"What's going on?" The huge man brought the sunlight as he shoved the door open without slowing his pace. "Daniel, are you all right? Karlee? Allie . . ."

The screams of a moment ago had settled and now the room seemed a tomb. Everyone looked toward the corner where the boy and Allie had landed.

The savage knelt beside the tiny unconscious woman, one arm around her, the other holding the knife she'd used to free him. His teeth were bared, like a cornered animal, and his knuckles were white around the handle of his weapon.

"Don't hurt the woman!" Wolf moved slowly forward. "It's me you want to kill, son. She's done nothing but be kind to you."

John's arm pulled Allie closer against him as his gaze darted from Daniel to Wolf.

"Come away from her, and I'll fight you barehanded against your knife." Wolf tried again. "But don't hurt her."

Daniel heard the clank of Wolf's hunting knife on the table only inches from where he and Karlee stood. The hairy man held his hands high showing he had no weapon.

"Come on, kid. This is your chance. Fight me. It's my scalp you want for your belt, not hers."

"Wait!" Karlee cried in near panic. "Don't you see, Wolf? The boy's not planning to kill Allie. He's protecting her."

"No." Wolf heaved his chest preparing to fight. "The kid's wanted to kill all of us, including her, since the moment he laid eyes on us. She may already be dead, and he's just an animal protecting his prey."

Daniel slowly felt behind him for Wolf's knife. If he didn't think fast Wolf, or the boy, would be dead.

"Stand up and fight me, boy!" Wolf ordered.

John swept the blade across the air at belly level. Hate darkened his eyes.

Daniel's fingers bumped into the huge hunting knife. Slowly, he gripped the handle and pulled it forward.

"Look, Wolf!" Karlee cried. "He's holding Allie against his chest just like she told me he did in the field. Only now she's the one knocked out. He's protecting her."

Wolf shook his head. "He just knows he can kill her any time. It's me he has to worry about now. She's done all she could to help him. His mind is Apache. And we're all his enemy."

Daniel straightened. "Stand guard, Wolf."

Wolf opened his mouth to argue as Daniel pushed away from the table and, with two steps, put himself in the center of the room between Wolf and the boy.

He held the long knife in his grip as he faced the shadowy figure kneeling a few feet away. Karlee reached to pull him back, but he shoved her hand away.

"I remember the night we first saw Allie." He talked

more to calm Wolf and Karlee than the boy. He knew the boy would wait for his chance, and the knife would give him pause. "She's a lady now, but there were some who thought she was a savage when Wes first brought her to Adam's place."

Daniel held up the weapon, balancing it on his open palm. "I'll not hurt you, John," he said in a low slow voice. "I need no knife."

The boy shifted his smaller knife to his left hand and grabbed the offering from Daniel's open palm.

"Wonderful," Wolf growled. "Why don't we give him all the knives?"

"Karlee." Daniel didn't move from in front of the boy. "Get all we have just as Adam did with Allie. He has to know we mean him no harm."

Karlee made a little sound of pure fear and turned toward the shelves. One by one, she handed Daniel the knives, big and small. One by one, he gave them to John.

The boy held as many as he could, then began to spread them around him within easy reach. Wolf moved close enough to offer Daniel a chair.

Daniel sat down without saying a word, extending his leg in front of him to ease the pain.

Allie moaned and finally moved in John's arms. She felt her head as she regained her senses. The moment she realized it was her brother's arm around her, she reached to hug him without the slightest hesitation or fear.

"John. You're all right." Tears ran unchecked down her cheeks.

"Run, Allie, run," he mumbled words he hadn't said in fifteen years.

She touched the scar on his chest where she'd seen blood all those years ago. "Come on, John. Let me take you home."

All the knives surrounding them were forgotten.

NINETEEN

KARLEE HELPED DANIEL BACK TO HIS BED, BUT HE allowed her to take very little of his weight. He managed on his own, with her only as a guide. When they reached the parlor, still dark from sheets over the windows, Daniel closed the door.

"Will you put the wet cloth over my eyes for a few minutes?" He sounded tired.

"Certainly," she answered formally.

When he was tucked into bed with the towel in place, she sat beside him and told him the details of Willow's childbirth.

"Did you get any sleep last night?" he asked when she finished.

"No." She removed the cloth from his eyes. "But I can manage. I have lots to do today. Would you like the blindfold replaced?"

"No." He caught her hand before she moved away. "Rest a while. We've both had a long night and a harrowing morning. Allie needs time alone with her brother. The twins are gone. The house is quiet." He pulled her closer. "Rest here."

Hesitantly, she stretched out beside him. "I thought you didn't want me so near."

"This seems a practical place with the house full. Had you rather sleep somewhere else?"

"No," she answered quickly. Too quickly, she thought. "Here is fine."

Daniel had to ask. The question had eaten away at him for two days and her behavior might never tell him the truth. "When I touched you a few nights ago, did you mind?"

"No." She felt the room suddenly warm. She didn't pretend not to know what he was talking about. "I didn't mind."

"But." Words stumbled from his lips. "I didn't want you to feel like you had to allow—"

"If I hadn't wanted to let you, I wouldn't have, marriage or not." She rolled on her side to face him.

"Good." Daniel closed his eyes, worry lines disappearing from his face. "I don't want you to ever do anything you don't feel right about. This marriage should be an agreement we both make, not one setting rules for the other."

"That sounds a fair bargain. I can ask for nothing more." Karlee rested her head on his heart and snuggled into place. "Being here beside you feels right somehow." She yawned. "It's felt right since the beginning."

"Sleeping next to you does take the edge off the loneliness," he admitted. "Once your feet get warm, it's comfortable. I see no reason we can't continue." He could think of two reasons pressing against his side at this very moment, but if she didn't mind, he should forget about how they felt in his hand.

"I find you comfortable as well." She tried to keep her voice steady.

They could have been poor actors rehearsing lines for all the meaning she heard in their words, but she didn't know where to start to make him care about her.

He cupped his hand over her hair and kissed her forehead. Then, tugged at her braid, loosening the tie and pulling her hair free. "Go to sleep, my wife. I'll wake you in a few hours."

Her exhausted body melted into the warmth at his side. She wanted to talk to him more, but all the hours without sleep piled atop her, weighing her eyes closed.

By the time he finished unthreading her braid, she was fast asleep. Slowly, he combed his hand through her thick hair, amazed at how good the strands felt to his touch.

She was his, he thought. Whether he wanted her or not, whether he ever slept with her, even if he didn't love her, she was his.

He bent and paused, almost tasting her lips now parted in sleep. Finally, he could resist no longer. It wasn't a kiss, but a taste, light and thorough across her mouth. He told himself he was just getting used to her. They were no longer strangers. It was time he stopped acting as if she'd go away when he blinked. Like it or not, she was here to stay.

Karlee turned toward him as she slept, cuddling into the safety of his arms like a child. She spread her hand over his chest.

Daniel watched her for a long while. His eyes were clearing and what he saw in the shadowy light astounded him. Her hair was the color of autumn, browns and golds and reds mixed together to make a color unlike he'd ever seen.

His hand migrated down her back, then up across her shoulder, placing her arm behind her as he reached her hand. He threaded his hand through hers thinking of how strange it felt to hold another's hand.

Slowly, very slowly, his hand crossed the front of her dress. He could imagine the softness of her breasts beneath the layers of fabric. He'd been surprised when she'd said she hadn't minded him touching her.

"Karlee?" he whispered. How could he ask to touch her again. He'd sound like a fool. "Karlee?"

"Yes," she answered thick in sleep.

The slow rise and fall of her chest filled his hand with the shape of her breast.

Daniel froze. All he had to do was move his fingers away. But his hand now weighed a ton. He tightened his grip slightly. She moaned in her sleep but didn't pull away.

He told himself he was on fire because he hadn't touched a woman in so long. But it was more. It was Karlee.

Carefully, he unfastened the buttons at her collar, hoping to make her more comfortable. When she didn't move in sleep, he allowed his fingers to drift along the outline of her breasts once more, gently testing their fullness and shape. Then he slid his hand along her back as though she were a sculpture he had to touch to appreciate.

Brushing her lips, he wanted more of the taste of her. His hand twisted into her hair as he lightly teased her mouth with feather kisses.

She stretched in sleep, lifting up to him as though in welcome.

Moving his hand over her, his kiss deepened. He wanted more of her, far more of her. Without thought that he might wake her, he parted her lips with his tongue and drank in the flavor of her.

Her body rocked slightly, shifting beneath his touch. For a moment, he thought she struggled. But by the time he could register the thought, she'd settled once more.

He couldn't get enough of the taste of her. With a sudden hunger his hand caressed the fullness along her hip.

She moved her leg over him, cuddling against him even closer. Now she was so near he could feel her breathing. He took the weight of her rounded breasts against his chest, knowing that she'd welcome his touch when he stroked her.

She seemed to sleep so calmly while he felt himself burning. The need to feel her skin beneath his hand, to hold her against him, to blanket over her, was driving him mad.

His hand slid beneath the layers of her skirt. With only a thin cotton undergarment to cover the warmth of her flesh, he moved his fingers along her thigh.

She made a little sound and would have pulled away, but he gripped her leg tightly with one hand while the other stroked her face. When she relaxed, he kissed her tenderly.

His fingers spread over the thinly covered flesh of her backside as his mouth moved from her lips to her throat. He found the place where her blood pulsed and tasted her skin.

She moaned in need now, and he laughed as he returned to her mouth more hungry for the taste of her then ever before.

Slowly, he withdrew his hand from her skirts and spread his fingers boldly over her breast, kneading her flesh through the layers of material. She arched toward his touch as her mouth opened, responding to his hunger.

He smiled against her lips, enjoying the way she conformed so willingly to his touch. He hadn't expected it. But then, he hadn't expected Karlee at all.

Through the thickness of his mind, he heard the sounds of talking coming from the kitchen. Much as he wanted more, now was not the time or place to explore further.

His touch softened to a gentle caress, the kiss lightened. Gently, he rocked Karlee back to sleep in his arms, allowing her to grow accustomed to his hands moving over her. When her breathing had returned to its slow easy pace, he tasted her lips one last time.

"You're mine," he whispered. But he could no longer add "whether I want you or not."

Karlee tried to push away the voice of someone waking her. She wanted to stay asleep and continue the wonderful dream.

"Karlee," Daniel whispered near her ear as he stroked her hair away from her face. "It's noon."

She yawned and stretched, feeling his body beside her. "I don't want to wake up," she answered. "I was having the most delicious dream."

"Dreams are dreams, but the reality is we have a house full of company." His voice softened slightly. "You can dream again tonight."

Karlee sat up in bed and stretched. "You're right, of course. Do you need help?"

"Besides being starving," he grumbled, "I'd like to get dressed."

"But . . ."

"If you'll find my clothes, I'll be out of this bed."

She stood and straightened her garments. "Of course. I'm a wrinkled mess too. I'll be right back."

Within a few minutes, she brought a stack of clothes. She placed his on the bed and moved to the chair with her pile.

"I've been wearing this same dress since I put it on two days ago." She pulled the garment over her head and tossed it on the couch. Next came the petticoat and undergarments. "It will feel so good to get into fresh—" her eyes met his just as she pulled the first button of her fresh camisole together.

"What is it, Daniel?" He seemed to have paled from a minute before.

"You're undressing in front of me," he said so quietly she barely heard the words.

Karlee relaxed. "Of course I am. I've done it several times before. Surely you're used to the sounds by now." She pulled on her bloomers.

Daniel reached for his pants. "Let me guess," he said as he dressed. "You've thrown your clothes in a pile on the couch."

"You're getting good." She rested her foot on the bed as she pulled on her stockings.

"And right about now all you have on is your undergarments."

"Good guess." She laughed as she finished buttoning her camisole.

"They're white, of course."

"Of course," she answered.

"With a pink ribbon laced along the top just above the bustline like a drawstring."

"I wove that in myself." Karlee's fingers stopped at the last button where the pink ribbon crossed.

She glanced up. His blue eyes were staring directly at her. "You can see!" she mouthed the words.

"I can see." He smiled.

Embarrassment warred with excitement inside Karlee. She quickly pulled on her dress. "I'm so thankful you can see," she mumbled beneath the layers of her garments. "I've been hoping and praying and . . ."

"Karlee?"

She didn't answer but turned away from him as she buttoned her dress.

"Karlee, it's all right."

She slowly raised her head. "I know it's all right. I just didn't know I was being watched."

"You've nothing to be ashamed of. You have a beautiful body."

"That's the first compliment you've ever paid me." She walked to the door, too embarrassed to say more.

"It won't be the last," she heard him mumble.

• • •

Karlee entered the kitchen hoping no one would notice how red her cheeks were, but her entire face felt as if it was on fire. She started lunch with little more than a smile to Allie and Adam.

Allie must have stayed close to John all morning, talking *with* him and not just *to* him for the first time. She'd even managed to get him to wear a pair of trousers.

Wes wandered in with a nod to Karlee before sitting down at the table. He tried to get his wife's attention so he could tell Allie all about the fine horse he'd bought for John.

Daniel entered without a word but fully dressed. He made his way slowly to the table and sat down across from Wes.

Karlee tried not to look at her husband's face while she served the soup. She told herself his caresses had been a dream and she'd been asleep, but she knew both were lies.

Adam broke the silence. "He's up and dressed. I guess the morning nap was the best medicine he's had." Adam pointed to Daniel but winked at Karlee.

"And he can see," Karlee volunteered.

"A little," Daniel answered as Adam forgot the meal and started examining him.

"A lot," Karlee corrected. She sat down at the only chair left. The one beside Daniel. To her surprise he made no attempt to keep his leg from brushing hers. To her shock, neither did she.

Everyone talked at once as they ate her potato soup and crumbly cornbread. Karlee had to give the McLains credit. They all thanked the cook politely, as though they didn't notice the poor quality of her skill.

"If you think you're able to make it on your own, I thought I'd head back with Wes and Allie toward home." Adam leaned in his chair. "I know Nichole will be wishing me home by now. I'll ask the doc in town to come by and change your bandage."

"There's no need," Daniel answered calmly. "Karlee will do it for me. She does a better job than the old doc does anyway." He absently slid his hand along his leg, brushing hers with his movement.

"Allie and I could stay another few days if you think there will be any trouble," Wes volunteered, even as his wife frowned.

"No need," Daniel promised. "Wolf's here in case trouble explodes the minute you leave."

Both older brothers laughed as if they half expected their little brother to find calamity the minute they weren't around, just as he did when he was a kid.

After lunch, the four left for Wes and Allie's ranch with no ropes around Allie's brother. It would take a long time to find the John Sheridan inside the Apache. A part of him would always be the free warrior.

When they were gone, Wolf insisted on going after the twins only to return a few hours later to report that the Buchanans wanted to allow Karlee and Daniel time alone. He also brought supper, saying it was the first installment on Adam's bill for delivering the baby.

Karlee laughed, knowing that, more likely, Granny thought the men starved from having to eat Karlee's cooking. Also, she and Daniel needed no time by themselves. Alone or with a house full of people wouldn't matter. Nothing would happen between them, she thought. They were simply getting used to one another, nothing more.

She dressed for bed, then tapped on the parlor door. She wasn't sure if she should ask to sleep with Daniel or not.

Daniel sat up in his bed reading, a blue ribbon twisted around his fingers. "What is it, Karlee?"

He sounded tired. He'd pushed himself to stay up all

afternoon moving around the house, forcing his leg to take his weight. Several times on the porch, Daniel and Wolf talked, almost arguing about something. Karlee hadn't caught more than a few words, but she remembered hearing Lieutenant Logan's name whispered as an oath more than once.

"I thought I'd change the bandage," she offered as she entered Daniel's room.

"All right." He lifted the covers off his wounded leg.

Karlee tried not to let her hands shake as she worked. "It's almost healed." She said the obvious. "How are your eyes?"

"They sting some and hurt when I touch them, but other than that, I can almost see to read." His words were impersonal. The fact that they were alone seemed to bother him rather than make him feel comfortable. He twisted the ribbon tightly across his fingers.

"I moved back into my room upstairs." Karlee tried to keep her hand steady as she wrapped the leg. If he wanted her to stay, he'd have to ask.

"That's for the best," Daniel finally answered.

He now seemed to be strangling the velvet ribbon in his fingers. She could almost hear him say, "I want no wife. I want no more children. I'll never love again." The ribbon had somehow reminded him of those promises.

Karlee finished and climbed the stairs to her room. For the first time since she'd been in Texas, she reached for the box beneath her bed.

Her letters.

No matter where she traveled, she always took the box with her. It was all she had left of her parents—their letters to one another while her father was away at sea. She'd read them so many times, the paper bent beneath her touch, as pliable as cloth.

Carefully, she lifted the first letter dated before she was born.

"*My darling, my love,*" it started.

One by one, she read the letters. They told a story of a young couple desperately in love. Again and again, her father begged her mother to sail with him. Over and over, she wrote of reasons she couldn't. Then, finally, in the last letter, she promised she'd go with him on the next voyage.

Karlee closed her eyes and remembered the last day she'd seen her parents. They'd left her on the dock crying in her grandmother's arms as they sailed. She'd waved until the ship disappeared over the horizon.

A month later, they were gone. Another month and her grandmother died. By Christmas, Karlee was alone. Totally alone. One unanswered question had haunted her from the day she'd bid them farewell. Why hadn't they taken her with them?

She scrubbed her eyes with her fists and hurried downstairs. She needed to feel the wind in her hair.

For a long while, she stood on the cold front porch and listened to the wind stir the branches. The air was humid, turning her hair wild with tiny curls, but she didn't care.

Finally, when she could breathe deep without choking back tears, she went inside.

Daniel's door was open, but his light was out. He was back in his dark world once more to sleep.

She tiptoed to his bed and made sure he was covered.

Without warning, his hand grabbed her arm. "What is it?" His voice was too harsh for him to have been asleep.

"I was just tucking you in." She pulled at his grip.

"I don't need a nurse," he answered. "I'm not a child who must be checked on at night."

"I know." She stepped away in the blackness. The dark mood that haunted him earlier remained.

"Then go to bed, Karlee. We both need time."

His words were almost a slap, but this time she wondered if the harshness were for her benefit, or his own. If they couldn't talk about what happened between them, maybe they did both need time. After all, they had a lifetime.

Karlee pressed her lips together, wishing she could see him. "Must you always be so short with me?"

The room waited in total stillness. "Yes," he finally said without explanation.

Karlee could barely see his outline. He still sat up in bed. He hadn't been asleep at all, and it was growing very late. Where was the man Wes and Adam had talked about who loved a wife so much? Who always helped people? Who protected his children with his life? Did he plan to display that kindness to all the world except her?

Karlee raised her head. She could live with that. She'd lived in houses where they openly hated her for inconveniencing them. She could live with his coldness.

"All right." She reached the door. "It doesn't matter to me, but I should tell you something."

"What?"

Karlee smiled, anticipating how much her words would bother him and delighting in the thought. "I've decided, Daniel McLain, to love you for the rest of my life."

TWENTY

Daniel took her words like a blow. "I don't think I ever asked you to love me."

"I know, I just decided to." Karlee's smile flashed shorter than a wink.

"Well, stop it. I told you from the beginning I could never love you. People don't go around loving folks who don't love them back."

"I do."

"I don't want your love, Karlee. I'm happy with how it is between us. I don't want to love anyone else or have anyone love me."

"Too late, I've made up my mind." Karlee crossed into the hallway. "Good night, Daniel. I love you."

"Don't say that," he yelled after her.

Karlee closed the door as she left but she could still hear him grumbling about her, calling her every name he could think of. She smiled. Despite everything, he was a man worth the loving, and she planned to do so even if he never spoke to her again.

He could close himself off from the world if he wanted to, but not her. She planned to love him even if it drove him mad.

Crawling into her bed, Karlee shut her eyes. It felt so good to love someone.

She reached for the pen and paper in the bottom of her letter box and began, 'My darling husband . . .'

"She's crazy," Daniel swore beneath his breath. "I've given her no reason to love me. Hell, I don't even like the woman." He opened and closed his hand. "All right. I like the way she feels. But that doesn't mean I want to love her, and I sure don't want her to love me. Can't she see that? Hasn't she heard a word I've said since the day I let her out of the trunk?"

Daniel rubbed his forehead. She had him talking to himself. The insanity was spreading. In no time he'd be yelling "clear the decks" and running outside every time he needed to use the privy.

He closed his eyes, trying not to think about the way she'd looked standing at the end of his bed while she changed clothes. Her skin seemed made of cream, and her breasts were high and pointed—and full. They were so full and rounded, made for a man to rest his head on.

Daniel slapped his forehead so hard stars danced in his eyes. He was going mad! Here he was thinking of a woman in a way he was sure wasn't proper for a man to think of someone he never planned to bed. He was a preacher, a reasonable man, not some lovesick cowhand who hadn't seen a woman in months.

But she was his wife. She was his! He'd about talked himself into believing that he could keep his hands off her. This morning had been a mistake. He told himself he could never make love to a woman he didn't love. It wasn't fair to her. But then she'd gone and said she loved him. Didn't he have any say about the matter?

Daniel dressed an hour before dawn. He might as well get up. He decided he'd probably never sleep again. He'd spent half the night thinking about her and the other half praying for forgiveness for his thoughts.

Limping to the kitchen, he made himself a pot of coffee. By the time Karlee came down, he was on his third cup.

"Morning."

She looked at him as though she'd had a full night's sleep, which infuriated him.

"Morning," Daniel grumbled. He was turning into a bear. He'd always thought of himself as even-tempered, but Karlee had managed to destroy that lifetime myth. She seemed determined to aggravate him. She'd worn a proper dress, but she must know how its snugness outlined her body. When she moved close, he had to fight the urge to reach out and touch her. She was driving him nuts on purpose.

Wolf stumbled in from his all-night outing, relieving them of the need to say more to one another. The hairy giant downed half a cup of coffee and sobered enough to fill Daniel in on details in town.

"We've got to get Jesse Blair's brother out of the stockade," Wolf said between swallows of his second cup. "I heard word Logan is worried about the man dying before the hanging."

Daniel glanced at Karlee, but she showed no sign of listening as she carefully burned eggs to match the bacon she'd already charred for breakfast.

"Some of Jesse's friends want to break in, but the place is too well guarded. There would be soldiers killed plus no telling how many prisoners." Wolf scratched his beard. "We have to think of another way."

"As a minister, I could go into the stockade," Daniel volunteered.

Wolf shook his head. "You're barely walking."

"I can handle it. Get me to the gate. I'll make it the rest of the way. Once I talk with Blair, we can come up with a plan to get him out. There has to be a way besides force."

"Jesse says he'll come in as a trade to save his brother."

Daniel rubbed his forehead. "They think Jesse's dead. They'd never agree to it. Not after Logan saw the body. We'd be no better off with Jesse in jail than his brother. Both the Blair brothers have to disappear."

Wolf laughed without humor. "Funny thing is the brother, Altus Blair, didn't even fight in the war. He managed to stay home and safe for four years, then got caught up in the aftermath. He's a carpenter by trade, with thick glasses and a cough that's been with him since he was a kid. Jesse told me Altus wasn't expected to live to adulthood, much less long enough to be hung as a traitor."

Daniel nodded. "He helped build the church and this house. I've heard a few folks mention that he was a good friend to the first preacher and his mother who owned this place."

"You think he knows about the guns?"

Daniel glanced at Karlee and shook his head. "If he did, why wouldn't he have picked them up? The house was empty for a month before I got here."

"Maybe he was afraid of Baker. If Cullen Baker and his men stashed them, Altus might have been afraid they'd come back."

"I'll find a way to talk to him," Daniel promised. "We'll see if he knows anything that might help us."

"Can't hurt to try." Wolf downed the rest of his coffee. "But I doubt the man will tell us much. Whoever knew about those guns is long gone, or long dead by now."

"Can you hitch the team for Karlee to go after the twins and the buggy for me to drive to the stockade?"

"I can do better than that. I'll tell the settlement of

Germans living in your barn that you need a driver and a wagon. They can get you to the stockade."

Wolf excused himself as Karlee put breakfast on the table. The giant professed how sorry he was that he wouldn't have time to stay and eat.

Daniel picked at his food. Halfway through the meal, he broke the silence. "I want you to go after the twins and stay out at the farm as long as you can without stirring up questions."

"All right." Karlee didn't pretend not to understand why. She knew there could be trouble in town. "If you like, I could drive over and visit with AmyAnn today."

"No." Daniel looked up at her for the first time. "I don't want you anywhere near the Blair place. I'll meet you back here just before sunset."

Karlee stood and moved close to his chair. "Be careful."

Daniel smiled up at her. "You should have warned me about that before I ate breakfast."

Karlee did as he'd instructed, staying to visit with Willow late into the afternoon. She pretended a great interest in learning to make pies, so it was easy to spend the hours in the kitchen. Granny had a habit of telling Karlee everything to leave out of a recipe as well as what to put in. Finally, loaded down with pies, Karlee pulled away from the Buchanans' farm.

When she neared home, she was surprised to find the house dark. She'd never have guessed Daniel would be gone so long.

She put the twins to bed and waited, thinking up places he might have stopped. His leg was not that strong, he must be exhausted, wherever he was.

To pass the time, she sewed another doll for the growing collection on the kitchen windowsill. The German widow, who lived in the barn, stopped by to visit. Karlee gave her two of the pies Granny had made and assured her she could stay as long as she needed.

It was after midnight when Karlee finally crawled into bed. She'd spent the evening listening for every sound, waiting for Daniel. But in vain.

At breakfast the next morning, she felt as if she'd slept on a bed of nails. The twins were happy to be home. They excitedly helped her make cinnamon toast and then were delighted when she said they could eat it in their tent.

While Karlee washed the dishes, she glanced out the window and saw Wolf approaching with his head low. Something was wrong!

She was out the door and onto the porch before he reached the first step.. "What is it?"

Wolf's frown made his lips disappear into his beard.

"Daniel didn't come home last night." Karlee tried to keep her voice calm. "I know something's wrong. What's happened?"

The big man pressed his lips together as though he could keep from telling her.

Karlee waited.

"He's all right," Wolf finally began. "At least as far as I know. When he went to the stockade yesterday morning, Logan detained him. At first, we thought it was just for a few hours. But when he didn't come out with the midnight shift change of guards, I knew it would be longer."

"How long? Why?"

"I don't know how long. There are men who've been in there for months for no reason. As for why, my guess is Logan knows Daniel's been helping some of the Rebs around these parts but can't prove it. To make matters worse, the guard said Daniel refuses to talk to anyone."

"But he's hurt. He hasn't done anything."

Wolf raised an eyebrow. "He's done more than you

think, but that's for him to tell you. I've seen him risk his life more than once to fight the injustice going on. It's almost as if he places no value on his life, only that of others. And if I know him, he won't leave that stockade until he can get Altus Blair out."

Karlee paced across the porch. "What can we do to help?"

Wolf rubbed his beard. "I don't know; I've spent my life trying to stay out of jail, not get in. The only way we're going to get Danny boy out is by smuggling him a gun, and there's not much chance of that. I can't get near the place. As a Ranger, the Army hasn't made up its mind which side I'm on."

"Would they let me see him?"

"Maybe," Wolf shrugged. "I've seen wives pass pretty freely through the gate. They'll check you for weapons, make you empty your pockets, that kind of thing. I've even seen them check the hem of a woman's skirt. Course, they don't do anything improper, but a lady might find it embarrassing."

"That doesn't matter." Karlee whirled. "I have to bake some fresh pies, then I'll be ready."

Two hours later, she was dressed in her most proper Sunday dress of black with a black cape hanging off her shoulders to her waist. Her bonnet bore no lace. Her only jewelry was a tiny cross. She looked very much a preacher's wife.

The twins were playing in the kitchen with Valerie on watch. Karlee wrapped two hot pies in clean linen towels and started out for the stockade.

Ten minutes later, she was arguing with the guard at the gate. Thirty minutes later, she'd been stuffed into a small room and the guard had taken her pies. Karlee straightened her clothes. They'd patted on her shoulder pads and pressed her hem to make sure she wasn't concealing something, just as Wolf had predicted.

She glanced up as Daniel stumbled through the doorway, almost falling. The guard slammed the door closed, leaving them alone in the tiny dust-filled room with not even a chair in sight.

Karlee straightened, bracing herself for his anger. He'd tell her she shouldn't have come. He'd think her plan was crazy. She wouldn't have been surprised if he'd refused to see her.

But Daniel didn't say a word. He raised his handcuffs and encircled her with his arms. For a long while, he just held her.

"I . . ."

"Shhh," he whispered against her ear. "They're listening at the door."

He rubbed his face against her hair. "You smell so good. It's been a long night without my bride. I'm so glad you're here, Darling."

Karlee knew he was talking for the guard's benefit. She needed to ask him about Altus but she didn't dare. "I brought you pie." She played along with his conversation. "You know I promised you I'd bake you a pie every day of our marriage."

Daniel chuckled and slipped his arms over her head so they could stand apart a little. Without a word, they moved to the furthermost corner. "I know." He watched the door as he spoke. "I saw the guards eating it when I came in. They were fine-looking pies. I didn't know you knew how to bake."

"I don't, but I'll bring you another tomorrow." Karlee put her arms around his neck. "I promise, my love."

Daniel rubbed his scratchy chin along her cheek. "I'm sure I'll be allowed to keep the next offering." He leaned close. "You really do smell good, Karlee. I can almost taste the spices you cooked with."

Karlee turned her head and their lips met. "Then taste

me," she whispered against his mouth for no one to hear but him.

He hesitated a moment, surprised at her boldness. Then, he joined in the pretend game she played. Kissing her like any newly married man would kiss his wife.

"Can they see us?" she whispered.

"Only through the bars at the door." He continued to brush her lips with his as he spoke. "But you can bet they're hearing every word."

Karlee turned her back to the door. "I don't care," she raised her voice slightly. "I had to see you and have you kiss me and touch me. I'd die without your touch."

Daniel's surprise at her boldness turned to shock. He knew her words would be repeated among the guards. A proper lady, a proper wife, didn't behave so wantonly.

Before he could answer, she cupped his hands in hers and placed them on her breasts.

When he would have objected, she closed her mouth over his and kissed him as he never thought she'd kiss. Boldly, wildly, passionately.

Daniel's control shattered. His fingers closed around her breasts as the memory of her standing nude before him flashed through his mind. If she wanted so desperately to be touched, he'd touch her.

He moved his hands over her breasts, suddenly wanting more. She was like some kind of wild creature, behaving so.

"Is this what you wanted?" he whispered.

"More," she answered.

His fingers spread wide to please her, knowing that the guard would see nothing in the shadowy room. As his hand crossed over the valley between her breasts, he felt metal block his path. He widened his hand and brushed the outline of a derringer.

She'd smuggled him a weapon!

"I missed you so much, Darling," she said as her hand

moved alongside his and began unbuttoning her blouse. "The days and nights are torture without you near." She unbuttoned enough for his fingers to slip into the dress.

"I feel the same." He kissed her lightly as his hand sliced beneath the cotton. "I promise I'll be home as soon as I can." He moved across the thin camisole and found the pink ribbon he remembered. "We have our lives to spend together." He tugged at the ribbon pulling the thin garment low. The small gun slipped into his palm as he felt her bare flesh on either side of his hand. For a moment, he paused, loving the feel of her warm skin.

"Hold me, my love," she cried. "Hold me once more before I go."

She pressed against him as he slipped the derringer into his vest pocket.

He kissed her then in earnest as she buttoned her blouse. With a sigh, he walked her to the door. He didn't know how this trouble would end, or how long it would take him to get out of this prison. But one thing Daniel knew without doubt. He would touch the valley of bare flesh between her breasts again. And soon.

TWENTY-ONE

Valerie met karlee a block from home with a twin in each arm. All three girls were crying.

"What is it? What's happened?" Karlee jumped from the wagon.

"Soldiers!" Valerie said between gulps. "They broke in the front door without knocking and told us to get out. They said they had orders to search the place."

"For what?" Karlee lifted the little girls into the wagon bed with a strong hug for each. "It's going to be all right," she whispered against their blonde curls. "Everything will be just fine."

"I don't know why they're there." Valerie tried to stop her own tears. "I just grabbed the twins and ran. They were throwing things and breaking things. When I ran out Ida, the old German, was trying to tell them to stop breaking things, but they weren't listening."

Karlee hugged Valerie. "Things don't matter," she whispered. "You and the girls do. You did the right thing by leaving." She thought of asking Valerie to watch the twins longer, but she'd imposed enough. The girls were now her responsibility. "Climb in, and I'll drop you at the bakery."

"No thanks." Valerie waved. "I can cut through the

houses and be there in half the time. I think I want to see my *madre* right now." She tried to smile. "Be careful."

"Don't worry." Karlee flicked the reins. "We'll be fine."

A few minutes later, Karlee left the wagon at the front door and walked into her house with a twin on each side of her. "Now don't worry, girls. These men are just playing hide-and-seek, and they have to learn it's an outside game."

She moved through the house listening to the racket from above. They must all be on the second floor. From the sound, she'd guess four, maybe five men.

Karlee grabbed a quilt and spread it out in the wide foyer where the sunlight shone in through the open doorway. She sat the twins down and collected all the dolls she'd made. "You and all your friends can watch the men leave," she tried to sound cheery.

A soldier stepped to the landing above. He was shorter than her by half a head and a few years older in age. His clothes and body were the bagginess of a man who'd worn the uniform too long.

She quickly straightened, blocking the seam in the paneling where the wall slid open. She had no idea what they were looking for, but she didn't want them finding the guns. Daniel had never mentioned his arsenal to her. Until this moment, it had never occurred to her as strange that a man who wore no weapon of any kind would have owned so many guns.

"What are you doing here?" the soldier yelled from the landing. "I thought I told everyone to leave. I'm Sergeant Whiteley, and I've got the authority if you want to see the papers."

"I'm Mrs. McLain and I live here, sir. I have every right there is to ask what you and your men are doing in my house, paper or not!" Karlee yelled back. "And there's no need to yell, Sergeant Whiteley! I have no problem with my hearing."

"We've been ordered to search, and search we will." He stormed down the stairs, his voice still a notch below an all-out scream.

She heard something familiar in his tone. A touch of home twisted in his words. "Then do your duty, but be careful what you break, or you'll answer to me, Sergeant."

He paid her no mind.

"Or," she added, "your mother back home in Indiana."

The stout sergeant turned and stared at her with tired eyes.

"You are from Indiana, aren't you?" Karlee had guessed right.

"Indiana Regular. First to fight, first blood spilled," he said proudly. "A Volunteer force all through the war, and I'm proud to say I was one of them."

"Well, I guess your mother would be real tickled to know you're down in Texas tearing up the home of a good preacher who fought with the Indiana Regulars as well." Karlee was guessing, but after all, Daniel was from Indiana, he must have fought with the state's regiment. "The reverend was wounded a few months before the war ended. He came home to find his father's farm had been raided by Rebs. His parents were both dead. And now he has you and your men as a plague."

The sergeant's face paled. "McLain fought for the North? I figured him a Reb for sure."

Karlee tried to remember what she'd heard Aunt Rosy tell of the McLain brothers. "He fought along with his brothers, Captain Wes McLain and Doctor Adam McLain."

The sergeant's face was starting to look sickly. "He don't favor his brothers, does he?"

"No," Karlee answered slowly. "Daniel has blond hair, but both his brothers are darker."

Men stomped down the stairs and into the study throwing things aside as they searched. Their shouldered rifles bumped into walls and tables with no care taken.

"Hey, men!" Whiteley yelled. "Be careful of the preacher's things. There ain't no use in us destroying the place."

The soldiers looked up in surprise and slowed their pace. They weren't raiders, only enlisted men following orders.

The sergeant leaned against the wall beside Karlee, unaware he was aiding her with her concealment.

He lowered his voice so the men wouldn't hear. "I knew a Captain Wes McLain back in sixty-three. With the chances he took, I never figured he'd make the end of the war. I remember one night a bunch of us was talking about the battle up ahead, and Captain Wes said he had it covered. If he was wounded, he had a brother who would fix him up and if he died, his little brother would preach him into Heaven."

The sergeant smiled. "I ain't thought of that night in years. I was so scared I couldn't think of nothing but cleaning my rifle. I must have cleaned the thing a hundred times before daybreak. I got where I could put it back together in no light at all."

Karlee watched the others as she listened to the sergeant. They had no skill at searching a place. She could have hidden the horse in this house and they'd never have found it. One soldier was playing with a half-finished doll. Another read the book titles slowly, mouthing the words as though he'd find the answer to a puzzle in them. A third had gotten on his knees trying to answer Starlett's questions as fast as she fired them at him.

The sergeant straightened to his military stance.

"What's this youngest McLain done that landed him in the stockade?"

"I don't think he's done anything," Karlee lied. "I couldn't love a man who was rotten. He's only a small town preacher."

"Did he tell Lieutenant Logan he was in the Regulars? Logan's looking for men who helped that thieving troublemaker, Cullen Baker. An Indiana man would never do that."

"He won't talk to Logan. Daniel thinks all men, Northern or Southern, have a right to be treated fairly. The war's over."

"But all he's got to do is open his mouth and Logan will know. He wouldn't dare hold a McLain without a darn good reason. There's bound to be several men among us who knows the family name."

"If Daniel talks, he'll be treated differently? The injustice lies with Logan, not my husband."

The sergeant saw her point. He'd spent most of his life in the Army following orders and it had got him nowhere. The Union Army had been sent down here to prevent trouble. Chasing after a ghost like Baker was just stirring more up. He'd seen Logan step out of line more than once trying to catch the man.

"Would your husband talk to me? I figure I owe him that much, being from the same state and all."

"He might." Karlee turned around and pulled the already loose ribbon from her camisole. "If you gave him this, at least he'll listen."

"I'm not promising anything, ma'am." He stuffed the ribbon in his pocket. "But I'll do what I can."

Whiteley turned toward the men. "All right, empty your pockets. We ain't taking souvenirs with us. Let's get out of here and leave this mother and children in peace."

Karlee watched them file out. She still stood in front of the hidden latch. They'd found nothing.

Several of the day-shift guards reported in sick the next morning to the stockade known as Sandtown. They complained of something they ate.

Daniel watched replacements come in reluctantly for duty. They didn't want to be here any more than the prisoners did. They probably wanted to be home with their families, not on duty in Texas.

He'd found Jesse's brother, Altus Blair, and the reports had been right. He was near death. Even if they found a way to break him out, he might not live through the rescue.

"You the preacher?" A stocky sergeant stopped in front of Daniel.

Daniel didn't answer as he turned and walked toward the far wall of the stockade. He wanted no trouble. He knew Logan was just looking for a reason to keep him here longer. Daniel figured, if he stayed out of trouble, the Lieutenant would have to let him go. He might think Daniel was involved in something, but he had no proof.

"I said, you the preacher named McLain?" the sergeant asked again.

Daniel tried to turn and walk away, not wanting to talk to anyone in this place.

The sergeant fell into step. "You are Daniel McLain, Wes McLain's brother."

Daniel stopped and faced the man but didn't speak.

"I was ordered to search your house yesterday. Your wife chewed me out right and proper for bothering you and her. Course, we didn't find anything—just like she said. But she threatened to tell my ma how I was behaving." The sergeant smiled. "No one's done that in years."

Daniel could almost see Karlee letting him have a

piece of her mind. He smiled to himself. Better that than a slice of her pie.

"I told her I'd talk to you." He reached in his pocket. "She gave me this little snip of ribbon to let you know I was on the up and up, and this ain't no trick."

The sergeant handed Daniel the pink ribbon.

Daniel took the ribbon but still didn't speak. He wasn't as trusting as his wife. The man could be playing him, hoping to help Logan.

"I fought with your brother in sixty-three. A braver soldier I never met, and that's a fact. My name's Whiteley. Been called Sergeant Whiteley for so long I plum' forgot my first name. Tell your brother Whiteley, and he'll remember me."

"Whiteley." Daniel nodded.

"Reverend." Whiteley nodded back as if they'd just been formally introduced.

Daniel straightened and tucked the ribbon in his pocket. "So, you knew my brother in sixty-three. You ever see that terrible scar on his left leg?"

Whiteley looked confused. "I don't think I ever did. I never got past that one on his face. He told me he got it in the first battle of the war, and before that day, he'd been the handsomest man in Indiana."

"That sounds like Wes." Daniel relaxed a little. The man was telling the truth. Karlee might have mentioned the scar, but he felt sure she didn't know when Wes got it.

"Are they treating you all right, Reverend? Getting plenty of food? Did you get issued a blanket? I can help you if you weren't."

Daniel decided he had nothing to lose by trying. "Whiteley, there's a man in here who didn't even fight in the war. He's been ill since he was a boy. He's about to die."

The sergeant shook his head. "I'm no doctor, McLain.

And if I was guessing, I'd say there's more than one in this place who fits that description."

"I know. I need your help getting this one out of here so he can die at home with his family."

Whiteley shook his head. "I haven't got that kind of power. If Logan wants a man in here, there ain't no way to get him out but maybe feet first."

"Then tonight we take him out feet first. Meet me at this spot at sunset." Without another word, Daniel turned away from the sergeant, wondering if he'd show up at dark.

Slowly, he walked back to the only building in the stockade. If he could call it a building. It served as a jail for the more troublesome prisoners.

As he neared the gate, he saw Karlee. She was dressed very properly as a minister's wife should be. She entered with a pie in each hand. He heard her say, "Now you'll make sure my husband gets at least one of these?"

The replacement guards nodded, their mouths already watering as they stared at the pies.

Daniel couldn't help but smile. He knew he'd never see a slice of pie, and the guards would pay for their theft.

"McLain? You want to see your wife?" As Daniel stepped to the door, Sergeant Whiteley moved in beside him. "They'll be listening," he whispered as he cuffed Daniel.

Whiteley had just proved his loyalty.

"I know. Thanks." The sergeant didn't close the cuffs uncomfortably tight around his wrist as the guard had yesterday.

Daniel walked into the small room and raised his arms to his wife.

Karlee moved into his hug. "They almost didn't allow me to see you today," she whispered.

He smelled of her hair and just hugged her, realizing he needed her near.

She finally broke the silence. "I brought you a change of clothes."

"Thanks."

"How much longer, Daniel?"

"I don't know. A day. A week. A month." He felt her tremble with his words. "At least I know the twins are safe with you."

Karlee buried her head on his shoulder. "Daniel, I forgot to tell you. I'm not brave. I never have been. I'm more the run-and-hide type than the stand-and-fight."

He couldn't hold back the laughter. "I doubt that. From what I've seen, I'd say you're about as brave as a wife could be."

"No, you got a lousy deal in this marriage. I can't cook. I'll never be a beauty. I head off on some plan and later wonder why. And to top it all off, I'm sure I'm a coward."

Daniel had never seen her like this. He wished his hands were free so he could hold her tighter. She was frightened, truly frightened. And to his surprise, he realized what scared her most was the fear that she might let him down.

"Honey, listen, you *are* brave." He leaned close, kissing the tear on her cheek. "I want you to pack the house, everything except the furniture and the kitchen, and of course what's upstairs. Understand?"

She nodded. There was nothing left except the secret compartment in the hallway.

He raised his voice a little. "Since my church burned, we may have to move. I guess the house belongs to the church and now there's no church it will probably be sold." His voice lowered against her ear. "Search carefully, pack everything."

"I will," she promised.

He kissed her lightly. "I'll be home sooner than you think. Logan's a hard man but I don't think he'll step to drumming up false charges."

He pulled away as he heard the door unlock. "Take care of the twins."

"I'll be back tomorrow," she promised as the guard signaled her out.

The weight of her problems settled over Karlee like an unwanted summer cold. She lingered longer at the bakery, talking to Valerie and her mother, than she'd planned. But going home without Daniel there didn't appeal to her. Valerie's mother had given Ida a job. The tiny German woman was like a worker ant. She seemed to carry ten times her weight and walked in almost a run from place to place. Each time she passed, the little woman smiled, proud of her job.

Valerie asked about John. She needed assurance that he wasn't being mistreated. Karlee promised to let her know the minute she got a letter from Allie and Wes. "John's all right," she hugged the girl. "He's with his sister. She'll see that no harm comes to him."

With the twins loaded in the wagon, Karlee finally started for home. She'd stalled long enough, there was much to be done. She'd understood what Daniel had been trying to tell her. She had to get the weapons, hidden behind the sliding door, out of the house.

She pulled to the back porch, noticing a stack of trunks beside the door. Fine, leather, hand-tooled luggage. Wolf leaned against the house looking like a hunting dog who'd been ordered outside.

"What is it?" Karlee asked, helping the twins down from the wagon.

Wolf shook his head. "About the time you think trouble is full and plenty, another scoop gets added to the batter."

"Wolf?"

Just as he opened his mouth to explain, a tall woman in white swept from the house as though she'd been taking another curtain call.

The woman glared at Karlee for a full minute, her plastered-on smile as wide as a medicine man's banner. "Why, Karlee Whitworth, don't you remember your cousin, Gerilyn? It has been years and years and years."

Karlee realized her time trying to forget her cousin hadn't worked. She'd recognize those cold blue-gray eyes anywhere.

"You ask me," Wolf mumbled for Karlee's ears only. "I should pack her up and take her back until she can add a few more years onto that greeting."

Gerilyn must have thought Karlee's sudden smile was because of her visit. She swayed gracefully down the steps and gave Karlee an almost hug and an almost kiss.

TWENTY-TWO

Gerilyn hadn't changed in the fifteen years since Karlee had seen her. Her hair was still the brown of deep chocolate, her face china white, and her eyes the soulless blue-gray of a winter river.

"Hello, Gerilyn." Karlee watched her hug each of the girls and give them an air kiss an inch away from their cheeks.

"Aunt Rosy wrote me that you came down to help poor Daniel. He must have had an impossible time finding someone adequate." She straightened the already perfect pleats in her traveling dress as she continued, "Then I was beside myself when I heard of the fire in town. With only you as help, I knew he must be near panic. I just had to come down and make sure my nieces were all right. Precious angels."

"They're fine, as you can see." Karlee followed Gerilyn into the kitchen. "We're all fine." The last thing she wanted to do was tell Gerilyn anything was wrong.

"And where is my poor dead sister's husband?" Gerilyn dusted a kitchen chair with her gloves before sitting down. "Didn't he get my telegram?"

"We've been busy here." Karlee didn't even know if there was a telegraph office anymore.

Starlett tried to show her aunt one of the dolls Karlee had made for her. Gerilyn wasn't interested. "Wait until you see what I brought you girls." She patted Starlett on the cheek.

"Now," Starlett chimed. "Show us now."

"No, not now, dear." Gerilyn smiled at the child's impatience. "Later, when I open my trunk. We'll have plenty of time."

"You're staying then?" Wolf asked from the doorway as if the end of the world had just been announced.

Gerilyn looked as though she smelled something disgusting. "Who is this man, Karlee?" She totally ignored Wolf's question.

"That's Uncle Wolf," Starlett answered. "Can we open your trunks now? Good things come in trunks. Karlee did. We want to see what you brought us."

Gerilyn wasn't listening, only thinking about what needed to be said. "No, child, I told you later." She realized her words were sharp for she ended her statement with another pat. "And, of course I'm staying. You don't think I traveled all this way to go back tonight. I'm sure Daniel will make room for me. After all, I'm his wife's sister, not some distant cousin."

"What'd you want me to do, Karlee?" Wolf looked as if Karlee only had to say the word and he'd toss the thin woman over his shoulder and haul her back to the dock.

Karlee lifted her head. "If Gerilyn doesn't mind watching the twins for a few minutes, I'll help you move her luggage up to my room and clean my things out."

Wolf grunted, but lifted the first of three huge trunks. "It ain't fair," he mumbled as he followed Karlee upstairs. "You shouldn't have to move anywhere. This is your house. Only, by the amount of traffic that passes through here, you'd think it was a Butterfield Stage Station. Company's a curse on the newly married. I wish they'd scatter and leave us be."

Karlee fought down a laugh. He obviously considered himself part of the family. He was right though. It was her room. But between Wes and Allie, and now Gerilyn, she didn't seem to be sleeping in it much.

As Wolf stacked the luggage, Karlee moved her few belongings into the twins' room. In truth, there was plenty of space.

"I'm getting out of here as soon as I bring up the last load. If you need me, check with Ida. I'll tell her to look in on you twice a day. All you got to do is tell her to get word to me. One of her boys will be able to find me. She'll be proud I trust her to watch after you all. She's lost three husbands, you know, so she's fond of trying to keep up with people. Probably working on her skills while she looks for number four."

Karlee giggled. "Thanks, Wolf. I'll be fine. I've been around Gerilyn before."

"But you didn't even tell that woman you were Daniel's wife." He hugged her good-bye as if leaving her at the battlefront.

"She didn't ask. She strikes me as a person who only enjoys the sound of her own voice. And my guess is she's not going to be very happy when she finds out about the marriage. I'm the 'poor relation' in my family."

Wolf headed down the stairs mumbling, "Appears to me any relations leave a fellow poorer after they stay a while."

Gerilyn spent the afternoon resting and unpacking. About four, she came down to complain about the noise the girls were making. "Can't they go somewhere else besides the porch right beneath my window?"

Karlee was ironing. "Where would you have them go, Gerilyn?"

"I don't really care," Gerilyn whined. "The moon seems far enough. I must spend some time telling you how to discipline those two or their voices will have calluses before they're half grown. And you really must do something about their hair. I can show you how to braid it properly in a style that becomes any little girl."

"I didn't know you knew such things, not having children of your own," Karlee ventured.

"One doesn't have to be a fish to know how to swim. Observation and a sharp mind are far more valuable than carrying a calf like some cow for nine months."

Karlee didn't comment. Talking to Gerilyn was a waste of time.

"Dear," Gerilyn said sweetly as if she'd forgotten Karlee's name. "Would you mind pressing a few of my dresses? Traveling does wrinkle them so. And use a cloth over the silk. I'll not have it looking too shiny."

"If I have time. I need to start supper soon. Would you like to help?"

Gerilyn gave a practiced laugh. "Oh, heavens no. I would like to talk to that brother-in-law of mine, however. I guess since he's got you here slaving away with the house and children, he's out running free. Lord knows he's had these twin burdens tied around his neck long enough."

"No, he's not running free." Karlee smiled. "He's at the stockade helping with a dying prisoner." She figured that was close enough to the truth for Gerilyn.

A few minutes later, Ida tapped on the back door. Gerilyn took one look at the little German dressed in a menagerie of rags and excused herself without an introduction.

Ida tiptoed into the kitchen as shy as ever. "I brought you some soup for your supper and bread made fresh from the bakery."

"Oh, you shouldn't have." Karlee accepted the gift. "You are too good to us."

"No, no child, you are a blessing to all of us. I have a job because of you, and both my older boys are working at a full man's wage thanks to you. And that hairy giant who comes here brings me more vegetables and meat than I can cook. He says he finds them, but I see him in the market. His heart is big, that one . . . as is yours."

"I'm glad we could help." Karlee was a little embarrassed at the praise. All her life she'd wanted to aid others but usually she had nothing to give.

"Mr. Wolf came by the bakery and told me a witch is living in your house." The widow leaned closer. "You want me to get rid of her? My boys could bury her where not even the wind will find her."

"No, Ida. She'll be gone in a few days. But the offer is tempting." Karlee wasn't entirely sure the old German was teasing.

"Wolf said this lady is blessed with the knowledge of knowing everything of no importance and the curse of constantly telling others. He says she tries endlessly to give everyone this knowledge, but no one will listen."

Karlee couldn't argue.

Ida raised one slightly bushy eyebrow. "They say the bone dust of such a woman will make a willow sapling grow into an oak."

"You don't really believe that, do you, Ida?"

The old woman's rounded shoulders rolled. "I don't know. We had such a woman in our village once. Not long after she died I started noticing a great many more oaks in the woods."

The twins ran into the kitchen, breaking the stillness that hung in the air like a ghost.

"Look, Karlee. Look what Aunt Gerry gave us. Dolls with china faces and lace and hands that look real."

Ida waved good-bye and winked with both eyes, making her eyebrows seesaw. She was doing it again, Karlee thought, she was brightening the day in her odd little way. Ida had been a blessing since she moved into the barn.

Kneeling, Karlee gave her attention to the girls and the fine dolls they carried. "They're beautiful," she said. "The most beautiful dolls I've ever seen."

"They're from Paris," Gerilyn announced from the doorway. "Now my nieces won't have to play with rag dolls. And, twin," She pointed toward Starlett. "don't ever call me Aunt Gerry. If you can't say my name correctly, don't say it at all."

"I'm Starlett," the girl answered.

"Whatever." Gerilyn occupied herself in checking to see how the ironing was coming along. "Just go play with your dolls somewhere other than under my feet. And Karlee, the lace won't droop if you put a towel in the sleeve when ironing."

All evening Karlee ironed and cleaned while Gerilyn gave advice and complained. After dinner, Karlee was thankful Gerilyn hadn't offered to help put the girls to bed.

Karlee finally had time alone with her little charges. Cinnamon hugged her goodnight while Starlett asked how long the aunt planned to stay. The newness of having an aunt had worn off fast.

Karlee stayed in the twins' room as long as she dared hoping to avoid more lectures. When she finally tiptoed onto the landing, Gerilyn had already gone to her room. Karlee blew out all the candles and slid the hidden panel open in the foyer. By touch she began taking the weapons out one at a time and moving them to the kitchen table.

There, by moonlight, she wrapped each gun carefully and packed them away in the largest of Gerilyn's new trunks. Karlee had planned to use her own huge trunk, but it was now packed and in a corner of the girls' room. Gerilyn had insisted on removing all the empty luggage from the small bedroom so there would be walking room. Now, the shiny new trunk just seemed to be waiting for Karlee. With the Germans living in the barn, she could think of no where else to hide the guns.

When the last weapon was packed, Karlee scooted the load onto the porch and shoved it back in the corner. With a tablecloth as a cover, no one would even notice it was there.

Midnight had long passed when she crawled into Daniel's bed in the parlor and tried to sleep. She'd have to be careful in the house with Gerilyn here. The woman must think everything was normal. She should suspect nothing. But Karlee wasn't sure how long she'd believe Daniel was only visiting the stockade.

As Karlee fell asleep she whispered, "Daniel, I love you."

A mile away, he thought he heard her words as he stood in the shadows with Sergeant Whiteley.

"We can't pretend Altus is dead." Daniel's words were low, meant only for the Sergeant. "If Logan gets wind of it, he's likely to pump the body full of lead. We're not doing the man any favor by getting him killed the day before he's due to hang."

"Well, I did some checking. Altus Blair ain't done nothing wrong in his life. He stayed here during the fighting, worked as best he could building houses even when he was sick and took care of his mother while his brother went to war. There isn't a person in this town who has a bad word to say about the man. They even say his best friend was that preacher who got killed just before you came."

Daniel agreed. "I have to help him. Logan must be wrong in his charges. Altus doesn't sound like the kind of man who would hook up with Baker and raid."

Whiteley shook his head. "Baker's men are mostly soldiers, trained to kill, not carpenters." After a moment, he brightened. "I got some good news. I heard word an hour ago that you'll be released come dawn. Seems several of the men are on sick call. Logan was ordered to cut the number of prisoners and delay any hangings until we have the men. He can't come up with a reason to hold you so you'll be walking come daylight."

"Thanks." Daniel smiled. "I figured I'd have to break out. Maybe I can do Altus more good on the other side of this fence. I don't seem to be helping him much in here."

"I'll keep an eye on him," Whiteley promised. "Don't worry. I'll make my rounds and then be back tomorrow."

Daniel nodded his good-bye and watched the stout little man head toward the gate. His shift was almost over. There was nothing left for Daniel to do but find a dark corner where he could try to get a few hours sleep. He'd talk to the sergeant again tomorrow, hopefully as a free man.

Just before dawn, the barrel of a rifle jabbed into Daniel's side. He was ordered in a harsh whisper to march to the gate. Several other prisoners waited with their few belongings tucked beneath their arms. One by one, they were checked through the guard station and told to be out of sight before the camp woke.

First light brushed the horizon when Daniel reached the check-out point. Just outside the entrance lay a line of stretchers holding those who left only after death claimed them. They now waited for someone from town to come for their bodies.

Daniel stepped through the gate and walked slowly past the bodies. No one had even bothered to close their eyes or cover them as they rested in eternal sleep.

Next to the last lay one small, withered man, his thick glasses still perched on his nose.

Daniel knelt. "Altus," he whispered as he removed the glasses and closed the man's eyes.

He ignored the pain in his leg as he walked home. Blair's brother was dead. Daniel had done nothing to help a man who had taken no side in the war. Now, if Daniel was going to stop more bloodshed, he'd have to act fast.

TWENTY-THREE

DANIEL FORCED HIMSELF TO CLIMB THE STEPS TO his house. "My house." He laughed. Without a church, this wouldn't be his much longer. Not that it ever had been. The preacher who built this place had been killed one night by what the sheriff claimed to be a stray bullet. The sheriff called in the Rangers to help with the crime and to insure the townsfolk would think he did all that could be done. After all, it didn't look good to have a preacher killed on the streets for no reason.

When Wolf investigated, he found the gun wall built into the preacher's new house. He suspected murder rather than bad luck. Wolf kept his find secret and wired for Daniel's help. They'd uncovered a great many problems in the months they'd been in Jefferson, but so far, no one had mentioned the hidden wall with enough artillery stored to restart the war in these parts.

What bothered Daniel more was the disappearance of the first preacher's mother. The night her son was shot, she seemed to have vanished. She'd been a quiet woman who kept to herself, but surely someone had seen her leave.

He sometimes caught himself glancing in corners, expecting to see her standing near or almost afraid to look up at an open window after dark for fear she'd be looking back.

Daniel shook off the feeling. This wasn't his house any more than Karlee was his wife. He slowly opened the door. No smell of coffee greeted him. Karlee wasn't up yet.

Painfully, he limped to the hallway and slid the panel open. The guns were gone. She'd done what he'd asked. Somehow, somewhere, she'd hidden the weapons. Until he knew which side they belonged to, it was safer if no one knew they existed. The searching of the house had been a close call. Too close.

He crossed to the open door of the parlor and saw his wife sleeping on his bed. With an exhausted sigh, he lowered himself beside her and rolled her into his arms as if he'd done so hundreds of times.

"Daniel?" she murmured.

"Shhhh," he whispered, pressing his face against the soft warm smells of her hair. "Go back to sleep."

She stretched, allowing him the length of her warmth and did as he requested.

Daniel plowed his fingers into the velvet of her hair and relaxed. The world could wait a few hours while he rested. He needed to feel her against him more than he wanted to admit. She'd slept in his bed as if knowing he'd return and find her. She anchored him to the only peace he'd found in months.

He brushed her hair back from her face. She was not a woman he'd have thought to court, even if he'd been looking for a wife. There was something a little unnerving about a woman tall enough to look a man in the eyes. Most women he'd felt like a giant around, always afraid he'd move too fast and accidentally step on them. Or put too much pressure in his grip when he touched them and crush their birdlike bones. But he didn't feel that way with Karlee. She seemed to fit by his side and in his life.

Running his thumb lightly over her full lips, he thought of kissing her. But he'd wait. He wanted her fully awake when he returned the passionate kiss she'd given him in the stockade. For now just holding her as he slept felt good.

He felt like he'd just closed his eyes when the shrill sound of a woman's voice shattered his dreams. "Oh, my God! Oh my God! Oh my God!" someone kept screaming as if it were a war hymn at benediction.

Daniel opened one eye to bright daylight as Karlee scrambled from his side. He wanted to pull her back, but couldn't clear his foggy mind fast enough to act on his thoughts.

The voice came closer. "Daniel McLain! You call yourself a preacher! You will rot in Hell! You and this worthless, homely cousin of mine!"

He put a name to the voice. "Gerilyn," he mumbled as one might identify a plague.

"How dare you defile the memory of my dear sister by sleeping with another woman so soon after she died? And with her children just upstairs. The sin is unforgivable!"

"Gerilyn." His voice grew stronger, and he managed to open both eyes.

"And you call yourself a fit parent. I've seen barn cats with more discretion."

"Gerilyn!" Daniel's voice didn't rise, but became deadly calm. "Enough."

"I'll not forget your sin so easily, Daniel McLain. You can't quiet me with a word."

He faced her, now fully awake. "Would you mind telling me, dear sister-in-law, what is so terrible about a man sleeping next to his wife?"

Karlee finally found the nerve to look at Gerilyn. The

woman's face drained of all color except the tiny round spots she'd painted on each cheek.

She raised one manicured hand. "You mean you married this . . . this . . ." Gerilyn shook her head so hard the perfection of her curls wilted. "You can't be serious."

Bolting from the room, Karlee didn't need to hear more. She'd heard it all before. It made no sense that a handsome, kind man like Daniel McLain would marry her. And Gerilyn was the one person who must never know the truth of why he had. So Daniel would have to stand and take a listing of all Karlee's shortcomings.

Running into the kitchen, Karlee covered her ears, not wanting to hear what they said to one another. What did it matter why he married her? He was stuck with her, and Gerilyn would never let him forget it.

She lifted the load of dirty clothes and hurried outside. Today was laundry day, and she might as well get started. The feeling that if she worked hard enough and long enough eventually she would matter, kept her hands moving. If she did the chores no one else wanted to do? If she acted like she didn't mind when they laughed at her? If she . . .

Karlee shoved the first load of clothes into the pot of water and lit the fire beneath. She didn't want to think. It didn't matter that her hair flew around her wildly or that she scrubbed her knuckles raw. All that mattered was that she not think about what Daniel was telling Gerilyn. Or worse, what she was telling him.

As Karlee lifted the first load of clean clothes and moved toward the line, her foot caught on the hem of her skirt and she tripped, tumbling the clothes into the dirt.

For a moment, she waited, expecting to hear laughter from the house.

But all she heard was the sound of the door opening.

Then Daniel knelt by her side helping her pick up the twisted balls of cloth.

"Don't," she whispered fighting back tears. "I can do it."

"Karlee?" He handed her a muddy shirt. "What is it?"

"I can do it. Don't help me." She tried not to notice the question in his eyes.

"I didn't tell Gerilyn anything except that we were married." Daniel was trying to guess the source of her distress. "And to mind her own business. But she never seems to hear that part of any discussion we have."

"It doesn't matter what you said." She grabbed the last of the once clean clothes. "Just don't help me. She'll be watching."

"I don't care if she watches." Daniel looked confused.

Karlee turned back to the pot and set the clothes down to be rewashed. "But I do. Don't you see, she'll say I couldn't do it right and you had to help me."

"Well, if she's watching, we might as well give her something to see." In one swift action, he swung her into his arms.

Karlee opened her mouth to protest as his lips closed over hers. His kiss was hard and determined. His arms tightened as he held her a few inches off the ground. She clung to him more from a need to balance than a caress.

Without releasing her mouth, he slowly lowered her back to earth. His hands drew her to him and she sighed as the kiss turned to liquid pleasure between them. Determination melted into desire. The kiss they'd both been thinking of, been wanting, since he'd been locked up could wait no longer.

Neither reacted to the slam of Gerilyn's upstairs window. They no longer cared. They were lost in one another.

Daniel moved his hands up from her waist to her arms

and lifted them to encircle his neck. Then, he twisted his fingers into her hair and tugged gently. As her head arched back, her body pressed closer. She felt him rock slightly from the tender blow against his heart.

He broke the kiss, out of breath. "That should show her you do something right," he mumbled.

She knew he wasn't thinking of Gerilyn's reaction, but of his own.

Pulled back, he allowed his fingers to linger as long as possible. "I only meant to kiss you politely. I'm sorry I got a little carried away."

There was no doubt in his manner that he was a man never given to getting "carried away."

She didn't know what to say. She'd never been sorry when he'd touched her and saw no need for him to be. "I love you, Daniel."

"Don't say that." He ran his fingers through his hair. "You're not making it any easier to walk away."

She tilted her head slightly in question.

He frowned. "Don't act like you don't know what I'm talking about." He stared at her with passion still darkening his eyes. "About the time I think I have a handle on how it has to be between us, you get just a little too close. And then you smell like you do, all fresh and newborn. And you taste better than any woman should taste. It's like I can't get enough of you."

When she didn't answer, he continued, "And the feel of you is maddening. Do you have any idea how good you feel in a man's arms? Soft as warm butter."

His voice hardened. "And what right did you have of kissing me like you did when you visited me? There could have been people watching. That wasn't exactly a polite greeting kiss, Mrs. McLain. I lost more than one night's sleep thinking about it."

Karlee shrugged, taking his criticism with a laugh.

"How did I kiss you? Like you just kissed me? And there *are* folks watching, now."

Daniel glanced at the barn. Half a dozen Germans smiled at him.

Stepping away suddenly, he seemed embarrassed at his own rambling. "I don't have time for such foolishness. I have to find Wolf before trouble breaks out. He needs to know what happened at Sandtown."

"I can get word to him," Karlee volunteered.

Daniel circled, staying a full three feet away from her. "Good. Send word for him to meet me here. I should be back by nightfall." He glanced up at the closed window. "I hate to leave you with Gerilyn, but there are things I have to do."

"I'll survive." Karlee smiled with limited conviction. They'd given Gerilyn enough to keep her lecturing all day.

Daniel squared his shoulders. "I seem to be always thanking you. In truth, I wonder how I made it without you."

She blushed. He couldn't have paid her a greater compliment.

He stepped a few more feet away. "Our marriage? It was a good bargain?"

She nodded. "A good bargain."

He was gone without another word.

Karlee finished the first line full of clothes before the twins woke up and her day truly began. Gerilyn stayed in her room until almost noon. When she descended, she was ready for battle.

She played the perfect guest until lunch was served and the girls were busy playing on the porch, then she opened fire.

Karlee didn't mind the insults about her cooking and the poor quality of her housework. She didn't even mind the digs at how poorly she dressed and how nothing could make her hair better. But, finally, as the afternoon wore on, Gerilyn hit on what did bother Karlee. Like a hawk, she spotted the vulnerable spot and flew directly toward it.

By supper time, she'd explained in detail why Daniel would never want to have children with someone like Karlee. After all, she was already so large. Pregnant, she'd be a walking mountain. And no man wants ugly offspring. Especially not a girl child who might take after her mother.

But it wasn't just Karlee's looks Gerilyn patiently explained in detail. A man might overlook the "large bones" and red hair, but the lack of grace and quick thinking could never be ignored. Not only would his female children be unmarriageable, but his sons would be slow and clutsy with two left feet and a heritage of clumsiness.

Karlee wasn't to blame, of course. After all, her mother, though plain, had come from a good family. But she'd married a sailor. The whole family had known it was a mistake from the beginning. He was huge with knotted muscles and the inability to stand with his feet together like normal men do. He'd had red hair and a laugh that shook the house. No man of breeding would have acted as he did from the moment he saw Karlee's mother. It was a disgrace, Gerilyn assured Karlee. Neither of them cared a wit what anyone thought. They were dancing fools, drunk on love. They married without even a formal wedding. And of course, no one was surprised at their offspring. Karlee was doomed to have the worst of both parents. Her father's looks and her mother's slow wit.

Gerilyn kept on rattling as Karlee set supper by the stove. The house guest didn't see any need to wait dinner on Daniel, but also didn't seem surprised Karlee insisted. Karlee could almost feel her mentally listing just one more in a long column of sins that she'd relate in a letter to Aunt Rosy.

The twins played quietly with their dolls. They'd been told once too often by Gerilyn not to mess up the new dolls she'd given them. So her china-faced gifts lay on the table while they played with the family of rag dolls Karlee had made them.

Karlee excused herself, claiming she needed to freshen up. She could hear Gerilyn's advice on grooming as she hurried into the hallway and out the front door.

It was not full dark yet, but gray clouds made the air thick with promised rain. The whole world seemed to reflect Karlee's mood. She could hear thunder far to the north as though it were rumbling, churning before stampeding. The breeze caught her hair and lifted it, combing the first raindrops through curls.

On the silent, shadowy porch, Karlee took her first deep breath all day. She felt as if she were bleeding from a hundred tiny cuts over her body. Leaning against the house, she tried to relax and gather the strength to make it through the rest of the evening. Part of her wanted Daniel to return, part didn't know if she could bear for him to hear all the things Gerilyn said.

Karlee faced the wall and pressed against the wood, wanting, as she had since she was a child, to disappear. Why hadn't her parents taken her with them? Had they left her behind because she truly was the worst of them both? She pressed harder, wanting to move into the wood and never be seen again. Tears bubbled from her eyes as she let the weight of all her shortcomings settle on her. She'd been so busy these past few weeks she'd almost forgotten who she was. What she was.

A hand rested on her shoulder, so lightly at first she wasn't sure when it had appeared.

"Karlee," Daniel whispered as he turned her around. "Don't lean into the wall. Lean into me."

She folded into his arms without a word. How could she tell him all Gerilyn said? He could probably see for himself.

His strong, powerful arms closed around her so tenderly, she wanted to cry all the more.

He held her as she fought to control her breathing. He didn't say a word or tell her to stop. He let her cry without question, without reason.

When she finally stopped, she wondered if he had any idea what a rare gift he'd just given her.

With his arm around her shoulder, they walked inside. She didn't miss the way he let her take a little of his weight almost as though it were too much for him to handle any longer alone.

"Jesse Blair's brother died early this morning," he whispered before they reached the kitchen door. "I've been out among the Rebs trying to stop a riot. If the doc hadn't convinced them Altus died of natural causes while in jail, I think they would have stormed the stockade."

"Are you all right?" She could see the tired lines in his face.

"I will be soon. There's a meeting tonight somewhere near the Blair place. Can you get word to Valerie and ask her to sleep over in the twins' room? I'll need you with me."

Karlee rested her hand on the kitchen door. "You forgot our house guest." She pushed, and Gerilyn came into view.

"How could I forget?" he mumbled against her ear. "We'll wait and leave after the house is quiet. You will go with me?"

She wasn't at all sure why he wanted her along, but she nodded.

The twins ambushed him, drawing his attention as Karlee set the table. No matter how tired or what troubles he thought he had, his daughters lightened his load. Starlett filled the room with stories she'd dreamed up, and Cinnamon managed to hug him more times than he could count.

He hardly noticed Gerilyn complaining and was thankful when Wolf appeared at the kitchen door and drowned her voice out completely.

When the hairy man was invited to stay for supper, Gerilyn looked aggravated, as though she'd been asked to dine with dogs. Her irritation seemed to jolly up everyone else in the room.

Wolf made an effort to be the gentleman, doing his best to show her that he'd been raised with proper Kentucky manners. But she didn't seem interested.

Before the bread was done and on the table, Gerilyn had reverted to her favorite pastime of belittling Karlee. She even tried to enlist Daniel and Wolf in her endeavor.

"Have you ever seen a woman with such hair?" Gerilyn chimed into the men's conversation. "Unbelievable color. Simply unbelievable."

Wolf growled at her, knowing there was an insult to his friend, but unsure where it lay hidden in her words.

Daniel didn't care what his sister-in-law said. What mattered was the way Karlee reacted. He watched as she pulled her hair back as if trying to hide it.

Gerilyn continued, "It's quite unfair, being blessed with a far from petite body and hair like that as well. Sometimes I think our Maker has no mercy. Don't you agree, Reverend?"

Daniel remained silent. He simply watched and remembered how he'd thought her hair had looked like velvet fire at dawn when he'd seen her standing outside in the wind.

Wolf wrinkled his brow and stared at Karlee as

though it had been he whose opinion were sought. "I always thought red hair was pretty, different from the run-of-the-mill. As for her size. She seems the right size to me. At least she's not skin and bones."

When Karlee glanced toward the hairy man, he winked.

Gerilyn looked down at her plate paying Wolf's praise no mind. "What is this, my dear cousin, a biscuit or a coal? I can't tell."

Wolf reacted immediately. "Why, that's a biscuit, Miss Gerilyn. You must be getting where you need glasses. That happens when a woman gets to your age. There's nothing to be ashamed about. Now look closely. It's a biscuit, nice and done, just the way I like them."

He leaned so close his shoulder brushed Gerilyn's. "If you ain't going to eat it, ma'am, I'll take it off your plate. I can't get enough of Karlee's biscuits."

He said it so convincingly, Gerilyn's jaw dropped in a very unladylike manner.

Daniel saw the game. He grabbed a handful of the hot dough-centered rocks and laughed. "Wolf's right. Karlee makes the best biscuits I've ever eaten." He'd pray later for the lie.

Karlee looked as surprised as Gerilyn as the two men almost fought over every dish she set on the table. They bragged and ate as if kings at a royal feast.

At one point, Wolf closed his eyes and moaned as he chewed a bite slowly. "This is the best fried ham I've ever tasted."

"No," Daniel argued. "I think the one she made a few nights ago was better. Though I'll have to have another slice to tell for sure."

Gerilyn kept nibbling at her food, at first convinced they were mad but slowly, like a first-year student among masters, she tried to see what the men saw in Karlee's work of art.

By dessert, the men had put on quite a show. They both asked for a large slice of pie.

As she stood to oblige, the door flew open and Valerie blew in with the damp rainy air. Her black hair circled her like a cape and she carried a bundle half her size.

"Evening," the girl said with a wide smile. "Ida's son told me you'd like me to spend the night with the twins tonight."

"If you'd like," Karlee grinned at the wonderful little girl who had become almost part of the family.

"I'd love to. *Madre* says she can teach me to cook, but I'm to ask you to help me with my sewing if you have a few minutes. I'm working on my graduation dress. I'll be finishing the eighth grade in a few months. At the rate I'm working on this dress I'll have to wear it at my wedding. *Madre* and Ida agree that you've got the finest stitch they've ever seen."

Gerilyn raised her eyebrow at Karlee. "I *truly* doubt that to be so, Cousin . . . a fine stitch from such a large hand?"

Valerie might not yet be a woman, but the hot blood of her ancestors thundered in her veins full grown and exploded before Karlee could answer.

"Well, of course, it's so, lady. You don't think my *madre* is in the habit of lying, do you?" She stood with her hands on her hips, ready for a fight.

Wolf's laughter shook the room. "Now calm down, little Miss Valerie. We usually don't like to scalp guests until after dessert."

Valerie stood her ground. Gerilyn tried to laugh, but kept the woman-child within her sights.

Daniel stood and pulled out a chair for Valerie near the twins. "Would you like to join us for some of my wife's delicious pie?" He bowed low as though seating a queen.

"No thanks," Valerie answered politely, her blood

cooling to kindness as fast as she fired when insulted. "After living around sweets all the time, I never eat them. Though I'm sure your wife's pie is as fine as her sewing." She directed the last words to Gerilyn.

Gerilyn was wise enough not to answer.

Karlee opened the pie safe. She was warmed by their lies, but not as easily fooled as Gerilyn. In gratitude to these two wonderful men, she cut them large slices of the last of Granny's pie. Karlee cut Gerilyn a small slice of one she'd made.

This time the men's praise was loud and genuine. They did everything except lick the plate. Gerilyn forced down a few bites, complaining that she must be under the weather for nothing had much of a taste to her tonight.

As the meal ended, Daniel stood and crossed to a small box on the top cupboard shelf. "I've been meaning to give you this, Dear," he said as he pulled something from the box. "You should have had it from the night we married."

Gerilyn watched with great interest as he held out his hand to Karlee. A gold band rested in his palm.

"Surely, you're not giving her May's ring?" Gerilyn cried. "Not my poor, dear dead sister's ring? It wouldn't be right."

"No," Daniel answered. "I gave May's ring up long ago to save a woman's life."

Karlee stared at the gift, speechless. Except for the tiny cross a teacher had given her once, she'd never owned a piece of jewelry.

Gerilyn had no such problem with talking. "Well, it's for the best. Karlee could never wear such a tiny ring as May's. Look at the size of her hands. Farm hands, my mother would have called them. Nothing but plain old farm hands. In fact, I'm sure no lady's ring will fit.

You're wasting your time to even try putting it on Karlee."

When Karlee didn't lift her hand, Daniel bent and gripped her fingers. He slid the ring on her third finger. It fit perfectly.

"This was my mother's ring," he said simply. "She was as fine a lady who ever lived. She'd be happy to know you now have her ring, Mrs. McLain."

Karlee stared down at the band of gold. Nothing Gerilyn could say would hurt her now. Daniel had just given her all the armor she needed.

TWENTY-FOUR

V ALERIE MADE DANIEL TELL THE STORY TWICE
about how he'd given away his first wife's ring to save
Allie's life. He told her every detail of how his brother
Wes had saved Allie from being treated like an outcast
because she'd grown up as a captive in an Apache camp.
Daniel described how men were at the door, planning to
take Allie back to a cage, when he set the ring beside
Allie and told her she wouldn't have to go if she were
married to his brother.

"Well." Daniel laughed. "We all know Wes is no
handsome catch with that scar running across his face,
but Allie must have seen the good within. She picked
up May's ring and slipped it on her finger as I pro-
nounced them man and wife."

Valerie sighed. "How romantic."

"Don't you miss the ring?" Gerilyn asked. "After all,
you gave it to my sister."

"No. I see it often when Allie and Wes visit. The love
she has for Wes shines just like May's love for me did."

"And Karlee's," Valerie added. "Tell me about how
the two of you fell in love."

Gerilyn leaned forward. "Yes, tell us. I'd be interested
in that story."

The tightening of Daniel's jawline was so slight only Karlee saw it. She waited along with the others to see what he would say.

"I'm afraid," he said slowly, "we'll have to save that story for another night. It's long past the twins' bedtime."

Valerie whined in disappointment, but stood and began gathering the twins. Gerilyn excused herself as Karlee wiped the table clean.

When all but Karlee and Daniel had left the room, Wolf pulled on his rain slicker. "I'll see you later." He looked at Daniel. "I've things to do before the meeting, but don't worry Danny boy, I'll be there."

"We'll both be there as well," Daniel answered.

Wolf frowned. "But . . ."

Daniel held up his hand. "It's time she knew."

"Whatever you think." Wolf opened the back door. "I'll see you there at midnight."

Without another word he was gone, leaving Daniel and Karlee standing alone in the kitchen.

Karlee glanced down at the ring as Daniel watched the rain.

"I'll put your mother's ring back in the box after Gerilyn leaves."

"There's no need to. It's yours now." His thoughts seemed to be far away. "There's an old buggy in the barn I could hitch up. It'll offer some cover in the rain if you still want to go with me. We're early, but the rain may slow us down."

"All right." She wasn't sure he wanted her along, but after all, he'd asked her. "I'll get my cape."

"Grab some towels, too, and a change of clothes. If we're soaked to the bone by the time we get there, we may want to change."

He pulled on his rain coat and disappeared into the sheet of water.

Karlee quickly collected their things and was waiting on the porch when he pulled the buggy close to the house. In truth, the buggy was old with frayed leather and a worn seat, but the bonnet was wide and deep keeping the passengers dry.

They drove out of town into the night. If Daniel hadn't known the road, he would have never found it in the rain for the land was liquid. Karlee felt like they were closed off from the world inside the buggy, truly alone for the first time. She relaxed against the crackly leather and snuggled near him.

Daniel, as always, didn't say a word. He seemed to enjoy silence the way some folks love music.

Karlee slipped her hand beneath his elbow. She wished she knew what he was thinking but realized she probably never would. She'd even tried to read some of his articles in the study, but found them far above her head. She'd been surprised at where his writing appeared, journals, magazines, chapters in books.

As they left the lights of town behind, she leaned against him and rested her head on his shoulder. The slow rocking of the buggy made her sleepy.

After awhile, he pulled the horse off into a grove of trees so thick the rain stopped pattering on the bonnet when they moved beneath the branches.

"I want to show you something," he whispered as if he thought she might not be awake. "But I'm not sure you can see much in this light." He fumbled for a lantern in the boot of the buggy.

Helping her down, Daniel held her hand while they walked beneath hundred-year-old branches bearded with moss. The light of the lantern made a yellow circle, casting more shadow than light.

"This is Caddo Lake." Daniel's voice was low, respectful. "The locals say it's haunted by the ancestors of the Caddo Indians who once lived here."

Karlee could hear the slosh of the water as it circled between the huge knees of the cypress trees. "It's beautiful," she whispered as though she might wake the ghosts.

"Legend has it that, years ago, a village was in the center of this area. The chief was warned by the Great White Spirit to move his people to higher ground. But he ignored the warning and went on a hunting party. When the party returned, the village was gone along with all his people and this lake was here.

"The Caddo said the earth shook and buckled. The current of the Father of Waters reversed suddenly, toppling trees, swallowing the settlement whole, and creating the lake from waters of the bayou."

She moved to the edge of the dark water. Twenty feet out, beyond the branches, she could hear raindrops hitting the surface, but here all was quiet.

"The locals say there are all kinds of dangers in this area. They warn people not to go near the lake without one of the old Indian guides, but I found this little cove and it seems safe enough. There's even a small German settlement on the other side of the lake. Their campfires look like fireflies on a clear night."

Karlee stared through the midnight hoping to see campfires on the other side, but the rain shielded them into the cove.

He hesitated and shifted, suddenly embarrassed. "I usually swim here and bathe. It's hard for a man of my size to get clean in a hip tub. If you wouldn't mind waiting in the buggy, I'll only be a minute."

It was too dark for her to see his face.

"Is there any reason I can't swim also?"

"You swim?"

Karlee laughed. "I'm a sea captain's daughter. Of course I swim."

"Then I guess there is no reason you shouldn't. It's

so dark out here, no one could see us if they were an arms' length away. The water's warm but deep."

Her eyes had adjusted to the darkness enough that she could see the shadows of trees banking the water. "I'll undress on one side of the buggy. I can swim in my underthings. I brought dry ones."

He didn't say a word as he moved to the other side and placed the lantern between them on the buggy's seat. She heard a splash and knew he was in the water before she even took off her stockings. She pulled the pins from her hair and placed them carefully beside the lantern so she could find them later.

"Daniel?" she whispered as she neared the water's edge.

"I'm here," he answered. "To your right. The bank drops off fast at the edge of the trees. The water may be over your head. Are you sure you can swim?"

"I'm sure," she answered as she stepped off the bank. The water covered her, warm and thick. For a long moment she floated downward, enjoying the feeling of surrendering to the lake. Then she touched bottom and kicked upward.

Karlee broke the surface, spitting and fighting her hair from her face. As she kicked to keep above water, a strong hand gripped her arm.

"Are you all right?" He pulled her close enough that she felt his words against her cheek.

Karlee laughed with pure delight. "Wonderful. Come on."

They swam out to where the rain met the surface. The downpour was so great, it became hard to tell when they were above water. Karlee hadn't felt so free in years.

Daniel stayed near, swimming at her side, touching her gently to steady her. They floated in the rain, letting the drops cool them as the lake warmed. The night hid their movements. She knew he was near more by sound than by sight.

They might not know how to dance, but as they swam, they danced in the waves. Their bodies brushed lightly in the water, naturally.

Without a word, they finally swam back to the bank. He pulled himself out first, then reached down to help her. Karlee couldn't help but wonder if she'd have the nerve to do what she'd done in daylight. Now, he couldn't see her body. Now he didn't have to look at her to be with her. Now, in the darkness she could be beautiful.

He grabbed a towel he'd hung in a branch. "Did you enjoy that?" he asked as he wrapped it around her.

"Oh, yes." She couldn't help but smile. "It was grand. Thank you for bringing me here." Her words sounded more formal than she'd meant them.

"You're welcome." He turned away and moved to his side of the buggy.

She could hear him getting dressed, but she didn't want the time together to end. He seemed suddenly in a hurry. He was a man who allowed himself very little time for freedom, she guessed. She felt honored that he shared the time with her. But why had he closed off so quickly? It was as though a clock had chimed somewhere in his mind and he had to go back to being the serious loner again.

Gripping the towel tightly, she maneuvered around the buggy. She could barely see him in the shadowy light as he buttoned his trousers. The white shirt he wore hung open. The lantern behind him put his face in shadow.

"Daniel? What is it?" She moved closer.

"Nothing." He turned from her. "We need to get dressed."

Karlee didn't move. She knew something was both-

ering him. The night had been so perfect. Now suddenly
he was cold and silent.

"Tell me," she asked and waited, wondering if he ever
would . . . if he could.

"No. Just get dressed." He didn't look at her.

Karlee placed her hand on his shoulder and waited
still feeling the closeness they'd had in the water.

He stammered, fighting for words as he finally faced
her. "I—I can't pretend any longer with you, Karlee."

Tears sprang to her eyes as the laughter died in her
throat. Just when she thought they were getting along so
well, he was going to tell her to go. Not even the shame
of divorce would make him stay married to her.

"I . . ."

He must have waited for this darkness, not wanting
to see her face when he told her good-bye. She pulled
the towel tighter. She'd heard it many times before, why
did the words hurt so much now.

"I've always been honest, with others, and with myself." He got the words out one after the other.

She couldn't speak even though she wanted to yell,
"Stop. Don't send me away, don't make me be nothing
again, mattering to no one. I've earned my place beside
you."

"From that day you smuggled me the derringer," his
voice grew stronger, "all I could think about was how
brave you were . . . and how much I wanted to touch
you."

"What?" She raised her head so quickly, water flew
from her hair.

"It may sound strange, even distasteful to you, but I'd
like to touch you." His voice lowered. "Not through layers of material. But truly touch you."

She couldn't answer. Somehow she'd changed trains
at full speed and had no idea where she was heading.

"Of course, if you object, I'd understand and respect

that." He turned toward the lake, paying little notice that the rain had almost stopped. "I've tried to think of other things. I've told myself it is wrong. There is far more between a man and wife than touching."

He stared into the night seeing only his falling. "There must be something warped in the way I feel. But I can find no sin in a man wanting to touch his wife. And the only dishonesty is not being straightforward about my request."

Karlee tried to breathe, but she felt like she was underwater again. "Why?" she whispered.

Daniel shook his head. "I don't know. I've never felt this way with a woman before. It's just that whenever you're near, I want you to be just a little closer. I want to feel you and hold you. The only times I've slept solidly in years have been the nights we've been together."

She moved beside him. "All right. Where do you want to start?"

He turned toward her and lay his hand over the knot where she'd twisted her towel together across her chest. There was no need for words. She understood.

Slowly, she let the towel fall. The thin cotton of her camisole clung to her like a second skin and seemed to glow as little more than spider web covering in the lantern light.

His fingers tugged at the ribbon, then unbuttoned the first button. His hands were warm. Hesitantly, he tugged at the second button.

Karlee closed her eyes. His hand gently spread the material away from the valley between her breasts. He moved his knuckles along the silken slope.

She shuddered, suddenly almost falling. His arms were around her instantly, bracing her against him.

"What's wrong?"

"Nothing," she answered and straightened away from him. "Please continue."

"You feel like warm velvet, you know." He lifted her damp camisole and peeled the material from her breasts.

She fought to stand still and control her breathing. If he wanted to touch her, for as long as he wanted, she'd not stop him.

His hand caressed her skin with such tenderness, she sighed. He wasn't examining, or evaluating, but worshipping. His hands circled over her, learning, memorizing.

As he passed his thumb over the tip of one peak, she sighed again and swayed toward him. His hands locked around her shoulders and held her so that they barely touched. He shifted, keeping a fraction from her as she felt the warmth of him so near. He was testing himself, seeing just how much he could endure, how much he could stand of being so close. So very close.

His knee sliced between her legs and she felt the brush of wool against the inside of her thigh. She sighed and would have reached for him, but he held her arms at her side. He shifted again and the buckle of his belt pressed against her belly. She felt the hardness of him press against her where a child would grow.

"Daniel," she whispered, but he held her from melting against him.

Slowly, as if torturing himself, he pulled her until the rise and fall of her breasts moved against his heart. The soft hair on his chest brushed her, and she lost her mind to the pleasure.

When his mouth finally covered hers, she was ready and hungry for his kiss.

His grip moved to her waist as her mouth invited him to taste deeper, and her arms lifted to his shoulders. She pressed against him, desperate for the feel of him after his heavenly torturing. She needed the pressure of his hands moving along her back and over her hips. The kiss continued. He slid her undergarments away from her slowly, enjoying each inch of flesh revealed.

The slight breeze cooled her skin, but his hands moved over her, warming her with his exploration. As she whispered her pleasure, he turned her in his arms, pressing her hips against him as his fingers spread wide on their journey from her throat downward. His mouth was warm on her neck while he took his time learning every part of her.

She whispered his name, a plea for him to continue. He turned her roughly to face him and kissed her so completely that thoughts no longer came to her mind.

He'd longed for this nearness since the night he'd first kissed her and he would drink his fill of her tonight. She moved to his every wish, taking all his caresses and kisses before offering more. He knew he was bruising her flesh, but he had to know fully the feel of her or he'd go mad.

Again and again, she moved against him, turning in his arms, giving him all of heaven he could hold. She learned with each kiss and when he returned to her mouth offered him more pleasure.

When he finally pulled away, he was out of breath and seemed shaken. "Get dressed, Karlee." His voice sounded unsteady. "We have to go."

He seemed to be fighting himself. He touched only her lips with the tip of his fingers as he moved away.

They dressed in silence and he helped her in the buggy. Before he raised the reins, he turned to her. "You must think me completely mad."

"Once more," she asked with her hand resting on his arm. "Hold me once more before we have to go, Daniel."

His control shattered. He pulled her wildly onto his lap and found her mouth. As the kiss deepened, he tugged at the buttons of her dress, shoving the material away in haste. His hands were as hungry as his mouth.

He bared her breasts so quickly she felt the material rip.

He could no more explain his need for her than he could have denied it. He'd thought the taste of her, the feel of her, would satisfy the hunger inside him, but all it did was make him want more.

When he ended the kiss, she lay across his lap, her head cradled in his arm, her breast bare. He gently caressed her left breast as though he had petted her so tenderly for years. And, as he knew she would, she responded to his touch with a little sound that made him want to give her more, far more. She felt so good in his arms, warm, welcoming. A gift he hadn't asked for but could never return.

"I take it you've no objections to your husband's touch?" He closed his fingers around her flesh and watched her arch her back in pleasure.

"No," she whispered almost mindlessly. "I've no objections."

Daniel pulled her close, hugging her to him. "Then promise to come to me again, dear gift. Come to me again as you did tonight." She was a woman of such fire and opinions, yet she molded to his desires without question.

He kissed her on the cheek and sat her beside him. There was no need for her to answer his request. He could see her answer in her eyes.

While she worked the buttons of her clothing, he drove toward the last stronghold of the Confederacy. The only place he knew of where men still fought a war already lost. His hands held the reins, but his thoughts were still holding Karlee.

TWENTY-FIVE

Daniel watched the shadows as he drove through the opening to a valley. He couldn't see anyone, but he knew they were there. Watching. Waiting.

A cliff rose on one side. The road narrowed so much that it would be impossible for him to turn the buggy around. He decided he should have told Karlee that the men surrounding Jesse Blair wouldn't have let him come alone even with Wolf vouching for him, unless she came also. They'd told Daniel he'd be shot if he entered the valley without his wife. Their reasoning was obvious; a man doesn't travel at the point of an ambush with his wife at his side. Despite Wolf's backing, Daniel was a Northerner.

A shadow materialized twenty feet in front of the buggy.

"Halt!"

Even though Daniel had been waiting, listening, he barely caught himself from bolting out of the buggy at the stranger's sudden appearance.

"Step down!" the faceless figure ordered.

Karlee squeezed Daniel's hand. Her calmness steadied him. He wasn't sure what he'd expected, but once more she was proving her bravery.

"I have to blindfold you both." The Southern voice softened slightly. "Don't worry. You'll come to no harm, Mrs. McLain."

The man covered their eyes and helped them back into the buggy. He didn't tie their hands as Daniel had expected. With a jerk, the man led the horse, pulling the buggy forward.

Karlee's hand slipped into Daniel's. She held on tightly as they moved. Daniel listened, trying to guess first one direction, then another. Trees brushed the bonnet of the buggy from time to time. The road turned from rocky to smooth, then rocky again. They twisted so many ways Daniel finally lost his sense of direction.

The horse slowed, then stepped forward suddenly. Daniel smelled the familiar odor of a barn. The wind ceased, and doors closed behind the buggy as it came to a stop.

"You can remove the blindfold now," a woman said in a voice low and kind.

Karlee was out of the buggy before Daniel could stop her.

"AmyAnn!" she shouted with delight and hugged the little mother as if there was no one else in the barn.

Several men stood around, unsure what to do. This wasn't the reception they'd planned. The women hugged and cooed over the baby as if a dozen men with rifles weren't circling them.

Daniel fought back a smile. Karlee seemed to think she was at a church social. Surely she must know the danger they were in. Unless Jesse brought his wife for the same reason he'd insisted Daniel's come. Assurance.

"Now which one of these men is your Jesse?" Karlee asked AmyAnn.

AmyAnn pointed to her husband.

Holding the baby up, Karlee stood directly in front of the man who once laid, almost dead, on her dining table.

"I wouldn't have recognized you, Jesse. You've gained some weight since your funeral."

Jesse nodded and lowered his rifle. "Yes, Ma'am."

"And this boy looks just like you," Karlee added. "The spitting image of his old man."

The father, barely into his twenties, grinned with pride. "We all think he does, Ma'am."

Karlee looked at an older version of Jesse standing next to the new father. "And you must be Jesse's pa?"

The man nodded politely.

"I'll bet you're mighty proud of little Rip here," Karlee said, as if just passing the time. "He's going to grow up to be a fine one."

These men might be outlaws, wanted criminals planning to rob and murder for their cause, but they were also Southern gentlemen and Karlee reminded them of that fact. One by one, she met each, introducing herself to them and them to her husband. One by one, the rifles lowered and disappeared from view.

When the door sliced open and Wolf passed in, he stood in shock. "What is this, a church supper?" He knew these men, he had fought beside a few of them. He'd had to pull every favor he could to get Daniel, a Northern preacher, allowed to walk in their midst, and now Karlee had turned the secret meeting barn into a parlor.

He moved to Daniel's side and whispered, "We'd better get started before your wife has them singing a round of 'Dixie.' "

Daniel held his hand out to Karlee. She joined him, still holding AmyAnn's baby in her arms.

Wolf cleared his throat. "Thank you all for coming tonight. I know it was at great risk for some of you. There's been talk about what to do in retaliation for Altus Blair's death. Before you decide, I want you to hear from Reverend McLain. He's my friend, and he went to

the stockade to check on Altus. He was there the night
Blair died. He's helped us before. I think we owe him
a few minutes."

Men who had argued bitterly against Daniel coming
now stood politely and waited.

Daniel never turned loose of Karlee's hand as he
spoke. His normally hesitant speech disappeared. "I'm
here, not as a Yankee, or even a preacher, but as a man."
He glanced at Jesse. "A man who'd like to see his children grow up in peace.

"We have to stop cutting into scars. We've all lost
enough blood. I saw some of you the night of the fire
working together side by side with men you profess to
hate. If we stopped the fire in town, we can stop the
flames of injustice licking away at what we all know is
right and fair."

Karlee listened in surprise as eloquent words flowed
from Daniel unrehearsed, as though straight from his
heart. He presented his argument for letting the war die
with Altus its last hero. He talked of a future for children
where North and South weren't divided. He spoke of the
opportunities here in Texas, and how he'd do what he
could to help.

Slowly, Karlee realized the man before her, with all
his shyness and gruffness toward her, was a gifted
teacher. Not a holy, hellfire and brimstone preacher, but
a man who believed in brotherly love.

She saw the goodness in him others must have seen
all his life. An open heart that would tolerate no injustice. A man almost too kind to live in his time. An intelligence strong enough to allow others to think for
themselves.

At first, she swelled with pride, then her cheeks
burned. How could this man be the same one who'd
touched her in the dark beside the lake an hour ago?
How could she ever hope such a man would love her?

He'd been either upset or injured all the time she'd known him. She hadn't really seen Daniel McLain. And what she'd experienced up to now must have been the low points in his life while the same memories had been mountains to her.

As Daniel ended his plea, he handed Altus's glasses to the oldest Blair. "Let the war end here. Let your son rest in peace so that little Rip never has to pick up the sword."

A tear rolled down the elder Blair's weathered face. Daniel gripped the man's shoulder in understanding.

An hour later, the Rebs agreed to consider Daniel's plea. Karlee hugged AmyAnn good-bye and allowed herself to be blindfolded and put back in the buggy with Daniel.

They rode in silence until the guard released them at a safe distance. Daniel took the reins in one hand and put his arm around Karlee in a natural gesture that almost made her cry. He didn't say a word as they drove home. She leaned her head on his shoulder and hoped he thought her asleep.

When they reached the back porch, he kissed her head and said simply, "We're home."

She climbed down from the buggy and went inside while he took care of the horse. She was dressed for bed when he came into the parlor.

Without a word she crawled beneath the covers and mumbled, "Good night."

Daniel sat down on the edge of the bed. "What is it?" He knew something was wrong.

"You were good tonight." She rolled to face him. "No, it was more than that. You were great."

He brushed her hair back over her shoulder. "You weren't so bad, yourself."

"What I did was nothing compared to what you did. You opened people's minds with your words." She swallowed hard, trying not to say the next words. "Folks probably wonder how you could have married me."

Then Daniel understood. "Karlee, you've had far too much Gerilyn for one day. You're a fine wife, and I'm a lucky man for this marriage. Now go to sleep."

"Aren't you coming to bed?"

"I've work to do in the study." He smiled down at her. "Thanks for an interesting evening."

Karlee closed her eyes and tried to go to sleep, but the way Daniel had touched her kept drifting through her mind. She wasn't sure what she'd expected, but sleeping alone tonight wasn't what she hoped for. She almost wished she could have been the wife who died after knowing the completeness of his love rather than the wife who lived and would never have but a part of him.

At dawn, she awoke still alone. She tiptoed to Daniel's study. He was sound asleep in his comfortable chair, his leg propped on the old box he used as a dresser. Books lay open around him, and a pencil still rested in his fingers. Papers were scattered across his lap and a blue ribbon wound its way across the mess.

Karlee moved closer, watching him sleep. The first rays of sunlight danced in his hair and across the handsome lines of his face. Asleep, he looked much younger. Young enough to still believe in loving.

He was resisting her, she thought, and himself. He had passion in what he said, and what he felt. He'd proved that last night at Caddo Lake. He wanted her, or at least he wanted to touch her, but he kept himself just out of reach. Because May had died, he'd condemned himself to a life without love.

She brushed his hair lightly. A curl circled around her finger. If he were waging battle over feelings for her, she aimed to make it a little harder for him. Karlee loved him more every day and figured she had a lifetime of love stored up.

Thirty minutes later, Karlee placed a cup of coffee beside his chair and knelt in front of him. She'd brushed her hair and scrubbed her face, but left on her night-gown. As she watched him sleeping, she unbuttoned her gown several buttons and leaned forward.

Her lips touched his lightly at first, bringing him into morning slowly. He moved with her, taking her kiss as a part of his dream.

She leaned forward, brushing her body over his arm as the kiss deepened. Her hand slid timidly beneath his open collar and covered his heart. It was pounding. He was alive whether he wanted to admit it or not.

Daniel jerked suddenly, fully awake. "Karlee!" His eyes reflected his surprise at her nearness.

"Good morning," she answered as she moved only inches away. "I brought you coffee."

Daniel frowned and plowed his hair back. She could see him growing distant. "Coffee is fine, but you need not wake me so personally."

"I thought you liked my kisses?" She wasn't being coy, simply asking a question.

He looked away. "I do," he answered. "But . . . I can't . . ."

"You can't what?"

He closed his eyes. "I don't know if I can make you understand. I'm not sure I do." He turned his face toward the window. "Years ago, I gave my love wholly and completely to another. To sleep with you, to have chil-dren with you would be wrong. Don't you see, Karlee? I've nothing to give you but a husband during the day. We'll never share the nights."

"But last night . . ."

"Last night was a mistake that kept me from sleep most of the night," he snapped. "I thought I could touch you and get it out of my system. I was wrong. The feel of you still lingers on my hands."

Karlee smiled. The battle was nearly over, and he didn't even know it. "All right," she said. "If that's what you want."

"That's the way it has to be between us." He sounded so determined, but his words were forced. "I've told you that from the beginning."

"I agree," she answered. "Only, since you unbuttoned me last night, don't you think you should button me up this morning?"

Daniel looked at her. First at her eyes, then his gaze lowered to her nightgown with a two-inch opening at her breasts. "I'm not a saint, Karlee."

"Yes, you are." She shifted slightly so that her gown opened more. "Saint Daniel. Ready to sacrifice your whole life for the love of one who died. Well, prove it. Button me up."

Daniel faced her and began at her throat as if the task she asked of him was nothing. But as his hands slid against the sides of her breasts, sweat broke out on his forehead.

"If I touch you again like I did last night, there'll be no stopping."

"I didn't stop you last night, Daniel."

He finished the buttoning, his hands shaking slightly. "Don't expect me to sleep next to you again." His voice was gruff. "After touching you, I don't think I could lie next to you without . . ."

"Whatever you want, dear," she answered sweetly. "I'll make sure you have it."

She stood and left, knowing she'd win. It might take a week or a month or even a year. But eventually, she'd win.

All morning, Gerilyn's barbs had no effect on her. Karlee simply remembered the way Daniel had touched her at the lake. If she were so deformed and ugly, he wouldn't have caressed her so. She could almost feel his strong fingers working fire over her skin.

Gerilyn didn't notice Karlee lost in a daydream. Her pattern of speech sped up, as though she felt the need to talk faster and get everything into the lecture.

Valerie stayed the morning, feeling a need to protect Karlee. They worked on the girl's graduation dress while Gerilyn pouted with boredom.

Finally, when Valerie left and the twins were down for a nap, Gerilyn asked, "How does it feel, Cousin, to be a hand-me-down wife? I know you've had seconds all your life. Well, now you have another woman's husband."

Karlee didn't answer as she poured tea.

When Gerilyn didn't get a response, she wandered on to another topic, having no idea her words had hurt Karlee.

"I think I'll venture down to the docks when it cools a little and see if there is a boat leaving in the morning. I've done about all the good I can do here."

"I'll dress the twins and go with you." Karlee brightened.

But her good mood soon faded as she walked through the market. Something was wrong. She wasn't sure what, but she could feel it in the air, in the way men greeted one another, in the absence of children and women outside and in the stores. Trouble was blowing in like a summer storm.

While Gerilyn checked on passage, Karlee stopped to talk with Valerie's mother. "What is it? What is happening?"

Valerie shook her head. "My *madre* will not speak of it. She says talk brings trouble walking in."

Ida passed with her arms loaded down with fresh bread. "That could be true, child. Listen to your mother."

Karlee busied herself with other conversation, knowing she would get nothing out of the two women. As she left the store, Valerie followed.

"I must know," Karlee whispered, hoping Valerie would confide in her.

"I'm not supposed to say. But you're not from around here and don't know what's going on." Excitement danced in the girl's eyes the way it does in only the young when danger is near.

They sat on a bench outside the bakery. "There is a man named Cullen Baker. He's plenty mean. Folks say he killed his first man when he was nineteen and liked it so much he keeps killing. He was a raider during the war, not caring which side he robbed and murdered. But since the war ended, he picks on mostly Yankees. So, some folks hide him out and think he's somehow good. But my *madre* says there is no good in him."

"But how is this Cullen upsetting the whole town?"

"Baker and his men robbed an army shipment a year back. They killed the guards and took everything, wagons and all. The rumor is one of his men betrayed him and kept part of the goods. Baker has bragged that he'll ride into town tonight and take back what's his. He says he'll kill anyone who helped the traitor."

"But he can't just ride into town. The sheriff, the troops."

"The federal troops don't have a cavalry big enough to chase him. Tempers have been boiling for months. They say there will be a riot tonight over the way the courts have been handing out justice." Valerie looked truly frightened. "Some even say bodies will hang from the trees come morning."

Karlee stood. "When you close tonight, you and your mother come home with Ida. I'll make room for you both at our place."

Valerie shook her head. "I don't know if *Madre* will do that."

"Tell her I'm afraid for the children because Daniel will be away." Karlee thought that wasn't far from the truth.

Valerie nodded. "I will tell her. *Madre* loves the little ones."

Karlee hugged Valerie good-bye and walked calmly back down the street to where Gerilyn stood waiting to know if she had passage. She'd wanted the twins to keep her company, but now crossed her eyes with exasperation.

"I thought you'd never come back, Cousin. You really should be more aware of the time you waste. If you were better organized, you could accomplish twice as much each day."

"I'll remember that." Karlee motioned toward the papers in Gerilyn's hand and quickly changed the subject. "Are you going?"

"Tomorrow, late morning. On a steamer I would call adequate and nothing more."

"Since it's your last night, I've invited company for dinner."

Gerilyn plastered on a smile that was almost believable. "I love dinner parties. But nothing too fancy, Cousin. I have to pack and really have little time to prepare."

"Nothing fancy," Karlee promised.

The afternoon was spent with Karlee trying to cook and Gerilyn packing. She asked Karlee to bring her three matching trunks up one at a time. As Karlee delivered each, she knew it was only a matter of time before Gerilyn realized one trunk was missing. She couldn't empty out the guns from her trunk inside the house with the children about. If she emptied them on the porch all the town would probably notice.

Karlee had to think of something. A idea popped full-blown into her mind as she dragged a loaded trunk from Gerilyn's room, down the stairs and across the foyer. It was a great plan.

She slid the hidden panel open quickly. Lifted the trap door carved in the floor remembering how Daniel had asked her to climb into the hole that first night.

This was perfect. Gerilyn would never miss the clothes, and if she did, she'd think one of her trunks was lost in transport.

Karlee opened the trunk, grabbed armfuls of carefully folded clothes and shoved them into the coffin-sized hole. In less than a minute, the trunk was empty.

Out of breath, Karlee closed the trap door, slid the panel shut and began pulling the now-empty trunk back up the stairs.

She'd only made it halfway up when Gerilyn appeared on the landing. "Oh, there you are, Cousin. I was just about to tell you I needed my last trunk."

"I have it right here." Karlee smiled at the brilliancy of her plan. What could possibly go wrong?

TWENTY-SIX

Daniel walked the streets of Jefferson, listening to the sounds of hate around him. It was bad enough that the Southerners resented the Yankees' presence while the Northerners thought the Rebs should pay for the war. But the hatred was deeper. Far deeper. A kind of wound that has festered so long no one remembered how it started.

Sometimes he felt like the world had gone mad with resentment and prejudice. It reminded him of a story he'd read once about a tribe long extinct. The culture considered itself to be a civilized lot. So when two chiefs had a quarrel, they would stand on either side of the river with their people behind them. To show his belief in his cause and anger with the other chief, the leader on one side would kill one of his own tribe. The other chief would do the same. Back and forth it went, until one leader was sick of how many of his people lay dead at his feet. That chief was declared the loser for he would kill no more of his own. Sometimes, according to legend, only the chief would remain. He'd killed his entire tribe to prove how strongly he believed in his cause . . . he'd won.

Somehow being right and getting revenge were more

important than saving those he loved. Like the ancient tribe, everyone in Jefferson seemed to have lost sight of what mattered.

Added to an already boiling pot were men of Cullen Baker's type, who preyed on the festering wound like maggots. Daniel was not happy to hear that Baker was coming to town to even the score between one of his former men and himself.

A nagging thought brewed in the back of Daniel's mind. Rumor was, Baker's former partner withheld part of a loot stolen from a federal troop shipment. The guns that had been in Daniel's hidden closet were all new Union-issue rifles. Maybe it was just coincidence, for nothing else matched the former preacher and owner of Daniel's home to Baker . . . nothing except a mother who'd disappeared and the stash of rifles.

He planned to ask Karlee what she'd done with the guns. The sooner he could get rid of them, the better. But when he opened the door of his home, a dozen people greeted him.

Valerie and her mother were cooking. Ida fussed over the children. Several of the young German men talked by the fire. Gerilyn sat at the table looking very much like she'd been committed to the state ward for the insane. His sister-in-law was dressed for a dinner party that obviously hadn't turned out to be what she'd expected.

Before he could close the door, Gerilyn jumped at him as if drowning. "Oh, Daniel!" She didn't seem able to say more.

Daniel nodded at everyone. "Welcome," he said, and caught Karlee's glance.

She smiled back a little shyly. "We've company for dinner, Dear."

Daniel almost laughed out loud. He must be getting used to her unpredictability. "So I see." He took time to greet everyone individually, moving about the room with Gerilyn following in his wake asking questions.

Finally, he turned and took her hands. "Gerilyn, don't worry. We'll have a great time even if all the china on the table doesn't match."

She looked at him as if he'd joined the craziness she wanted him to save her from. "But don't you see, everything has to match. One just doesn't set a table with two kinds of dishes. It's simply not done."

For the first time, Daniel saw her for what she truly was. She never meant to be cruel and hurtful with her constant advice. She had lived by all the unimportant rules of society for so long they'd become her Bible. Informing people of their shortcomings was more important than their feelings. Proper manners more cherished than kindness. The social code had somehow replaced the Ten Commandments.

Daniel put his arm around her shoulder and led her toward the hallway. "It's all right, Gerilyn. Don't think of this as a dinner party." He needed to calm her. There were enough problems this night. "Think of it as an indoor picnic."

She took a deep breath.

Daniel clasped both her hands in his. "Now, I know everyone will be depending on you to guide them in setting the table and organizing the line for eating. With this many people, it will be chaos without your help." He patted her hands. "But first, why don't you go upstairs and change? You wouldn't want to be overdressed."

"Oh, no." Gerilyn lifted her chin, silently fighting her way back to known ground. "There is nothing more gauche than being overdressed at a party. A picnic, you say?"

"A German peasant picnic. They held them inside on rainy nights." He made up the tradition. "Neighbors

would help cook the food. Some would even eat on ta-
blecloths on the floor. It's a custom passed down from
village to village during the winter months when folks
only long for picnics."

"Really? I never heard of such a thing."

"Oh, it's very much a German custom. We should feel
honored they are willing to share it with us, outsiders to
their ways." Daniel smiled, feeling rather proud of himself for his fib. "But many of our guest are young and
dearly need a gentle hand guiding them on what's
proper. For I'm sure, as you know, even a picnic must
have rules."

"I'll do what I can, now that I understand the custom."
Gerilyn straightened her bony shoulders. "An original
idea, but my cousin should have informed me earlier.
And the dress is . . ."

"Very peasant looking." He watched a light come
back into her eyes.

As she climbed the stairs, he added, "Karlee didn't
send out formal invitations. She wasn't sure how they
should look. Perhaps you could show her an example.
Your guess will be better than anyone's."

"I'd love to. I'm sure I could design something very
proper. Though at this late date it would serve more as
a keepsake than an invitation." Gerilyn disappeared into
her room. "But first I have to get dressed and back down
there. I'm sure she has no idea how to organize a serving
line."

Daniel leaned his head against the wall and laughed.
Gerilyn was back.

Karlee joined him. Before he could put up his guard,
she leaned against him and kissed him. Her body lingered a moment, pressing him against the wall as if she
could hold him there.

"I'm sorry about the surprise company." She brushed

her cheek against his. "But Valerie and her mother were frightened."

"And . . ." Daniel knew there would be more.

"And I invited them to spend the night. They've already put their things in your parlor bedroom. And Ida offered to cook supper, so I asked her to sleep in the twins' room." She felt his day's growth of beard with her fingertips. "And her children came in because the talk is the streets will not be safe tonight. So I told them they could sleep in the kitchen and dining room after we've eaten."

"And . . ."

Karlee laughed. "There are no more 'ands.' I hope you don't mind."

"Only one question, Wife. Where do we sleep?"

Karlee frowned. "I guess my good idea got a little carried away."

He lifted a handful of the hair that she now wore down. "I like your peasant look. And as for sleeping, I'll be out most of the night. You can have the chair in my study. I've spent many a night there. It'll be comfortable, if you haven't given away all our blankets as well."

Before he could ask about the guns, the twins surrounded them, and Karlee was pulled back to the kitchen.

An hour later, the dinner party was a great success. Gerilyn arranged the settings and the tables. She even insisted on blending china with pots to create an almost campfire atmosphere. In a shawl tied with a belt at her waist and with a handkerchief twisting through her hair, Gerilyn looked almost human, Daniel thought.

When the meal was over, he took the twins to his study to read to them while the women cleaned up and Ida's sons moved bedding in from the barn. Gerilyn sat at the kitchen table finishing invitations for everyone to keep. She talked of having such a party, on a grander scale of course, when she returned home.

It would be dark by the time the house settled down, Daniel thought. Daniel only hoped the town would settle as well.

As he read, the twins cuddled on either side of him in the chair. Slowly, one by one, all three drifted off to sleep.

Daniel felt the girls being lifted from him by Valerie and her mother, but he didn't bother to open his eyes. He thought he'd rest a few more minutes before leaving to find Wolf.

An hour must have passed, for the room was in darkness when he felt Karlee kiss him.

Her lips were feather light against his as she leaned over him stretched out in the chair, his feet propped on the old square chest.

She hadn't listened to his warning from this morning, but Daniel didn't stop her. He saw no harm in what she did, and he was still too much in sleep to care. Her lips were soft and warm. He loved the fullness of them, tempting him so lightly with their honeyed touch.

Carefully, she raised her skirts and stepped one leg over him. He felt her knees slide beside his thighs as she settled over him.

He stirred when her hands moved into his hair and her mouth found his once more. The kiss was no light touch now, but hungry. The warmth of her was intoxicating, comfortable, inviting. Liquid desire floated over him as she warmed him with the blanket of her body.

Daniel awoke all at once, aware she sat astride him, leaning down against him.

He opened his eyes and pushed her a few inches away in protest. The sight before him in the shadows shook him to the core. She was so beautiful and so bold.

Dressed from waist down, but above, she wore only

her camisole, unbuttoned dangerously low. Her hair danced around her like midnight fire, making her skin perfection. She was a warrior, fighting for what she wanted. He found himself drunk on her bravery. He'd only known women who were meek, never aggressive.

"Karlee, no . . ." he began, but she kissed him once more. "We can't . . ." He mumbled into her mouth half-heartedly. "I—I . . ."

She wasn't planning to lose this battle, he thought. He'd never seen a woman behave so boldly toward a man. She'd learned quickly how to please him, how to warm him, how to drive him mad. This morning he'd pushed her away, but tonight, she'd returned stronger, more determined.

Knowing this was her first time made her assault on his senses even more irresistible. He rewarded her efforts with the kind of deep kiss that made her melt against him. Karlee warm and willing in his arms fulfilled a hunger that had dwelled within him since the first time he'd touched her.

She wasn't using the feminine ways of a practiced lover, but only the raw, pure longing that had been between them since their first kiss. His mind might tell him to stop, yet the hunger in his body drew him into the feast. He kissed her with a wildness that shook the very center of his calm life.

When she finally straightened, she whispered in his ear, her breasts almost brushing his face. "You said I could come to you when I wanted to be touched again."

"But . . ."

She straightened above him and unbuttoned her camisole the rest of the way. The material hung open a few inches, curtaining her perfection. "I want you to touch me, Daniel."

A hundred reasons why he should stop came to mind.

The riot, the house full of company, his promises not to make love to her.

None mattered as he shoved the camisole aside and her full breasts were freed from the cotton.

"Please," she asked, in a whispered voice that seemed to scream through his mind. "Don't pull away from me this time. Love me, Daniel. If only once. Make love to me."

When she leaned to kiss him once more, his arms closed around her and pulled her against him. All the logic in the world couldn't deny the need he had for her.

His kiss was now hungry, almost violent in haste. His hands were starved for the feel of her. He twisted her so that her head rested against the arm of the chair as his mouth moved to taste her fully. She moaned softly and arched her back as his mouth closed over flesh.

Giving and needing at the same time, she crossed through the walls he'd so carefully put up. Denying her would have been denying breathing. She reacted to his every move. Her reaction pumped adrenaline into his blood. She was perfection in his arms.

He couldn't get enough of the feel of her, of the taste of her. Had it only been hours since he'd touched her at the lake? It felt like a lifetime. Frustrated, he stood, lifting her with him.

As before, she drove him mad by welcoming his every touch, his every taste. She was a river, running white water through his veins.

"I can't make love to you in a chair." His voice was low with desire and frustration.

The study was cluttered with books and papers, the desk piled a foot high. He felt like he was on fire with need. Every room in the house filled with people.

He lowered her feet to the ground, leaning her against the wall. His body pressed along the length of her letting her know how dearly he wanted her. She'd shattered the calm reserve he'd spent years building. If making love to her was what she wanted, she'd never have to beg again.

His hands knotted into her hair while he pushed against her and kissed her with the need of a lifetime for a mate. Her body was made to fit his and she took his hunger as a gift.

He moved his hands from her waist and closed his fingers over her breasts. They were full and silk. He caught her cry of pleasure in his mouth as his palms pressed over them.

She was breathless when he broke the kiss, but he didn't lean away. She closed her eyes and rested her head against the wall as his hands moved over her. At the lake he'd been hesitant, unsure sometimes, but now he knew her body. He knew what she wanted and loved hearing the sounds of her pleasure.

Somewhere above, a child cried in sleep. Painfully, Daniel forced himself back to reality. He heard movement. Someone was up.

"This is insane," he whispered against her mouth still tasting her as he spoke. "We have to stop." He knew she'd do nothing to help his quest. "I have to stop."

Karlee nodded and rocked slightly, her body pressing against him, allowing him to feel her fullness against his heart. She was a woman made to be loved, hard and fast, soft and slow, all night long. He knew as soundly as he knew his name that she would never withdraw from him or help him stop holding her. He caressed her breast and heard her moan. He'd already taken her beyond reason. In another moment, he'd be there as well.

He cupped her face in his hands. "You are so perfect. Right or wrong, we will finish this between us." He held her still until he knew she was listening. "I promise, I'll make love to you so completely, Karlee, you'll beg for sleep."

Without hesitation she answered, "Or *you* will." Her breathing, against his throat, grew shallow, causing her breasts to rise and fall against him.

He grabbed her hair and leaned against her once more. "I'm not sure if it's me having you, or you having me, but I plan to bed you. If you have no objection, Mrs. McLain? When we have a bed, of course."

"I've no objection," she whispered as he pushed away from her. "With or without a bed."

For a long moment, he stared at her, his eyes hot with passion even in the darkness. There would be no more bargains or games between them. She'd open to him willingly the next time they touched. And he'd make love to her as he'd never made love to a woman in his life. She was a part of him, as essential as breathing. A part he could no longer deny.

TWENTY-SEVEN

KARLEE PULLED ON HER CLOTHES WHILE LISTENING to the sounds that had brought Daniel to his senses. Someone moved from room to room, carefully opening and closing doors to keep from waking anyone.

Her body still shook with need. She wasn't sure what she'd expected when she crawled onto Daniel's lap and kissed him while he slept, but an all-out declaration to bed her was what she got. She had little idea what it would be like to have him make their marriage real, but if it were anything like what they'd felt so far, it might kill them both.

He was such a kind man, reading to his children, giving a welcoming word to all. He even made Gerilyn feel as though she belonged tonight. Not because he liked the woman; he just didn't want to see her unhappy. But there was another side to Daniel McLain. A side she wondered if any woman had ever seen, even his first wife. Gerilyn talked of how they had been best friends, and he always seemed to carry May around as if she were a china doll.

Karlee couldn't imagine him plastering little May to the wall and pressing against her while he took her breath away with a kiss. If she hadn't been there she wouldn't have thought he'd ever do such a thing. A newly discovered passion pounded in him stronger than a heartbeat. Karlee found it exciting and impossible to resist.

"Are you all right?" Daniel's words startled her.

Karlee finished buttoning her blouse. "Yes, thank you." Her hands were shaking, her voice formal. She wanted all of this wild animal within Daniel, not to tame, but to satisfy. And she wanted the gentle Daniel, as well, to stand beside.

"I didn't hurt you." Worry flavored his words as he moved toward the door. "Did I?"

"No, Dear."

He extended his arm, and she moved beneath his gentle embrace.

"I never want to hurt you." He kissed her forehead. "It's more than you make me feel alive again after years. You take me to a place I never knew existed. I feel like I'm in a full run when I'm around you, and you're matching me stride for stride."

A latch clicked beyond the study. Daniel pulled her close.

"Someone just opened the front door," she whispered against his throat.

"I know." He rubbed his chin against her cheek. "And they had to have used a key for I locked it earlier."

They waited, listening.

"Stay here," he ordered.

Karlee nodded but followed him out of the study. The hallway was dark as a tomb. She touched his back for guidance and moved with him toward the porch.

She heard the latch close when he touched the door. Someone had stepped outside, leaving it ajar.

Slowly, he opened the door and moved onto the wide porch. Karlee followed, bumping into him when he stopped suddenly.

"What is it?" She peered around Daniel.

On the center of the steps, five feet away from them stood Ida, still as a statue. The light from the street lamp slashed across her face. Terror had frozen her features.

"Ida?" Karlee started around Daniel, but his arm swung to hold her back.

When she glanced up to understand why, silver light sparkled off a handgun with the barrel pressed against his temple.

For a second, nothing before her seemed real. The shadows hid the gun's owner from sight. Karlee tried to move, but Daniel's arm held her in place.

"Don't scream." Ida's aging voice drifted across the stillness. "Please, Karlee, don't scream, or the entire household will die."

Karlee made herself breathe. Screaming hadn't occurred to her. Fighting had. She hesitated, knowing she had to pick her time. She heard the slight jingle of spurs, the creak of leather, a restless breathing of several men hidden in the blackness around her.

"What's going on?" Daniel asked, his voice almost casual. "What do you want here?"

The shadow of a stout little man appeared from the murkiness beside her. "Just stand real still, Preacher. We don't want to hurt no one here."

"Whiteley?" Karlee whispered.

"Evening, Ma'am." He tipped his hat almost politely. "Sorry to wake you. But, you see, we got some business with your husband and this old woman in rags here. Some business we got to take care of tonight."

"You're working for Baker," Daniel interrupted.

Whiteley pulled up the trousers of his new civilian clothes. "You guessed right, Preacher. I've been inform- ing him of when shipments of supplies would be easy pickings for years now. We've made quite a haul.

Enough for me to retire and live easy after tonight. Only one unfinished detail I have to attend to."

Karlee felt sick to her stomach. She'd trusted this man. "Your mother wouldn't be very proud of you tonight, Sergeant Whiteley," she said before she thought.

He laughed. "My mother's been dead for twenty years, Ma'am, but when you mentioned being from Indiana, I figured it was my way to get your husband to talk. We had to find out if Altus was telling any secrets on his death bed. If he talked to anyone, it would probably be a preacher. He was always chumming up to them. Even built this house for the last one for almost nothing."

"What does Altus have to do with you?" Daniel jerked his head away from the gun, but two men rushed from behind him.

They shoved Karlee out of the way, and each grabbed one of Daniel's arms while the owner of the gun moved his weapon to point at Daniel's mid section. "Make any sudden moves, and I'll gut-shoot you," a whiny voice almost giggled with the threat. "I like to watch 'em die when they're gut-shot. They wiggle around and complain before finally enough blood leaves them to quieten 'em down."

Whiteley laughed. "I ain't got time for a visit, Preacher, but I might as well tell you Altus joined us when we started raiding Union supplies. He weren't like the rest of us. He weren't in it for the money. Altus saw raiding as his one chance to fight in a war he'd already missed. Soon after he came onboard, we made a grand haul. But he didn't take to the killing. We tried to tell him, killing is just a part of war, whether they're fighting back or on their knees, begging for mercy. But Altus didn't see it that way. So, it seems he kept part of the shipment. I've come to claim it."

Whiteley motioned to one of the men still in the shadows. "Gag the woman. I don't trust her to stay quiet."

A man stuffed a rag in Karlee's mouth and tied it around her head, twisting hair into the knot. Then he jerked her arms behind her and tied them as well.

Karlee gave him a swift kick in the shins for his efforts. The man twisted the ropes tighter and jerked her to the edge of the steps. If she moved again, she'd be tumbling down the steps.

"Altus didn't tell me anything." Daniel tugged at his human chains. "Let my wife go back inside. We know nothing about a shipment."

"That's what Altus kept claiming up until his last breath the other night in Sandtown." Whiteley shook his head. "He was hard to get to after the raid. Melting into the hills with his brother every time he got word Baker was close. I couldn't do anything with Logan breathing down my neck. We tried making the last minister talk. He said he'd rather take a bullet. So Miller obliged."

The whiny man in front of Daniel snickered. "Took one in the head, he did. Brains splattered ten feet across the road."

Ida let out a little sound of sorrow and melted as though her mind and heart refused to work any longer. Karlee struggled to help her, but rough hands held her tight. The men let Ida fall as though she were no more than a dried leaf tumbling along the walk.

Daniel tried to pull free. "What makes you think I know anything about a shipment robbed almost a year ago? I wasn't even in town."

"Guns!" Whiteley's voice grew angry. "Brand new rifles. We figured it out. They have to be here or at the church. We've search everywhere else, and the church burned. When I searched here the other day, all I had with me was new recruits. You could still have them hidden. Save us all some time. Where are they, Preacher?"

"How would I know . . ." The man in front of Daniel lifted the Colt and slammed it across Daniel's face.

"That ain't the right answer, Preacher," he hissed as he wiped Daniel's blood from his weapon.

"Easy!" Whiteley snapped. "Don't kill him before we get the answer." He glared at Daniel. "We ain't got much time. Where are the guns?"

Daniel knew any answer would result in his death. He glanced at Karlee, thankful she was gagged. She was the only one who knew and if she told, they were all dead. "I have no idea," he answered honestly.

Karlee wiggled and kicked, trying to talk around the gag.

Whiteley didn't miss the exchange of glances between them. He smiled. "You're crazy about this redhead, ain't you, Preacher?"

"She's my wife," Daniel answered losing his iron control. "Leave her alone!"

"Of course. We'd never want to hurt her." He motioned for the man holding her to move. "We'll just take her with us. We'll be back at sunrise. If you've got the rifles ready for us, we'll give her back. If you don't, Miller ain't never shot but one woman. He's always wanted the chance to kill another."

Karlee kicked and wiggled as they dragged her to the wagon.

Miller giggled in Daniel's ear. "I'll think real hard where to kill her. It wouldn't be right to splatter her face or bloody up her clothes. I heard once that if you stab a woman in the back right in the center, they go limp and don't even scream. She won't be nothing but a rag doll if I do it right."

Rage overwhelmed Daniel. He no longer cared if Miller shot him. He would not lose Karlee. Wildly, he pulled free of one of his captures and slammed his fist into the man on the other side. His mighty arm raised again and swung a second time.

The butt of a Colt plowed against his temple as Daniel's fist lifted a man off the floor.

Another blow slammed into his skull, and all went black.

Karlee watched him crumble and felt her heart shattering like crystal. If he dies, her mind screamed, I die. Amid the raging fear whispered an understanding. If he'd loved May a fraction as much as Karlee now loved him . . . if she lost him . . . oh God if she lost him!

Men raised her off the ground and tossed her, face down, into the wagon bed. She fought wildly until she could no longer get enough air in her lungs.

When she settled, Miller patted her behind. "Good girl," he whined. "Ain't no use fighting. If you get free, we'd just have to kill you early, and you wouldn't want that."

He patted her again, a little harder than before. "I ain't never had me a preacher's woman. What'd you reckon' she'd do if I rode her a while? If I cut her first, she'd be all limp. She wouldn't mind nothing I did."

He pulled a knife from his boot and slid it an inch along the center of her back, cutting through material as he passed. She felt the cold blade of the knife tickle her spine. He passed the knife back and forth, almost breaking the skin, almost ending her torture.

"Forget it, Miller. She's a good woman, and it's bad enough we got to kill her come morning," Whiteley answered. "You keep your hands off her."

"Right." Miller laughed as his hand spread across her hip. "I won't touch her if that's what you want, Sergeant. But you got to promise I get to be the one to kill her. I got it all thought out."

"I promised, didn't I? Now shut up."

Karlee twisted, rolling away from him. But he scooted

with her until he had her wedged into one corner of the wagon. Every few minutes, he'd glance toward Whiteley. When the sergeant wasn't watching, he'd pat her again as if playing some child's game.

Karlee knew she should be terrified or humiliated by the way the slimy little man played with her, but all she felt was rage. If she got free for one minute, Miller would be dead. She'd kill him and splatter *his* brains, if he had any, without a second thought.

Karlee almost laughed. The men kidnapping her might be a little surprised to learn that all this preacher's wife was thinking of was revenge.

After a few miles, the wagon turned off along the bayou.

"You think we oughta go in here without a guide?" Miller sounded frightened. "I heard tell the bayou is full of creatures, some living, some long dead, that'll bother a stranger."

"There ain't nothing in here but a few gators, Miller. We're meaner than they are."

Branches blanketed the wagon, hiding it from anyone who might ride past on the road.

"Get the woman out and tie her to one of the trees," Whiteley snapped. "And don't bother her none, Miller, or I'll break your right arm so you'll have to kill her left-handed tomorrow."

Miller took the threat seriously. He pulled her from the wagon and roped her to the tree without touching her more than necessary.

Karlee tried to shout insults at him, but the rag filtered the words into mumbling.

"I know you want me to pester you some. Women like it when I pester them." He slid greedy little hands from the rope at her feet up to her thigh. "But Whiteley ain't in no mood to be crossed."

He moved away, leaving her alone in the dark. She

could see the men bedding down by the wagon. She wished they'd been dumb enough to light a fire. The sounds of water lapping against the shore blended with a thousand whispered calls in the night. After a few minutes of staring, the shadows seemed to come to life, moving about the fringes of midnight black like ghosts of the long lost tribe of Caddo lingered there.

Karlee twisted within ropes. Rage kept fear away. If she could get free, she'd make them all pay.

The ropes held.

Finally, she gave up her useless quest and relaxed against the rough bark of the tree. Closing her eyes, she tried to remember the last few minutes she'd been in Daniel's arms. He'd admitted he wanted her. He had called her his.

If she survived this, she'd never nag him to love her. Just caring about her and wanting her near would be enough.

Karlee pushed the night sounds from her mind and tried to remember the way he'd felt against her. He'd been wild and demanding in his passion. He seemed as surprised by his hunger as she was. It was as if it were the first time for him as well.

Something splashed in the water ten feet away. Maybe only a fish? Maybe an alligator? Karlee refused to let fear consume her. Eventually, these fools would make a mistake, and she'd be ready. For the first time, she had a life to get back to.

She wasn't going anywhere but back to Daniel.

TWENTY-EIGHT

DANIEL SMELLED BLOOD AS HE CAME TO. HIS OWN blood, running down the side of his face. He felt for the cut along his forehead, shoving away a cloth that tried to stop the flow.

"You're bleeding." Ida patted at the wound once more.

"It's nothing." He tried to clear his head. "We have to find the rifles before they get back. It'll be our only bargaining tool for Karlee."

The sadness in Ida's eyes made her look even older. "It doesn't matter," she whispered. "They will kill us anyway. Just like they did my boy."

Daniel held her by the shoulders, forcing her to look at his face. "You're the late preacher's mother. The one who was Altus's friend. You're the woman who disappeared after the preacher was shot."

Ida nodded. "I knew whoever killed my son would come after me next." Her accent evaporated as she spoke. "Since I'm German, it was easy for me to disappear into the settlement. For months, I told myself I wanted nothing to do with this town or its secrets. But the night of the fire, I came back like everyone else to help. I saw the way you fought for the church my son and Altus built. I could no longer stay away."

"And the children who live in the barn with you are not yours." Pieces were beginning to fit together for Daniel.

Ida held her head high. "They are now. My only son was shot down months ago. In the settlement out by the lake, I found children whose parents died in last winter's fever. Most of the young orphans were taken in by families, but the half-grown children were left to fend for themselves. I knew the boys would turn to robbing and the girls to worse. They are all mine now. They're all I have."

Daniel wiped the tears from her wrinkled face. "Did Whiteley know who you were?"

Ida nodded. "I think I looked familiar to him the day he searched the house, but he didn't put it together until tonight. He caught me leaving."

"You were looking for something, but not the guns."

"I knew of no guns. I looked for a deed to prove the house mine, if such a thing exists. Karlee said you told her the house belonged to the church, but my son bought it the week we moved in. The week he died. Only I can't prove it without a deed. I didn't care at first, but now, with the children, I need a place."

"I'll help you look later, I promise, right now we have to find the guns." Daniel stood and helped Ida to her feet. "Karlee must have hidden them somewhere close. With Gerilyn and the twins here she couldn't have taken them far."

"You've seen this stash of weapons Whiteley talks about?"

Daniel walked with her into the foyer and slid the panel aside. "Until yesterday, they were behind this wall. Altus must have built it when he did the house. Probably the only other person who knew about this hiding place was your son." Daniel hated to ask, but it was necessary. "Was your son involved in the raids?"

Ida lowered her head. "A mother only wants to believe the best of her boy, but I think he was part of it for a short time. I may be German, but he was born in Tennessee right after I arrived in America. He was a man of God, but he was a Southerner, too. I think he thought raiding the supply wagons would stop some of the killing."

Daniel listened as he moved through the downstairs rooms searching every place large enough to store even one rifle. He paid no notice of the boys sleeping in each room. He did, however, tap on the parlor door and wait until Valerie said sleepily, "Come in."

As Daniel rummaged, Ida explained to Valerie and her mother what had happened. They followed in Daniel's wake searching everywhere he had in case he overlooked something the size of a rifle.

When he reached the kitchen, frustration echoed in his tone. "Where could she have hidden them?"

Ida's girls, who used the kitchen area by the fireplace as their bedroom, sat up and watched him as though he were no more than a part of their dreams.

"I've already looked in the barn and the upstairs for the deed," Ida answered. "I'd have noticed one rifle, much less many."

"Look again," Daniel ordered. Valerie and her mother darted off, willing volunteers.

Sleepy Germans followed him as though he were the Pied Piper. The children mumbled among themselves while they wiped the sleep from their eyes and pulled on robes.

After opening the last cabinet, Daniel slammed his fists on the counter, rocking the walls with the blows. "I have to do something! They have Karlee!"

He ran blood-covered hands through his hair and

reached for a towel. "I'm going after her."

Ida's frail fingers reached out to stop him.

"Don't worry. I'll be back before dawn." Daniel patted her hand. "I'd tell you to go somewhere safe, but I'm not sure any place in this town is safe tonight."

Ida's older children moved around her, a youthful army. "We'll make sure that all in this house are protected," one of the older boys said. In German, the young man began deploying his troops.

Never in his life had Daniel wished his brothers were closer. Wes and Adam were organizers, fighters. He'd always been the thinker. Even when he'd been wounded in the war, he was helping load men onto a wagon when shot, not fighting.

As he left the room, he asked one of the boys to hitch up the buggy. His leg was still too stiff to trust himself on horseback for hours, and when he found Karlee, he'd need something to bring her home in. He didn't even know if she knew how to ride.

As he opened the bottom drawer in his study, he realized how little he knew about her. He'd never asked, and she was not a woman who talked about herself. Did she ride? Could she shoot? Had she ever told another man she loved him? Why hadn't he taken the time to ask?

Daniel pulled out a gun belt Wes had given him for Christmas the year he'd turned eighteen. He'd shot the gun a few times at targets, but he'd never strapped on a weapon.

He was a man of peace. But they had Karlee!

Daniel belted the holster and checked the bullets.

Karlee watched the men. She could see them in the moonlight, but she knew they couldn't see her hidden in the shadows of the tree. As they slept, she sawed the rope against the bark, praying she could get free before they woke up.

Finally, the rope began to fray. Her wrists were raw and she felt near exhaustion, but frantically, she worked. She couldn't be sure of the time, but she guessed it was less than an hour before daylight when she freed her hands. The men would be waking any minute.

If she tried for the horses, they'd catch her. Assuming she could find the road, she'd never make it to town before daybreak. All Whiteley would have to do was ride by and pick her up. If she tried to go across country, she could be lost for days.

There was only one way to freedom. The river.

Karlee moved to the water's edge and slipped off her clothes. She buried them in the brush and mud. She'd worry about her lack of dress if she ever reached safety.

Slow as an alligator, she slipped into the water and began to swim toward the direction of town . . . she hoped.

Daniel thought he'd go mad looking for her. The Union had posted troops on every road into town waiting for Baker, but none remembered seeing Whiteley or any other men leaving in a wagon.

At the third post, Daniel ran into Wolf and told him what had happened.

Wolf reported vigilantes in flour-sack masks had broken into the local jail, kidnapping several men they claimed were murderers and about to get away with the crime because of the courts. Every lawman in the city was busy hunting them down.

To make matters worse, ruffians were looting, knowing their chances of getting caught were slim. They'd already broken into the bakery and several other businesses that had survived the fire. Wolf made sure they left the bakery empty-handed, but they'd still managed to damage the front of the store.

"Thank God, Valerie and her mother were at your place," Wolf said before he realized they might be no safer there than anywhere.

"I'll get my horse and look west for Karlee. If I know men like Whiteley, they'll be headed for the least populated area to make camp. They won't want to go far, only far enough from town to feel comfortable. The west blockade had the fewest soldiers guarding it. If I don't find anything, I'll meet you back at your place an hour before dawn."

Daniel nodded. "I'll search every barn in town, then move to the docks. If Whiteley stayed in town, there aren't that many places he can hide a wagon with a woman tied up in it."

Wolf gripped Daniel's shoulder. "Don't worry, we'll find her."

Daniel nodded wishing he believed everything would be fine. "I have to," he answered. "I'm not sure I can live without this woman."

Wolf grinned. "We'll find her. 'Til then, keep an angel on your shoulder, preacher, and your fist drawn until I'm there to cover your back."

Daniel smiled as Wolf repeated the old oath his brothers always said when leaving. "I'll do that."

Dawn danced off the surface of the bayou. Whiteley's camp was in a full panic. They were all running around like squirrels in a well, as if they'd somehow just misplaced Karlee.

"Where is she?" Miller yelled in frustration. He beat his bony fists against even bonier legs. "She couldn't have gone far in the dark."

Whitely studied the ground looking for clues. Others paced to the water's edge and back.

"Maybe a gator came up from the bank and ate her," Miller reasoned. "These cuts in the rope look like they could've been made by gator teeth."

"What about blood, you idiot? If she were eaten, there'd be blood everywhere."

Miller thought for a moment, then smiled a toothless grin. "Maybe the gator was real hungry and licked up all the blood when he finished. Kind of like a cat cleaning himself."

Whiteley slapped Miller on the side of the head with the butt of his rifle. "Shut up! You're as dumb as a wart on a dead frog."

Rubbed his scalp, Miller tried to act like he took offense at the remark. "Well, you got any better ideas?"

"She'd be too scared to go running through the dark and ever'body knows a woman can't swim." He picked up the gag lying a few feet from the tree. "She's hiding around here somewhere. Spread out, men! We'll find her."

Ten minutes later, all they'd found was Karlee's skirt and blouse.

"She done drowned herself!" Miller whined. "What a waste of a good killin'."

Whiteley shook his head. "A woman don't strip and hide her clothes before she kills herself."

Miller's eyebrows wrinkled together. "Then she's running around here naked!"

"Not likely," the sergeant replied as he scratched his head in thought. "I don't think preacher's wives are allowed."

Miller brightened. "Maybe the gator spit her clothes out after he ate her."

Whiteley swung the butt of his rifle again, but this time Miller ducked. He was still smiling when the return flight caught him unexpectedly.

"Forget about the gator," Whiteley ordered. "We can't

go into town without the hostage. The preacher wouldn't give us the guns even if he has them."

"What are we gonna do?" Miller rubbed both sides of his head. "What are we gonna do without the woman?"

The sergeant shook out the clothes and held them out toward Miller. "Get dressed."

Three blows later, Miller decided it could be a plan after all. He was still mumbling about the gator when he lifted his skirt and climbed into the wagon.

They made it to within sight of town before Whiteley saw something in the road that made him pull up short.

One man, covered in hair and wearing a Ranger badge, stood before them. He looked like a giant. If God sent an avenging angel, this surely was one. Twin Colts hung from his waist, and a rifle rested against his shoulder.

"Morning, Sergeant Whiteley!" Wolf growled. "I almost didn't recognize you in civilian clothes."

"This ain't your concern, Captain Wolf." Whiteley was in no mood to visit. He'd tangled with the giant a few times in saloons. Rangers like him considered being outnumbered six to one as about even odds.

"There's where you're wrong, Sergeant. You see, Daniel McLain is as close to a brother as I got. I'd take it real unkindly if any harm came to his wife."

"We ain't got his wife." Whiteley shook his head so hard everything before him blurred . . . except the giant.

Wolf's rifle leveled at the men in the wagon. "I'll see for myself, but first, everyone out."

Whiteley knew the six of them could all fire and kill Wolf before he could get more than two, maybe three of them. But he was too close to retirement to chance being one of the two or three. Besides, everyone in Texas knew Rangers were too mean to die. He'd heard rumors of a Ranger being wounded a half dozen times and still firing until his gun emptied.

Whiteley raised his hands and stepped down. One by one, the others followed. They were good at following orders, but not acting on their own.

Wolf took all their weapons and tossed them into the tall weeds fifty yards away like he was scattering half-pennies. When he was satisfied they were harmless, he moved to the back of the wagon and peeped inside.

The sight before Wolf made him laugh so hard he almost shot himself in the foot.

Miller swore loudly as he lifted his skirt and climbed out of the wagon to join the others.

"Where's Karlee?" Wolf asked when he finally gained control of himself.

"Miller lost her!" Whiteley shouted like a child caught in a playground fight. "I told him to tie her up, and he lost her."

"Gators ate her." Miller tried his theory again. "Must have spit out the dress."

Wolf leveled the rifle once more. "I'll kill you all. Then when you're resting in the ground, I'll dig you up and shoot you again if you harmed that girl."

"We didn't touch her." Whiteley sounded offended that Wolf would even think such a thing. "The gators didn't eat her, neither. She just got away. I figured we'd try to get the guns by making the preacher believe that Miller was her in the wagon."

Wolf reached in and tossed a rope to Miller. "Tie them up better than you did Karlee, or I swear I will feed you to an alligator myself." Miller didn't move so Wolf added, "You know a gator doesn't like to kill you fast. He'll keep you alive for days chewing off one arm or leg at a time."

Miller moved so fast he looked like he was dancing. When he finished tying the others, he held his hands out for Wolf. "You'll have to tie me."

Wolf grabbed Miller's roll of clothes and tossed them

as far as he could. "Nope. You ain't going anywhere dressed like that but to jail. All right, men. Start walking."

"I can't go to jail in this!" Miller whined. "I'd rather die!"

Wolf cocked the rifle.

Miller's face paled. Quickly, he dusted the skirt off and started walking toward town with the others.

TWENTY-NINE

EVERYONE IN THE HOUSE WAS READY. THE TWINS were tucked away safely upstairs with the younger of Ida's children. Any boy over twelve had been given a window to guard. Each had some kind of weapon and was told to start yelling the moment he heard anything. The girls turned the kitchen table over and hid behind it. They took turns watching the back door. They would throw every piece of china and pot at anyone trying to enter.

Gerilyn sat at the top of the stairs with an umbrella. She'd proclaimed herself the general of this army of children. From the way she shouted orders and arranged everyone, Daniel would have thought she'd seen combat.

The Reverend Daniel McLain, in his proper black coat and vest, stood waiting on the porch. The Colt strapped to his leg looked like a part of him. He had no intention of allowing one of Whiteley's men past the front door. Ida's menagerie of children were not naive little souls who frightened easily. They were fighters, or they wouldn't have survived this long. They'd lived through an ocean crossing with little food, no room and a body count of almost fifty percent to fever. They'd lost both parents and camped out on Caddo Lake, where most grown men were afraid to go alone.

Yes, Ida's children would fight, but Daniel knew that, if they had to take to arms, he'd be dead.

Full daylight came and still no sign of Whiteley with Karlee or of Wolf.

"You think Wolf found them?" Ida asked from her perch on the huge pile of Gerilyn's luggage.

"Maybe." Daniel was afraid to hope. Last night he'd thought he'd go mad searching for Karlee.

The town came alive like a Saturday night drunk who had to teach Sunday school. Mumbling, cranky, resigned. Daniel could hear the sounds from the dock a half-block away, voices shouting and wagons rolling. Valerie and her mother had left to check on the damage to their store. He'd told them not to return until the trouble was over.

The world turned despite Daniel's problems. He'd thought of notifying the Army or the sheriff about the kidnapping, but he could no longer be sure who was involved with Baker. If he told the law about the rifles, he or Ida might be arrested. These days, there was no predicting what would happen.

During the night, he'd heard several men mention they'd seen Baker about town. From the rumors, Daniel pictured a gentleman who changed his demeanor and language at will. He was reported to have played cards last night with Union officers, who had no idea who he was, and supposedly joined in a saloon fight near the docks that left two men dead. Baker was a man of many talents and one flaw. He never allowed anyone to best him. He never backed down or backed away.

Footsteps, running fast, drew Daniel's attention from his thoughts. Valerie hurried toward them, her colorful skirts flying.

"Daniel!" she cried. "Daniel! Come fast."

He stepped into the light of morning, fearing more for her than for himself. "What it is?"

"Karlee!" Valerie folded at her waist, trying to breathe. "She's in the water."

Daniel stilled, his body numb with fear. In his mind's eye, he could see Karlee floating in the bayou, her red hair circling her. Dead.

Valerie gulped air. "She won't come out, and she won't let anyone near her in a boat."

Daniel breathed.

"Hurry," Valerie cried. "She looks like she's been swimming for hours."

"Go!" Gerilyn yelled from the doorway. "I'll handle this front."

No pain from his leg reached his mind as he ran the half block to the docks. A crowd had gathered around, almost pushing one another in the bayou in their efforts to see.

The sight of a preacher wearing a gun made several women gasp as Daniel stormed onto the dock like a warrior.

"Where is she?" he yelled to no one in particular.

"Out there, Preacher," a man answered. "We told her to swim in, but she won't."

"I offered to row out to her, but she wouldn't hear of it," another added. "She keeps yelling for you."

Daniel stared hard at a head of wet, red hair bobbing up and down in the deep water.

"She's gone crazy," someone mumbled, and several agreed.

"Trying to kill herself. A loveless marriage, I'd guess. She'd only known him for a few days before she married him."

"I knew she weren't right when she let all them worthless Germans live with her."

"Heard tell she arrived packed in a trunk."

Daniel paid no attention to the talk. He no longer cared what anyone in town said. All he cared about was Karlee and why she wouldn't come into shore and out of danger. She was a strong swimmer. As strong as him. But she stayed away.

He raised his hand and waved.

Karlee did the same.

And then he saw it! Her bare shoulder. And he knew why she kept her distance.

Without saying a word, he unstrapped his gun belt and dropped it on the dock. Then he pulled off his coat and tied it around his waist. His boots landed next to the Colt.

As he moved to the water's edge, he caught Valerie's eye. "Find a blanket. I'll be needing it."

She nodded and vanished into the crowd.

Everyone watched as he dove into the choppy water and swam out toward his wife.

Daniel reached her in long steady strides. When he stopped in front of her, he smiled. "Good morning, Mrs. McLain."

"Reverend," she answered politely.

"May I offer you my coat?" He wrapped his coat around her as he folded her into his arms. "Welcome home."

"I'm sorry about this." Karlee pushed hair from her face. "I know I've embarrassed you greatly. It appears everyone in town is watching."

Daniel began to swim to shore. "It doesn't matter," he answered as he pulled her along. "You're safe."

When he reached a place where he could touch bottom, he pulled her to him and carried her the rest of the way. Valerie danced into the shallow tide and handed him an old packing blanket for Karlee's legs.

When the water was at his waist, Daniel stopped, unable to resist any longer. He kissed her full on the mouth in front of everyone.

Several of the women in the crowd gasped as if about to faint. Many of the men cheered.

Her lips were cold, and she shivered in his arms. "Let's go home," he whispered. They left the dock without explaining to anyone what had happened.

Karlee laid her head on his shoulder and closed her eyes. She didn't have to go anywhere. She was home.

When they reached the house, everyone talked at once, asking about Karlee and telling of Wolf coming by with men tied on a rope.

"Wolf wants you to meet him at the sheriff's office as soon as you can," one of the older German boys told Daniel.

"Tell Wolf Karlee's safe, and we'll be there directly." Daniel sat Karlee down in the rocker by the fireplace. "After I get my wife warm."

When he looked up, Gerilyn stood behind the children holding an armload of dry blankets and several towels. Prepared as always, she hurried forward, dropped her load by the fireplace and wrapped Karlee in one of the quilts.

"I was so worried about you, Cousin. It must have been horrible beyond words." She grabbed a towel and patted Karlee's hair. "Remember now, dear, a lady never talks about such unpleasantries. I'll stand beside you. After all, you're blood. But for fate it could have been me who those terrible men kidnapped." She clenched her hands to her heart. "I won't allow anyone to disgrace your name, no matter what happened during the kidnapping."

"Nothing happened. Except that I broke free and swam to town. I thought I'd get here early and could grab something to cover me before anyone saw me. But that didn't happen."

"That's the spirit, dear. Block it all from your mind." Gerilyn gave her a hug and almost touched her cheek with a kiss.

Daniel stood protectively behind the rocker. "I need to ask you and Ida a favor, Gerilyn. I know you're loading up to leave, but would you mind taking all the children down to the dock? I'm sure they'd enjoy breakfast at the bakery."

Gerilyn nodded soberly. "Of course, I understand. You need to talk to Karlee. I guess you've a husband's right to know the details." She patted her cousin's shoulder. "Chin up, dear. You'll survive this shame. There's no need for you to give a thought to suicide, though that's the path many in your situation would take."

Ida rolled her eyes then glared at Gerilyn for a moment before she shooed the children from the kitchen. As she left, with a twin on either side, she winked at Daniel. "Keep her warm," was all she said, but Daniel got the message.

Finally, they were alone. The house was quiet and no longer in any danger of attack.

He locked the back door and shoved the table against the entrance leading to the foyer.

"Expecting more trouble?" Karlee gripped her coffee with both hands and leaned toward the fire.

"No. For once I'd like not to be expecting anything or anyone." He crossed to her. "I'd like to be alone with my wife."

Karlee looked down at what a mess she was. "I'm sorry for embarrassing you, but while I swam last night my camisole ripped away and the bloomers fell off when the drawstring came untied."

He moved about the room as though he wasn't really listening. When he returned she noticed he had an armful of candles and the tin of matches.

"If you're worried about me killing myself, forget it.

Murder may have crossed my mind a few times in the past ten hours but never suicide."

Daniel spread a quilt on the floor in front of the fire and lit the candles one by one circling the quilt. Then he stood and slowly peeled away his wet clothes.

"What are you doing?" Karlee asked.

"I'm going to finish what we started last night in the study." His voice held a hint of formality, but he was smiling all the way to the twinkle in his eyes.

"But it's eight o'clock in the morning." Karlee couldn't believe what he was thinking. "The children are up. Everyone in town is awake. Folks don't do what we were doing in daylight. It isn't natural."

"I don't care." He stopped unbuttoning his trousers and pulled her against him. "I'm going to make love to my wife. Unless my wife has any objections?"

Karlee stared at him, wondering if he'd been drinking or maybe he'd been clobbered in the head once too often. This was not like Daniel.

But he certainly looked like Daniel. "No," she whispered. "I've no objections."

"Good." He pushed the blanket from her shoulders. "Then first I'd like to look at you in all kinds of light. I want to see you. Really see you."

Karlee stood in shock as he removed the wet coat he'd placed around her in the water and gently lay her down on the quilt.

Her damp body glistened in the sunlight. Firelight warmed her side, and candlelight sparkled in her eyes. When she would have curled up, he gently spread her arms above her head and lifted her hair so that it offered no covering.

After a few half-hearted efforts to cover herself, she lay still before him letting the light warm her. His large hand spread across her abdomen. She drew in a deep breath and released it slowly while his hand pressed against her.

"I want to see and touch every part of you. I want to make love to you, Karlee."

When she looked up, he was staring into her eyes, his thoughts unreadable.

Without another word, he leaned over and kissed her. His chest warmed her like a blanket. She closed her eyes but the image of him before her remained. She was floating now as she had in the darkness when she'd been too tired to swim. His hands passed over her, keeping her warm, keeping her alive.

She'd dreamed he was there in the night, moving beside her while she swam. Touching her softly as he was now. Silently telling her of his love.

Slowly, in the morning sunlight and crackling firelight, he stroked her. He didn't need to tell her that he'd been frightened for her life, that he'd gone mad searching for her, that he'd felt her absence like a blow. She knew.

Her fingers slid into his damp hair as she pulled his mouth to hers. "I love you," she whispered as she gave herself willingly to his caresses.

The night in the study had been wild, the morning tender and loving. He took his time, caressing her fully, bringing her to a level of need that made her mindless.

She rocked beneath him, wanting more. But he was in no hurry, driving her to the edge of sanity again and again. When his hands were finally not enough, he moved his mouth over her. Tasting her, kissing her, devouring her.

She wanted to touch him, to please him, but all she could do was react to his lovemaking. She lay unaware of anything but him. She rocked slightly to his embrace and moaned with pleasure. When she made a sound, he'd repeat any action until desire washed over her. Her body felt like it was on fire with need.

His rough hands moved so gently over her tender flesh she shivered. He pulled her against him but didn't stop his discovery of her.

He was her world, and she was his. He felt her happiness as his own and she felt his desire in the very core of her. The loneliness they'd suffered made their closeness far sweeter.

Suddenly, he pulled away and stood. For a long moment, he stared down at her.

She saw the passion in his eyes. A wild animal ready to run with her into a paradise he'd never known. A man looking at what he cherished most . . . her.

He pulled off his trousers and knelt beside her. Without a word, he put his warm hand on her thigh and encouraged her legs to open.

As she opened, he stroked her gently, completely.

"Are you frightened?" His voice rumbled with need.

"No," she whispered as he lowered over her, entering her swiftly and fully.

Karlee felt the pain and opened her mouth to cry out, but his lips closed over hers, swallowing her cry. The kiss now was deep, no longer with longing but with passion. He took her breath as he took her body, without resistance.

She moved with him, and the pain disappeared. He dug his hands into her hair and shifted in the timeless dance of lovemaking. She joined him, wanting more. He moved faster, giving her his weight with each thrust.

All the years of being alone, of never being touched, of never being loved melted away. Her heart pounded wildly, beating to the rhythm of his movements.

He carried her in passion's fantasy higher and higher, until the world shattered and pure pleasure bolted through her body.

He shoved into her, once, twice more, before she felt him tense, and she knew the bolt had struck him as well.

For a few minutes neither of them could move. They lay wrapped in one another's arms. He rolled to his side, drawing her with him.

Karlee laced her arms around his neck and rested her head on his shoulder.

Daniel stared at the fireplace for a long time. Finally, he found the energy to stroke her hair and kiss her forehead lightly. His fingers slid lazily along her back.

As much as he'd denied it since the moment he saw her, he loved her. He'd fallen hard and landed solidly on his heart. A heart he thought long since made of stone.

"I love you," he whispered as his mouth took hers with the sweet taste of satisfaction.

His hand slid over her body lovingly, caressing, cherishing.

"I know," she answered almost asleep.

THIRTY

WHEN DANIEL FINALLY MANAGED THE ENERGY TO move, Karlee was sound asleep. He unfolded from her wondering if she had any idea how perfect she was for him.

Somehow in this insane world, she'd come into his life. Her unpredictability kept him guessing. Her self-doubt only made him want to cherish her more. Her unwavering love wrapped him in a warmth that thawed all his emotions.

And her passion . . . there were no words for how her passion made him feel. He only knew that if he made love to her every morning and night of his life, he'd never get enough of the feel of her, the taste of her, the need for her.

He moved the table back in place and, after he dressed in his study, collected a pile of clothes for her.

When he returned to the kitchen, she hadn't moved. The light still danced on her body, making her look like some heavenly creature who'd tumbled to earth.

He warmed a pan of water and sat down beside her. Slowly, he began washing her. She'd mumble in her sleep from time to time, but she accepted his touch as so much a part of her life she didn't awaken.

Gently, he dressed her, knowing that tonight he'd repeat the action in reverse. When he finished the last button on her blouse, he glanced up and saw her watching him.

"How long have you been awake?" There was no apology in his tone.

"About the bloomers, but you were having such a good time, I didn't want to interrupt."

"I think I like undressing you more," he whispered as he pulled her into his arms. "I was trying to let you sleep a while longer."

"I need to fix breakfast." She kissed him lightly.

"I've had breakfast," he answered, leaving no doubt as to what he was talking about. "And I must say, Mrs. McLain, you do some things in the kitchen quite well."

"Thank you, Reverend. It was my pleasure."

"And mine."

He pulled her to her feet and kissed her soundly, loving the way she never pulled away from him.

When he raised his head, she saw a fire smoldering in his eyes. "Would you like another serving?" she asked boldly.

"Yes," he laughed, "But I'll starve myself until tonight. Right now, I'd like to make sure the men who tried to take you away from me are rotting in jail."

"I'll comb my hair and go with you." She moved away from him and was halfway across the room before she turned. "And Daniel," she giggled. "It was wonderful."

He tried to look stern but knew he failed. "You're not supposed to talk of such things."

She disappeared without promising, but he didn't care. He planned to love her, not judge her.

A few minutes later, she came back with her hair in a proper little bun. He pulled on a fresh jacket as a tap sounded on the kitchen door.

Karlee threw the lock before he could stop her.

Gerilyn walked in, her face so pale her powder looked pink. She was closely followed by a tall, rather thin gentleman who held her elbow in a tight grip.

"I know I promised you time, Daniel. But I simply must pick up my luggage. It seems to be scattered all over the porches. This gentleman insisted on helping me."

She turned to the man behind her. "I'd like you to meet my brother-in-law, Daniel McLain, and his wife . . ."

Daniel took one step toward the door as the stranger sauntered inside without waiting to be invited.

"Reverend McLain." He nodded as he stood beside Karlee.

Daniel hesitated. "Have we met, sir?"

"No, but that was my error. We should have met last night. I'm Cullen Baker." As he spoke, he pulled a small derringer from his vest pocket and pointed it toward Karlee. "And I assure you though this gun is small, it will make you a widower. I've come for my rifles. Your sister-in-law was kind enough to show me the way."

Gerilyn let out a very lady-like scream and fainted. No one moved to her aid.

Daniel appeared almost calm. "You'd better have two bullets in that weapon, because if you kill her, you'll have to kill me as well."

Baker looked sarcastic. "How touching. A man who loves his wife. Well, maybe I'll grant your request. One could go first." He moved the gun until it pointed at Daniel.

"I'll show you the rifles!" Karlee interrupted.

Baker smiled. "That's better." He pointed the gun back at Karlee, guessing Daniel was less likely to charge if there was a chance the bullet would hit her. "Where are they, Mrs. McLain?"

"On the porch. In a trunk that's shoved into a corner."
Karlee took a step closer to Daniel. "Take them and go."

Baker motioned for both of them to move ahead of
him as he casually stepped over Gerilyn's body. "I
would have come by last night, Mrs. McLain, but I
didn't think it necessary. Now you see, I not only must
get my own guns, I resent you putting half my men,
dumb as they are, in jail."

When Daniel walked through the door, he saw his gun
belt hanging over the railing. But Karlee stood between
him and the weapon. If he moved for the gun, Baker
would have time to get off a shot.

"They're in the trunk." Karlee pointed to the finely
tooled leather trunk. Someone must have removed the
tablecloth.

Baker watched them both as he worked the latch.
When he lifted the lid, Daniel moved closer to Karlee.

"Take the guns and go, Baker. We have no quarrel
with you."

The outlaw reached into the trunk and pulled out a
handful of lacy petticoats. He dug deeper, spilling lin-
gerie across the porch.

"What is this?" He was not a man who tolerated being
double-crossed.

Daniel knew time had run out. He shoved Karlee aside
and stood facing Cullen guessing the man would demand an answer before killing him.

"The guns!" Baker snapped. "I'll burn this house to
the ground before anyone takes anything from me!" He
threw a handful of underthings on the ground.

Gerilyn flew from the doorway, rage awakening a
warrior as her underthings drifted like colorful snow-
flakes across the porch.

Daniel rushed forward into Baker's direct line of fire.
Karlee screamed. For only a fraction of a second, Baker
hesitated.

Daniel had his opening. He slammed into Baker, sending the derringer flying. With two mighty blows, Baker swung backward and tumbled into the trunk.

Karlee slammed the lid and strapped the latch. Gerilyn pounded on the trunk as if beating Cullen senseless.

When she stopped, all was quiet, all was still.

For a moment Daniel, Karlee, and Gerilyn stared at one another, afraid to believe it was over.

"How dare that man handle my private things!" Gerilyn attacked the trunk once more pounding as she lectured him on what was proper.

"He could have killed you," Karlee cried. Suddenly fear overwhelmed her.

Daniel pulled her close. "No, darling. He could have killed you. That alone would have killed me. I'm a man who has always believed in peace, but you're worth fighting for."

She forced her tears away. "What do we do with him?"

"We'll let Gerilyn handle him for a while." Daniel smiled. "I'll hitch the buggy and get the rest of her luggage. After she's on board, we'll take him down to the jail and let them figure it out."

They walked toward the steps. Karlee stopped suddenly. "But wait! If the guns are not in the trunk, they must be . . ."

Daniel followed her thoughts. "In one of the other trunks?"

Karlee nodded.

"Why don't we just leave them there? Gerilyn can turn them over to the Army in New Orleans."

"Shall we tell her?"

Daniel glanced over at the wild woman still pounding on the trunk and yelling. "No, let her be surprised. I've learned a few unexpected turns in life can be very interesting."

An hour later, Gerilyn was aboard telling everyone all the details of a story "too terrible to talk about."

Karlee took the twins and walked back home, thankful to no longer have company. Daniel delivered the trunk to Wolf at the jail but didn't stay around to watch the unpacking.

It was almost dark by the time he finished his errands and made it back to Karlee. When he opened the door, he smiled. She was sitting on the floor with the twins, teaching them to make clothes for their dolls. Supper was burning on the stove. He was home.

She didn't say a word as she went about being the best wife she knew how to be. He hardly noticed the cornbread that crumbled in his hand or the coffee still full of grounds. He read to the twins, then she put them to bed.

When she came back downstairs, Daniel was waiting for her.

"I wanted to ask you something," he said, suddenly nervous.

"All right." She trying to guess what bothered him so.

"Will you marry me."

She smiled. "I thought I was married to you, Daniel."

"I know, but I wanted to ask you so you'd know you'd been asked right and proper."

Karlee understood. "And what is the bargain you offer?"

"A forever kind of marriage. A true marriage. I don't have much. This house isn't mine. The church burned, and my income from the articles is never enough. Most folks would say you're getting saddled with a ready-made family. But I promise to love and cherish you for the rest of my life."

"Then I'll be your wife." She answered. "My home will be your arms."

He hugged her tightly. "Come along, Mrs. McLain."

They walked, arm in arm into the kitchen. She was looking up at him and for a moment she didn't see all the people standing quietly around the table loaded down with presents of all sizes, wrapped in shiny paper with pink ribbons on each box.

"What's this?"

"It's your birthday, my love." He grinned.

EPILOGUE

DANIEL HEARD THE CHURCH BELL RESOUNDING through the clear summer air. He closed his eyes and took a deep breath thinking how he'd missed the sound.

He marked his place in the Bible with two ribbons, one blue velvet, one pink satin, and stood from a desk now void of all clutter. Glancing up, he noticed Karlee standing at the study door and wondered how long she'd been watching him.

Her beauty stopped his breathing for a moment. How could he have ever thought her hair a hindrance, or her body too thick? She was perfection. Just the memory of how they'd made love in the hours before dawn made him wish for the privacy of night once more. She was a woman who took him into her heart and body so completely, he became lost in the pleasure of her.

"You still love her, don't you?" she asked so quietly it was almost a thought. Her eyes held only a question, not a demand for denial.

Slowly, he straightened, pulling himself back to the present, making his mind see her now and not as she'd looked at dawn with her body bare and damp after their mating. "Yes." He circled both ribbons around his hand. "Do you mind?"

Karlee smiled. "No. She's part of you, part of what made you the man I married. If you stopped loving her, you wouldn't be my Daniel. She can be your first love as long as I can be your last."

He closed the few steps between them and kissed her tenderly. He couldn't keep his hands from moving over her, longing for the feel of her closer. "I do love you," he whispered against her ear.

"I know." She leaned into him as she always did, a perfect fit against him.

He knew she loved him, she'd told him so since before he even wanted her to say such words. But it was the way she touched him, always offering more, almost daring him to take more, that drove him mad. They'd been married four months now and, when he made love to her completely and fully, he saw her smile as she fell asleep, exhausted and satisfied. She somehow knew he'd never get his fill of her. She knew he'd always want more of the nearness of her, the feel of her, the taste of her.

He leaned, very properly, and kissed her on the forehead as his hand, hidden between them, moved over her boldly. She grinned, taking in a deep breath so that her breasts brushed lightly against his starched shirt. Daring again, he thought. An invitation. The challenge he'd grown accustom to.

Cinnamon shattered the silence as she ran down the stairs and out the back door, yelling, "Clear the decks!"

Daniel pulled himself back to the world.

Starlett followed her sister. "We're going to be late, Cinn. The bells are already ringing." She disappeared through the kitchen.

Daniel and Karlee didn't move. They both seemed to need another moment of closeness before the day began.

He wondered if she knew how deeply he wanted her? How much a part of him she'd become? He wasn't sure he'd ever find the words to tell her, but he planned to spend the rest of his nights showing her.

He couldn't resist tasting her lips briefly before moving away and pulling on his coat. "Are you going to miss this house?" His voice was slightly off balance as he forced conversation that lay far from his thoughts. There was no need to talk of the desire growing between them. They both knew it would be satisfied in the midnight hours.

Karlee shook her head. "My home is anywhere you are. Ida needs to live here, and we have a place waiting for us."

Daniel took her hand. "It'll be different, helping start a land-grant college. Some say it will take a few years. An agricultural and mechanical college at that. Sounds like a strange school to need a theology professor."

"Maybe they'll just call it A and M." She took his hand. "They'll surely change the name as it grows."

They walked out of the house without looking back. The wagon was loaded with their belongings. The twins were already on board, sitting atop Karlee's old trunk.

No one said a word as they drove toward church. It had been months since the fire. Daniel had the frame of the new church up with the bell tower finished. He'd even put benches for pews for his last service in Jefferson.

He knew Karlee worried about how the town would accept a preacher's wife who swam nude, but he didn't care. They hadn't accepted him before, and he could find no shame in loving her. He'd give his last sermon to a congregation of three if need be.

As they turned the corner Karlee let out a startled cry even before Daniel looked up the street.

The framed walls marked the boundaries of the church, but people stood all around. What would be the inside was packed with families, while many others waited out on the grounds and sat on blankets and boxes all the way to the boardwalk.

Karlee straightened with pride as Daniel helped her down. She looked very proper as a minister's wife in her finely tailored traveling suit. She walked to the first pew while Daniel stepped forward and unfolded his notes. When he glanced down at her, she winked in a most unminister's wife's way. He fought down a grin and cleared his throat.

As Daniel McLain began to speak, no one noticed the hairy giant in the back who laughed.

"Inspired," Wolf mumbled as he watched Daniel talking only to Karlee. "Makes a man want to believe in love."

He slipped away, not wanting to overdo his first time in church.

"Maybe I'll shave." He scratched his beard. "Maybe I'll make up my mind to fall in love one of these days."